EXILE

THE SCIENCE OFFICER
BOOK 14

BLAZE WARD

KNOTTED ROAD PRESS

Exile
The Science Officer Volume 14
Blaze Ward
Copyright © 2024 Blaze Ward
All rights reserved
Published by Knotted Road Press
www.KnottedRoadPress.com

ISBN: 978-1-64470-421-9

Cover art:
Illustration 120840815 © Tiziano Cremonini | Dreamstime.com

Cover and interior design copyright © 2024 Knotted Road Press

Reviews
It's true. Reviews help. Even a short one, such as, "Loved it!" So please consider reviewing this book (and all of the ones you've read) on your favorite retailer site.

Never miss a release!
If you'd like to be notified of new releases, sign up for my newsletter.

http://www.blazeward.com/newsletter/

Buy More!
Did you know that you can buy directly from the Knotted Road Press website?

https://www.KnottedRoadPress.com/shop

ALSO BY BLAZE WARD

The Jessica Keller Chronicles

Auberon

Queen of the Pirates

Last of the Immortals

Goddess of War

Flight of the Blackbird

The Red Admiral

St. Legier

Winterhome

Petron

CS-405

Queen Anne's Revenge

Packmule

Persephone

First Centurion Kosnett

Encounter at Vilahana

Consensus at Aditi

Hegemony at Dalou

Princes at Ewin

Empire at Gloran

Domain at Yaumgan

Additional Alexandria Station Stories

The Story Road

Siren

Two Bottles of Wine With A War God

The Science Officer Series Season One

The Science Officer

The Mind Field

The Gilded Cage

The Pleasure Dome

The Doomsday Vault

The Last Flagship

The Hammerfield Gambit

The Hammerfield Payoff

The Bryce Connection

The Science Officer Series Season Two

Alien Seas

Buried Among the Stars

Captain Navarre

Dragoon's Honor

Exile

Corsac Fox

Flight of the Corsac Fox

Hard Bargain

Outermost

Dominion-427

Phoenix

Princess Rualoh

CONTENTS

THE HUNTERS

PART I

Katya listened to the two men in her main conference room finish their briefing.

Usually, she was in charge. *Kymni Gauntlet* was her ship, after all. An Enforcer for the Jarre Foundation. A Battle-cruiser-scale warship that might be comparable to a Mark II Warmaster on a good day.

Neither of these men were part of the Foundation, but she'd been hired and specifically put under their command for this job. And, truth be told, she hadn't put up much of a fuss about it, either.

After all, the man they had been hired to go kill had betrayed the Foundation. Had lit out and gone completely rogue, even by the standards of *Concord* piracy, which still impressed her all these years later.

The shorter of the two men finished talking and turned to look her direction. Katya perked up. She hadn't been ignoring him, but half the words out of his mouth for the last thirty minutes had been rage and profanities directed at their new target. The man who had caused the three of them to be here, now, today, in this room, at this moorage, ready to go kill people.

"What do you think, Captain Velichkov?" he asked her.

Short for a guy, and bulky rather than muscular. Bald-shaved head with that stupid goatee that was supposed to make a fat, middle-aged man look aggressive. At least according to certain theories those men told themselves. On Valko Slavkov, it looked more like a pull tab to open his mouth for a piece of candy that would pop out.

Still, he was one of the wealthiest men in this meta-sector of space. Board of Directors of H & W Heavy Industries. Usually a Jarre Foundation rival, if not outright enemy.

Things always got strange when the pirate clans decided to make common cause.

Katya shrugged.

"I'm not sure that a Metcalf-style vessel will be all that effective against someone like Zakhar Sokolov, but it will certainly impress the hell out of people," she replied. They were paying for her expertise, not her flattery.

"No?" the other man asked.

Kliment Cunningham. Banker from Walvisbaai Indus-trial. Still pissed about *Nidavellir*. Almost as angry as Slavkov was for getting his sand train stolen. Particularly when it had subsequently been used to destroy the Walvisbaai platform at *Nidavellir*.

"Arsenal ships are capable of fantastic saturation attacks," Katya agreed. "Lay down an impossible number of torpedoes in a short period of time, overwhelming any defenders and generally scoring an easy kill. Since you don't want this target taken alive, that's a bonus. But nothing demands that they stay put after we start attacking, so we might end up in some bizarre stern chase across half the galaxy after they run.

Metcalf megalaunches are less impressive and more expensive then. Still might work better, though."

She let them have that bit. Katya would exercise as much nominal fleet control as one might, as the biggest ship when you put four different packs of war dogs together to hunt a rabbit. Or a fox in this case.

It would still be a freaking mess that she would have gladly missed, save that that that damned fox had embarrassed the Foundation. Insulted them, even.

Made the rest of his old comrades look bad, which was something they were never going to get over.

But even *Kymni Gauntlet* wasn't enough warship to take on his new vessel alone. Thus, the rest of the clans. And their ships. Possibly enough firepower gathered in one place to make even the *Concord* sit up and take notice.

But Slavkov and Cunningham were both that pissed. And that wealthy. That willing to challenge even a hegemonic power like the *Concord*, if it got them what they wanted.

"Did you have other suggestions, Captain Velichkov?" Cunningham asked dryly.

"No," Katya said simply. "We have an overwhelming force. Hopefully, surprise, if none of your spies have double-crossed us at the last minute. Zakhar Sokolov is a dead man."

"Just so long as we all understand that part," Slavkov growled.

Katya nodded. During battle, he'd be over on one of his own ships, rather than on her bridge, issuing orders and making stupid demands. Probably aboard *Obsidian Hawk*. Cunningham would be on that Metcalf beast, *Blackstone*, probably making Geno Goranov's life miserable.

Not hers. She could always ignore them, because Katya

was pretty certain that everyone who didn't fly a Jarre Foundation flag would ignore any orders from her as a matter of course.

Which was why these two had decided to bring an entire pirate fleet to hunt down one Galleon. Even a Galleon would be massively outclassed, though Sokolov had a rep in the industry for being able to pull off impossible feats.

Having Eutropio Navarre along with himwas even worse, since nobody really knew where that one had come from.

Didn't matter. They were all going to die. Ugly, too.

"I understand," Katya nodded to Slavkov, ceding him the final word on the topic. "We'll be there. I expect the rest of you to pile on."

"We will, Captain Velichkov," he growled. "We will."

PART II

Zakhar studied the face in the mirror. He didn't wonder when he'd gotten old, because he had a map in front of him, every wrinkle, scar, white whisker, and age spot highlighting all the light-years involved.

Occasionally, he had to stop and trace the line of decisions and inflection points that had gotten him to this exact moment, but it reminded him of the old Mayan saying that you walk backwards, facing the past, while the future in front of you is an unknown that only becomes clear in the moment it becomes that same past, lost behind you forever.

He wore burgundy today. Not green. *Excalibur* was circling around outside the edge of *Concord* space with the precision and care of a captain with a lot of bounties on his head and a number of people who wanted to arrest him and ask some pointed questions. The life of an exile.

How he came to be in possession of a massive cache of stolen *Concord* warship blueprints was only the most recent crime in his file. It was still a damned thick folder, when you got right down to it and made a list.

Hell, at this point, he wasn't even sure he could remember everything, but Zakhar had no doubts that someone had it all documented somewhere.

Twenty years as a formal sailor. Twenty more as a pirate. Or whatever he'd been in the half-dozen years since Hurricane Aritza had exploded into their lives and pretty much tumbled everything.

Zakhar adjusted his tie and nodded to the stranger nodding back. Today felt like one of those starting-over-cold moments. Zakhar had known enough of them in his time to recognize them when they arrived, though he'd never been able to predict them.

Merely ride the wave, looking backwards with Mayan certainty.

He turned to the hatch and the monitor next to it.

"Yeoman, what is your status?" he called, walking towards the hatch.

Suvi appeared instantly. And wearing burgundy like him, instead of the green that had been her thing for more than a century. A subtle joke on the galaxy, but one he appreciated.

They weren't *Concord* Navy any more. Any of them. So many retired veterans. Or chased out hooligans. All exiles.

She smiled. It felt infectious, so he allowed it.

"Dragoon is being grumpy at the ground team," Suvi said with big, emotive eyes.

"That's because they're leaving the ship to visit a planet we've none of us ever been to," Zakhar reminded her. "Not like this behavior is out of context for her."

Suvi laughed.

"Del is prepping for flight, also grumpy," she continued. "Javier is currently standing in the middle of the Gun Bunnies, explaining to Bethany that he does not require the services of a Ship's Librarian to scout the resort. She's mostly arguing out a sense of leaving him without adult supervision, I think. Afia is rolling her eyes so hard it might be painful. Sascha is stretching and doing kata. Hajna is currently pretending to take a nap."

"Let Djamila know I'm leaving now and will be down to see them off," he said, keying the hatch and heading out into the corridor.

Excalibur was a long ship. Tall, too, but not that wide. A whole bunch of decks stacked on top of one another to allow huge cargo bays, as well as excess crew and passenger space that was hardly ever used these days, mostly because they weren't wanting that many strangers aboard.

"Is *Ophiuchi* really that dangerous a place?" Suvi asked from a corridor monitor as he headed aft.

Zakhar knew she could follow him clear to the flight bay, shifting pieces of her consciousness between avatars in real time.

"It is not," he said as he hit the stairs down.

Warships had lifts, but war-sailors hardly ever used them. Too easy for something to kink in battle. Or even normal operations. Then you're trapped until someone comes to rescue you, usually after the battle.

They all used the stairs instead. Lots of good exercise, going up and down constantly. Kept a sixty-year-old man trim and hungry.

"However," Zakhar said as he hit the first landing. "*Drako III* is a complicated mess for navigation. One reasonable gas giant, sitting square in the middle of the star's habitable zone, with more than fifty moons, rings, and that pair of blue storms that everyone thinks are eyes when they look up. The ships that first terraformed this system saw all that real estate and decided to blow their entire budget in one place, so you have more than a dozen planets below us capable of sustaining life."

"And one resort that frankly looks a little tame," Suvi offered.

Zakhar laughed.

"Compared to a hollowed-out asteroid gambling den starship, I suppose so," he said. "However, it is surrounded by a wilderness that folks like to go camping in, rather than dancing and crap games. Back to nature. Most crews need something like that after long enough inside a steel box, though you've got the nature settings in your converted cargo holds. Not enough, though."

"Do we need to install a river and two lakes?" she asked. "Throw in a small forest?"

"Honestly, I think Javier's idea for a winter wonderland has the most promise," he replied. "Maybe you should look into all those design plans that you stole and see if we could build a jungle or alpine resort ship as well. Instead of skiing, a rock-climbing wall. Instead of skating, maybe a lake deep enough to cliff-dive?"

There was a pause long enough to be for his benefit, since Zakhar knew how fast she calculated.

"Got some ideas," she offered.

"Set me up a meeting in a few days," Zakhar nodded. "Make sure Bethany is with us for her perspective."

Then he was at the bottom and exiting into the flight bay.

PART III

Djamila left off grousing at her men when she heard the hatch open.

Zakhar entered the launch bay and she felt half the weight of the galaxy slide off her shoulders in ways that she knew would have been alien just a few years ago.

It still made her smile.

Javier smothered a grin as she glanced over, then shrugged.

"You will still treat it like a hostile planet encounter," she said sourly.

"No," he shook his head. "You will. You folks are crazy. I get that. It gets you out of bed in the morning and running laps around the ship in full combat gear and weights. Whatever, lady. I'm going to sleep late. Hike some. Maybe fly-fish for fun in the afternoon, before returning to a pitcher of fresh margaritas in my cabin. This is my vacation from being in charge, okay?"

Djamila wanted to say something, but kept her composure. If nothing else, it would largely keep him out of her way so the men could do some updated alpine and wilderness training in new environments.

There was only so much you could do on a ship, after all. With the two Pathfinders generally keeping Javier from being eaten by whatever local wildlife that might be that desperate, he'd be out of her hair.

Then, after a couple of days of scouting and preparation, Zakhar could start cycling crew down for some well-deserved leave time, too. Most had missed out at *Sovereign Nakhimov*, and even the ones who had gotten time had been limited to short blocks, instead of sleeping in a strange bed. And maybe waking up next to a stranger.

Not that she did, but Djamila understood that others saw that as a positive outcome.

She turned to Galal. If the team had a sergeant, he would fill that role, but those six men were all equals. Galal wasn't much smarter than the rest, but he was the smartest.

"Get everyone loaded, checked off, and ready to depart," she ordered, ignoring those men as they suddenly broke into a dead run for Del's shuttle. Hauling gear and hauling ass, like she was keeping score.

Today, she'd decided not to, but didn't tell them that. Merely turned to find herself alone with Javier, Afia, and Zakhar. Even Bethany had given up on Javier and returned to her library.

Zakhar grabbed her by the shirt and pulled her down into a kiss that left her less flustered than it might have, once upon a time. The other two grinned and waited.

"You want me to find you a fishing hole?" Javier asked as she gasped and recovered.

"Maybe," Zakhar replied evenly. "I'd like to be on this planet long enough to matter, you know."

"Hey, we needed to get gone after a bank job," Javier snarked. "Talk to the tall babe about that."

Djamila was always surprised to discover that she could, in fact, blush. Javier, fortunately, still seemed to be the only person in the galaxy capable of causing it. Which was good.

After she'd turned herself into a creature called *Jamie*, in order to seduce Jabril Qadir and get close enough to him to confirm who he was, she was also looking forward to some time off.

To maybe discovering who this Jamie woman might be, that she could occasionally replace the hardass Dragoon of *Excalibur*.

Weirder things had happened.

She turned back to Javier.

"Do we have any particular plans here?" she reconfirmed.

"Downtime," he nodded, turning deadly serious. "We've been going like hell for a long time, and the crew needs a respite. That includes you two as much as me and Afia. I'd like to hang out here for a week or three of doing nothing at all, so everyone has a chance to reset. We've still got something of a run to get home to *Altai*, but we're tired and a little cranky. Especially you."

Djamila kept her comments to herself. He wasn't wrong. And she was looking forward to getting to a place she could actually call home, a thing she hadn't known in decades.

Afia stepped up and imposed her immense will on the group.

"You do know that *Ophiuchi* has, like, crap for resupply capabilities, right?" she asked, looking at the two men.

"I'm happy with fresh fruit and whatever dried grains they can ship," Zakhar offered. "We can shift over to *Blue Amsterdam* or *Mauta* after a week and put you back to work. You take a few days off first, though. Worse come to worst, *Quari Station* or *Drako Transit* will have the basics we can pick up. Not like we didn't resupply pretty well last time around. Suvi assures me that she can go a while just from supplies aboard, if we can feed the organics."

Djamila nodded. She'd had a number of conversations with Javier's daughter on this trip, one of the few people she could really let her hair down around. Even if it was coming in gray in places these days. And still helmet-short.

She trusted Suvi to give them an honest assessment of things when they needed it. Afia, too.

"You folks got anything else before I go on vacation?" Javier groused.

Djamila bit her tongue. They all needed a break. Emotionally. Intellectually. Physically.

Ophiuchi would be perfect to take her boots off and sit next to a nice fire in the evening, possibly with a mug of rum and hot chocolate.

She needed it.

"No," Djamila said, looking for confirmation from Afia and Zakhar. "Let's go."

Javier liked the resort that Bethany had found for them. Five dozen cabins, each arranged in clusters of six around a central campfire pit, with a main building over near the landing lot where you could pick up whatever you'd forgotten to bring. Or have someone else cook you dinner.

Not that he cooked much, living on a ship with his own, personal French Bistro, but it would make a nice change to have peasant food. Simple stuff.

The basics.

This particular stretch of *Ophiuchi* was something of an alpine uplands that Afia compared to her home in the Yukon Protectorate. To him, images of a Swiss spring came to mind, looking at an even mix of evergreen and freshly budding deciduous every direction. Lots of undergrowth.

Maps had a couple of lakes connected by various rivers and streams, none of them particularly warm at this elevation, but he didn't need jungle. Had, in fact, put his foot down when Bethany had first found him a tropical resort on a northern sea shore with all the damned jungle he could have wanted.

And the need to inspect his shoes for critters before putting those boots on each morning.

He'd had enough scorpions for one lifetime, thank you.

Air was a nice, crisp ten degrees today. Mostly overcast. Threat of rain later. Snow on the higher elevations in the distance, and a few patches deep in shade.

Just about perfect.

He had on a sweatshirt he'd picked up on...somewhere. College sportsball team doing sportsball stuff plus a number. Not like he cared, as long as it fit and kept him warm. Couple of layers underneath, because they'd had to hike a fair distance from the starport to a local taxi after Del had dropped them off and gone back to the ship.

At least the gear had been delivered when they got here. He was getting too old for a backpack retreat.

Better to have Suvi fly some heavy-duty cargo drone from point to point, carrying heavy shit for him.

The Gun Bunnies took up three of the cabins. Djamila had a fourth with Sascha and Hajna in a fifth. Him in a sixth, possibly with Afia crashing here as he had two beds and a fold-out, depending. Eventually, they'd overflow to take up two more clusters, but the owners of the place had been thrilled to have guests in a spring off-season and had made Bethany one hell of a deal if she wanted to reserve the whole place.

Might, so he'd taken it. Kept the riffraff out. The other riffraff.

Javier had just gotten his boots off and poured himself a finger of some local hooch to toast the start of his vacation when his comm let out that godawful screech that indicated an emergency alert intended to wake a sailor from a drunken stupor and have them halfway to their station before their brain locked in and began to process.

Even after all these years, Javier dropped the glass on the hardwood floor and went for his comm with one hand and his pistol with the other.

The joys of a life of piracy. And other stupid pursuits.

Suvi appeared on the screen, but it was a recorded message. Burst transmission from orbit. He recognized the signs.

"Don't have long to talk," she announced. "Trouble is even at this moment coming out of jump in some sort of ambush box and I'm about to get crazy. Based on numbers and transponders, they know who we are and where to find us. I have identified Walvisbaai Industrial, H & W Heavy Industries, the Belfast Group Holdings, and Jarre Foundation warships operating in close concert. You should assume ground forces headed your direction and take evasive action immediately. I'll be back for you, but I'm not sure when. Love you lots."

The Dragoon kicked the door in, which was stupid because he hadn't locked it, but he understood where her brain was at this moment. He'd gone the same way and they had pistols pointed at each other for a second before he nodded and holstered his.

"You heard?" he asked, confirming.

"We have to move," she replied.

"Lucky we're mostly packed," he agreed. "Afia headed up front getting last minute supplies, or has she left?"

"She's buying a few things for now," Djamila said. "I'll task her with picking up some food we can eat immediately, before getting into the food packs in our gear. Plus cans of things for later."

"Deep woods survival training gone a shade too realistic?" he asked, feeling better that whichever dumbshit had pulled this stunt hadn't waited until they had more crew down here and folks scattered all to hell.

Not that it mattered much, since Suvi never left the ship and there would always be a command-grade officer present. Either him, Zakhar, Piet, or Mary-Elizabeth.

But if they were attacking in orbit, there was indeed a high probability of them dropping commandos in order to take prisoners.

"We were prepared," Djamila said simply. "You and Afia will be earning your badges."

He hated the sound of that. Too much like basic training a lifetime ago, when they'd dropped his ass on an island for a week and expected him to survive. At least he had already known how to hunt for geoducks. Nobody had expected him to gain weight that week.

More the fools them.

"How long until we depart?" he asked, quickly scanning his room and locating his boots.

Spare clothing. Some electronics so he had something to read. Not much else.

"Ten minutes," she announced, pulling a folded-up something from her pocket and handing it to him.

Then she was gone.

It turned out to be a backpack, once he got it open. He opened his larger bag and crammed things in with an eye towards needing to be warm and dry later.

Trouble had found them on *Ophiuchi*.

How?

THE HUNTED

PART I

Suvi never slept. It was a function of being a *Sentient* warship in service, going back to her time as a Probe-Cutter with a number. Not even a name. Just her and Captain Ulfsson against the galaxy. At least until Dad had saved her from the wrecker. And given her a name.

Now, she was upgraded. First-Rate Galleon, rebuilt and *improved* by someone with a lot of money and few scruples about keeping her boyfriend safe. It was still a little weird to think of Behnam Sherazi as her step-mom, but Suvi didn't mind. She kept Javier smiling in ways that none of the folks in Suvi's current crew could manage.

What's that?

A flicker of movement in her mind as two ships came out of jump. Bracketing her. Light-speed wave arrival announced Jarre Foundation, Zakhar's old bosses, and H & W Heavy Industries. One of the *other* pirate clans.

Chances of them both arriving randomly at the same moment were right up there with Suvi's JumpDrive spontaneously turning into a cash register. Two more ships appeared a flicker later. Not quite a box, but close enough.

Surrounding her on all sides.

Lucky for everyone, she thought at a speed that Humans simply weren't prepared to comprehend, let alone match. To them, an eyeblink. To her, almost twenty minutes of research and analysis.

Suvi brought everything fully online from standby. Didn't bother with the weapon systems or torpedoes, because eight more blips had appeared in the last tenth of a second.

Pretty damned tight timing for an attacking fleet, so they must have staged out about a light-hour then synchronized clocks and programmed a timer-jump.

And it was an attacking fleet. Belfast Group Holdings warship. Oh, there you are, Walvisbaai.

Everyone has come to play, haven't they?

Zakhar had the bridge, having just relieved Piet. Folks taking some extended downtime in orbit, even as Javier and Djamila had gotten to the resort and were probably settling in.

Pity that she was about to ruin their day off, but trouble never slept. And had apparently snuck up on them at *Drako III*, though they really hadn't been maintaining the sorts of Operational Security that one might in this situation.

Not that many First-Rate Galleons left in service these days, with folks who could afford it building the new Warmasters instead.

Good thing she'd been upgraded from a II to almost a III, based on the theoretical designs Djamila had recovered from whoever had stolen them from the *Concord* in the first place.

Nothing had dropped into her frame of reference that she couldn't take. Except that there was a whole, flipping fleet of them, boxing her on all sides and probably already getting twitchy to do something, as soon as Human reflexes could catch up with machine speeds.

She had less than a second at this point before someone lit her up with targeting scanners and fired torpedoes. Swiveled their turrets around and opened up with everything to bash down her shields and maybe start ripping hunks off her hull.

Some asshole had calculated the technical meaning of *overkill*, then built in a fifteen percent margin of error above that.

Shit had just gotten real.

Lucky for her, Dad and Zakhar trusted her. Every other *Sentient* vessel in the galaxy was built with all manner of blockages and lockdowns intended to keep a ship like her from running amok. Because sometimes, something in the hardware broke and shit happened. Look at the loser who'd lived here before her.

Zakhar had put her on her honor to not have anything preventing her from acting, if she determined the need.

That was about to save his life, because in three-tenths of a second, it was going to start snowing outside. If she had to stop and ask permission, he'd probably be just coming up to speed as the first Pulsar bolts started shattering hull plates, before he could order shields raised from navigation deflectors to armor plating. Then a zillion torpedoes starting to lock and slalom down on her.

Suvi considered her options. Took a snapshot of everyone present and composed it for Djamila and Javier. Put together a quick burst transmission and overrode the planetary comm network to deliver it.

They'd be on their own for a time, but Bethany had picked out a spot on the edge of a vast wilderness, once Djamila had requested a proper training ground. Javier and Afia were going to bitch about it, but that beat being captured or killed.

There wasn't even time for the message to reach the ground, confirm itself as delivered, then bounce a signal back up to her in orbit, because she had one-tenth of a second for Humans to come into present synch and start trouble.

Lucky for her that there weren't any other *Sentient* ships to face today, so she'd had all that time to scan, plan, and react.

Time to get gone.

Excalibur blinked out of existence.

PART II

Katya blinked in surprise at the image. Like a sudden strobe of light, *Excalibur* had been there for an instant, then gone. Just like that.

"Pilot, what happened?" she demanded.

Anton Kovachev was bashing fists on his screen and cursing.

"They were there," he snarled. "All lined up for a Pulsar broadside. Then gone. How the hell did they do that?"

Katya nodded. She had theories, but her crew didn't need to hear her speculate.

"Scan for them," she replied. "Assume an emergency jump and calculate where it landed."

She turned to her Gunner next.

"Mihail, contact *Blackstone* and *Obsidian Hawk* and update them," she ordered. "When Anton has a plot, we'll transmit it and move most of the squadron out. Send a note to *Para Bellum* to deploy their troop carriers. We've got spies on the ground that will provide coordinates in flight and we need to drop heavy on whoever it was that was the lead team.

Sources suggest that's usually Navarre and Sykora, with guards, so drop the entire battalion as a force and let Dragoon Naoumov overwhelm them. Move it people!"

Katya sat back in her chair and fulminated at the universe. *Excalibur* was a First-Rate Galleon. That meant *Sentient*. Could it have reacted that quickly to the ambush to flit out before anyone had even gotten a weapon lock?

Not impossible. Nobody knew where Navarre had come from, save that he'd worked closely with Sokolov for years at this point. Legends suggested that *Excalibur* had once been the *Neu Berne* flagship *Hammerfield*, but obviously someone had paid a lot of cash to refurbish the ship, since it was apparently on a long haul across a quarter of the galaxy, supposedly trading.

She'd read the reports of piracy that they'd been involved with along the way, so Katya wasn't fooled.

"Call from someone identifying himself as the flagship," Mihail offered sarcastically. *Obsidian Hawk* in this case.

She located the channel and confirmed encryption before opening it.

Slavkov. Already pissed and bright red, like a tomato with a stem for a chin.

"Where are they?" he demanded.

"They jumped as quickly as we arrived," Katya offered. "Did one of your people sell us out and warn them we were coming?"

Even Katya doubted that, but better to cast aspersions of guilt back in his face before he accused the Jarre Foundation of leaking. They'd been the closest to Sokolov in the old days.

That just meant that they had the rustiest ax to grind on the man today.

Slavkov sputtered to a halt.

"Find them!" he snapped.

"Got a predicted plot," Anton called loud enough for Slavkov to hear. "Serious level of chaos on the jump, moving from this deep in a gravity well, but only two possible valence outcomes above four percent probability."

"Transmit that to the squadron," she ordered, still watching Slavkov's image. "Then order everyone to jump in ten seconds and come out firing."

"Firing?" Slavkov countered, maybe a bit surprised at the vehemence in her voice.

"Last time was a surprise," she reminded him. "This time, they'll know we're coming."

PART III

Javier had done the math and grabbed two cans of beer from the fridge, in spite of the extra weight. Wasn't like he cared if they got charged for it later, because he was pretty sure that whoever came gunning for them was about to drop troops on the resort and he wasn't about to get his damage deposit back later. He just hoped that they had sufficient insurance for invasion and occupation.

Or other acts of an angry God.

Gun Bunnies and Pathfinders had all ascended to that higher plane of existence that almost looked orgasmic on their faces.

Time to go kill shit.

Afia had gotten the same message that he and the Dragoon had, because she arrived with a bag of things that quickly got doled out to the team, then the eleven of them were hightailing it across the quad towards trees. As the shortest person here, Javier was always amazed to watch Afia's legs churn to keep up, but she did. Like him, a backpack loaded her down, but didn't seem to slow her one bit.

A duck, paddling like mad.

From one of the crates, Demyan had produced pistols and belts, so he and Afia were armed like the crazy ones, following Hajna into the brush at something approximating a hard jog. Distance first, on the presumption that anyone landing knew where to start.

Only question would be if they dropped at the airport, a handy clearing in the nearby forest, or did some crazy-ass paratrooper shit right into the resort itself.

Just how pissed were these yahoos at him anyway?

If it was either of his ex-wives, he might have expected orbital strikes as a prelude to occupation forces, so hopefully nobody had tracked down Holly or Fryda as consultants.

The fun part was that they would be entirely out of contact for a time, with the Dragoon collecting his and Afia's comms and tossing them into Faraday cage bags to isolate them until later.

Dumbest thing you could do was call home and let the bad guys triangulate on your signal. At least everyone had been prepared for what was coming, even if the Gun Bunnies had been looking forward to one night in real beds first.

No beds tonight. About six hours of sunlight, depending on cloud deck and mountains. Maybe four.

How far could they go in four hours on a hiking trail?

Farther than one might expect, because he had crazy people setting the pace. And angry people chasing.

Time to haul ass, so he did.

PART IV

Zakhar noted the sudden change of scenery on his screens with a touch of surprise. A bit of consternation. And maybe a bit of insouciance.

"What just happened?" he drawled.

Piet and Mary-Elizabeth were off-duty right now.

Zakhar's screen lit up with a God's Eye View of *Ophiuchi* orbit. And a whole bunch more dots than had been there five minutes ago.

"Trouble," Suvi replied. "We were suddenly the guest of honor at a pirate jamboree. I emergency jumped before anyone could open fire. Sent a note to the folks on the ground. Currently, we are one hundred and eighty degrees around our planetary orbit at the same altitude while I determine how good our foes are."

"That's *Kymni Gauntlet*," Zakhar noted, recognizing one of the dots. "Jarre Foundation's principal enforcer. Battlecruiser by firepower, did you get a scan?"

"Negative, Captain," she replied ruefully. "Elapsed

response time from light-speed wave was exactly one second, and even then I felt like I was pushing my luck."

"No, you did right," he agreed. "That's enoughlocalized firepower to crush even *Excalibur*. You assume they were after us?"

"*Obsidian Hawk*, *Ice Eagle*, and *Fire Wyvern* all fly H & W Heavy Industries flags, sir," she replied. "*Yorrick* is from Belfast Group Holding Company. *Blackstone* is Walvisbaai. The other ships were smaller, and an even-enough mix of those four."

"All the pirate clans, I see," Zakhar nodded. "Well, we always figured that they were that pissed at us for the Land Leviathan and *Nidavellir*. Looks like someone finally put up the cash to do something about it. What is your status, Yeoman?"

"Operating outside normal parameters, Captain," she said, turning formal. "Standing emergency orders have been stretched to the utter limit here, but flight was necessary to protect the crew."

"Exactly…" he started to say when she interrupted.

"Stand by," Suvi called. "More signals coming out of jump. We've been tracked again. Departing."

And they vanished.

PART V

Suvi had ramped up the paranoia three notches already. Not the sort of party a nice, nerdy girl like her felt comfortable at, when every skeevy weirdo was going to be hitting on her.

Only half the punks showed up this time, but that was a matter of guessing where she'd gone, and somebody over there knew their business.

More ragged coming out this time. Not boxing her in clean, nor all dropping at once. Still, more of them than she could handle, especially if the other half were less than three light-seconds away.

For a flash, she considered dropping some torpedoes, just to make the brush-off clear, but didn't figure she should be wasting ammunition right now, even to express her pique.

Instead, she jumped. And started the process of arranging all of her turrets on different facings, so she could take a few potshots at those punks the next time she saw them.

Suvi had no doubts that this had just turned into a fox hunt.

Then she was alone.

Well, not alone. She had Zakhar in command. And had already sent a crew alert. Folks were scrambling out of beds, showers, or wardrooms to get to wherever they needed to be when all hell broke loose.

This was the first time since *Surayya* that it had been anything more than a drill. And that had been pirate bullshit, too, except for the part where Javier pulled a fast one to destroy an entire crop of pirates and make the galaxy a better place.

"As you were saying?" she prompted.

The best part about having Zakhar in command was that he listened. Understood the situation. Only then did he issue orders.

Much as she loved Javier, he still tended to shoot from the hip too much.

Zakhar watched the new screens and digested details, his mouth moving ever so little as she watched him count and name things under his breath.

"Jump immediately to your next destination," he ordered. "Then plot three more, randomly, based on the first three chords of Piet's latest symphony, and execute them as quickly as the drives can recharge."

Suvi actually had to blink at that. Then call up Piet's files. THEN figure out how to take three First Violin opening chords and turn them into navigational data. Took almost a tenth of a second, but she had something.

At least she thought so.

Then the logic of his craziness hit and Suvi smiled.

She had no idea where she was going. And didn't care, as long as she didn't hit anything in the crazy chaos of near space around *Drako III*.

Well, she did cheat and modify the math on number three. Mostly to make sure she dropped hard into a blind spot on the far side of *Drako III* from both *Ophiuchi* and *Blue Amsterdam*. Down in tight where nobody could see her and she could do something silly like dive into the clouds if she needed to.

Boom. Boom. Boom. And boom.

She came out with the sun of *Drako's* star on her back. Brighter than hell, but warm on her skin, mixed with the sorts of odd chemicals in *III's* atmosphere that almost made it feel like a bubble bath as she settled in.

"Good enough," Zakhar said with a grin as she updated his boards. "I doubt that they will find us here, at least for now. Have you shut down all external transmitters?"

"Affirmative, Captain," Suvi responded. "We don't even have aft running lights."

"Leave it that way," he nodded.

She watched him study the scan logs. Then he looked up and stared at infinity. Or something. Wasn't anything on her bridge, because his eyes weren't focused.

He drew a breath that felt portentous, then looked back down at her screen.

Javier had talked about it, but Suvi didn't think she'd ever really seen it happen before. Or maybe he'd just never pointed it at *her* before.

Zakhar Sokolov turned on that **Captain thing**, as Javier described it. Suvi automatically snapped to attention, even in her little music hall. Head up. Chin back. Shoulders back. Boobs thrust forward. Spine painfully straight, even as a projection.

Serious shit.

Wow.

"Yeoman, you will confirm that the ship and crew remain at Alert-2 status," he ordered, voice dropping a third until it hit her mind like a beanbag filled with warm ooze. "You yourself will default to War-status-1. I repeat, War-status-1. Confirm those orders."

Suvi paused to take a breath so her voice didn't crack.

"Crew to Alert-2, Captain," she said carefully. "Ship to War-status-1."

She'd never gone there, except in her carefully controlled training scenarios.

Zakhar had just unlocked her to do anything she felt necessary in order to preserve the vessel as a fighting unit, up to and including the loss of the entire crew if she felt it necessary.

War crimes had been committed by ships with stricter rules of engagement in place.

She had none. Nothing at all to stop her.

Absolutely frightening as hell.

"Send a message to reroute senior officers to the forward wardroom," he continued, voice more like a laser drill barging its way through an asteroid than a man speaking. "We will have a strategy meeting shortly, where we will begin by reviewing the last...seven minutes of real time operations, while we plan out what we will do to rescue crew currently trapped on the planet. And what we will do about the enemy fleet that is currently blockading the planet. Yeoman, you have command until relieved by a qualified senior officer."

Suvi sat there with her mouth hanging open as he unbuckled and rose from his station, then climbed down from that command throne and exited the bridge.

Man. Talk about making an exit.

She shook her head once, to get her shit more or less back together, then started working her way through all the contingency notes related to turning *Excalibur* into a Goddess of War.

It was about to get messy.

PART VI

Afia was used to carrying a lot of weight. She didn't do that silly-ass morning run around the ship with the Dragoon's Gun Bunnies all that often, but she did believe in treating the machines in the gym as a goal rather than an enemy. Javier was the one who would break before she did, though he might simply pass out between steps rather than admit that she'd walked his ass into the ground.

Boy was like that. She loved him anyway.

"Hajna," the Dragoon called quietly. "Current location?"

"Seven kilometers traveled," the tall blonde replied. "Roughly five kilometers as a crow flies. I'd like to get outside a ten-kilometer ring as quickly as possible, in case they move fast enough to hit the resort looking for us."

"Break here," Djamila said. "Galal, climb a tree and read the sky with passive sensors for enemy forces. Demyan and Tom stand by with SAMs deployed."

Afia shook her head, but didn't say anything. Surface to Air Missiles. Small and fast. Launched out of tubes those two boys immediately extended on their shoulders facing opposite directions as everybody else went lateral to get the hell out of the way of backblast if they fired.

Might bring down Del's Nameless Assault Shuttle if they hit just right. Anything smaller would be terminally wounded.

Afia started to squat, then flipped forward onto her knees and stretched out the tops of her feet instead. At least she still had the good boots on for this sort of terrain. Tomorrow, she might have been in nothing but a skirt, depending.

Everybody else thought it was chilly around here. None of them were from the Yukon Protectorate. Positively balmy to her. Probably actually gonna drop close to freezing tonight, though.

She pulled out a canteen and drank some water. There would be streams and ponds along the way, and they had treatment to kill anything growing, so the best place to store water was inside her body for now.

Galal went up the tree like a squirrel, then parked his butt in a crotch and pointed a handheld scanner at the sky, rotating through.

"Dragoon, we have trouble inbound," he called down. "Picking up at least four shuttles dropping in a linear formation that puts them down close to the resort parking lot, depending on how they handle deployment."

"How big?" Djamila replied.

"Assuming infantry scoped to environment, possibly as many as six hundred troops," Galal said. "That assumes no vehicles and minimal gear."

"Dial that down to four hundred," Djamila said. "They didn't know where we were going until they arrived, because we only knew in the last fifty hours. Standard infantry with some training, but not specialized mountain troops. Lock in with at least one command post and three to five company-level bivouacs."

"Call it four, Dragoon," Galal replied. "I confirm four large shuttles coming in at high speed. They look identical by class and lifting capacity."

Afia felt the tall chick's eyes on her and looked over.

"We'll need to move rapidly to get outside their expected ring," Djamila said simply.

"As long as I can rest later," Afia nodded. "Can burn up a lot of energy now, then crash. I presume you'll start full guerrilla tactics tomorrow?"

"I doubt that they'll be deployed and organized enough for that in less than three days, unless someone went and hired a proper mercenary army," Djamila grinned. "In that case, they might have put troops in place quietly and jumped us on arrival at the resort. This feels more like an ambush sprung as soon as they knew where we'd stop, after chasing us across space."

"*Concord* finally pissed enough?" Afia asked. "I know Suvi said all the pirate clans come for our souls, but would they gather that kind of fleet, this close to *Concord* space?"

"I'm guessing that they all gathered individually," Javier spoke up. "Looking at what Suvi sent, you've got four flagships up there, so somebody hired all four clans to throw a party."

"Four?" Afia asked, turning to look at him.

Man was in better shape today than when she'd met him. Aging like a fine wine she'd been planning to enjoy a bit of in a new bed. Sweaty right now, in spite of the chill, but he had that hardness in his eyes that got her motor running.

"Went back and looked at Suvi's notes.," he nodded. "*Kymni Gauntlet* from Jarre. The folks they would have sent after *Storm Gauntlet* back in the old days, had Zakhar gotten crossways with his bosses. Based on signals intelligence, throw in *Blackstone*, *Obsidian Hawk*, and *Yorrick*, all flying squadron leader transponder codes. Or something similar. Four chefs in the kitchen instead of one. Hopefully, Suvi can take advantage of that."

"Can we?" Afia asked.

"I'd be surprised if they all brought ground troops," Djamila interrupted. "Four identical shuttles suggests one vessel configured as a troop transport. Possibly the sort of thing where you drop hard on a target city or station, in order to capture all the wealthy folks for ransom later."

"Not that we ever did anything like that," Afia grinned.

Javier grinned back. The Dragoon actually blushed, which surprised her.

Of course, they'd been in the pirate business. And sometimes that had involved capturing folks and selling them on as labor force to farming communities or mines, where they could work off a debt.

For those folks who didn't have a big ransom in the bank already.

Javier would have gone down that path, but for his ability to fast-talk with the best of them.

"So, ground troops that know what they are doing, but probably not configured for alpine assault," Javier said. "What does that gain us?"

"Predictability." Djamila's smile turned utterly feral as Afia watched. "We can get outside their control, then sneak back when they start chasing us, scouting their ground operation and determining how much damage we can do to it."

"Eleven of us against four hundred?" Afia asked.

"Seems fair," Djamila nodded. "They can probably get

reinforcements from orbit if they remain in place long enough. And suffer sufficient casualties."

"We expecting to get ugly on them?" Afia asked.

"That is up to them, pipsqueak," Javier said abruptly. "If they came hunting *Excalibur*, then they are also coming after Navarre. That name means something. And I intend to remind them of that."

Afia couldn't help but shiver at that tone.

Javier was gone.

Eutrupio Navarre squatted next to her now.

Harder. Colder.

MEANER.

Them boys had just opened a can of worms and not realized it.

Or not been prepared for how quickly Suvi and Djamila could react in an emergency.

Afia nodded. Combat Engineer time.

And, she reminded herself when the scar across her belly twinged as she shifted, she did owe Walvisbaai for opening fire on an escape pod and nearly killing her, but for Ilan Yu turning into a hero the first time.

"I did not bring sufficient explosives for combat operations," Afia announced quietly. "Nor enough raw materials to construct the same."

"Lucky for you that I did," Djamila smiled. "You never know when the beavers are going to get out of hand."

She held a hand down and literally lifted Afia in the air to stand up. Javier unfolded on his yoga legs and Afia took a deep breath of pine needles and spring rains.

Yup, time to go get stupid out there.

THE HUNT

PART I

Marine Dragoon Benedict Naoumov studied the immediate terrain and scowled sufficiently that the senior officers around him all flinched.

Nobody had listened, up in orbit, when he'd laid out that Djamila Sykora had once been a member of the Dragon Watch, a *Neu Berne* Assault Marine and one of the deadliest people he'd ever encountered.

Or rather, they had politely nodded, patted him on the head, then ignored his advice to put ground troops in place on the surface before launching any orbital ambush.

From Group Leader Anton Marte's report, they'd missed their targets by seventy-three minutes, based on the one woman being in the room with a shopkeeper up front at the moment an alert had sounded.

"Seventy-three minutes?" Benedict confirmed.

"Aye, sir," Marte nodded. "I'm reasonably certain that we came out of jump at that moment. I still don't understand how they were able to react that quickly."

Benedict nodded. He had four good Group Leaders, but

they'd all gotten soft without realizing it. Slack. Too many operations against civilians who didn't put up much fuss when you had a hundred guns pointed at them suddenly.

He could see the need for a serious break in operations, in order to spend two months in a desert or something after this. They'd blunted that fine, killing edge at some point, and only realized it when they ran into something they couldn't cut.

Benedict paused to take a breath, rather than take it out on these four. They were the Group Leaders running the assault teams, and he needed them sharp.

"We are dealing with elite combat troopers, Marte," Benedict replied. "At least as good as anyone under your command. At LEAST. Since the resort is otherwise empty and apparently paid for, we will establish a primary command post in the parking lot and sleep rough. Each team will take up a cardinal point on the compass, clockwise from north, and fortify against infiltration and assault. There are a few hours of daylight left, then they will go into laager. Scouts will deploy immediately. Take half of your teams and have them aboard the shuttles for hot drop when a target is located. We want prisoners, but not at any cost. The other half have base duty tonight and we will rotate in the morning. MOVE!"

The four Group Leaders took off at a run, no doubt happy to get away from his rage. He turned to Arla Ancher, his Command Troop Leader. Noted the sly look on her face.

"Thoughts?" he asked in a quieter voice, noting that only the Command Troop—his bodyguard, really—remained close, as the rest of the force started answering orders and moving. Sandbags. Lights. Gun nests. Tarps.

Tents would go up later, once a perimeter was secured.

And the resort was remote in such a way as to ensure privacy and quiet. Exactly wrong for base security. Fortunately, it was also at the end of a road, so he could chop down some trees and build a command post off to one side, which some enterprising soul might turn it into a general store or something after he left.

Assuming he didn't burn everything to the ground later.

"We have two options, Commander," Arla noted, constantly looking over his shoulder like she expected a sniper or attack. He was no better. "If they run, we might not be able to track them down, given the scope of the wilderness surrounding us. At that point, we have to stay on top of things in case they call for extraction."

"Alternatively, they decide to come back after us," Benedict countered. "That's why we'll be half and half, instead of sending two full teams out and holding two. Folks are more likely to work to save their team, in spite of everyone being on the same side here."

"What do you need?" she asked.

"Skip the command post and go straight to digging a bunker over there," he said, pointing to a spot outside the resort along the ground road to approach. "Clear back some, but not all that far. Drop trees and drag them into a box we can use for cover, then get a roof tarped over it and a floor to keep us dry. We might get lucky tonight and the scouts get a trail we can hound, but we need to be prepared for a week or ten days on the ground."

"We gonna be in place that long?" she asked.

Benedict could see the others get a little twitchy at that thought, too. They were used to lightning raids. In and gone in twelve hours at most. Long before the cops could arrive to try to arrest anyone.

"The money folks have made arrangements with the local power structure," Benedict told them. "As long as we keep everything contained up here and don't bother the natives, they'll leave us alone."

She didn't seem convinced, but Benedict hadn't been surprised himself. Of course, the alternative had been a pirate fleet that felt the need to maybe take over your whole government for a month, holding hostages and causing a lot of grief.

Easier this way, if everyone ignored one another.

"Git," he ordered, turning once in place to study the trees.

And wondering how long it was until they developed eyes.

PART II

Katya was back in her office. Fortunately, this command staff meeting was entirely virtual, so she didn't have to smell the others using up her life support resources. And could dial down the volume when Slavkov went off on another one of his tirades. This one was just about done now, but it had taken him a bit to get it all out of his system.

"Where can they be?" he finally demanded.

"We have about forty options identified," Katya replied. "Under normal circumstances, we could quickly patrol all of them until we located that ship. However, given the situation, it is more important to maintain the formation where we can support one another. A ship like *Obsidian Hawk* would be fairly quickly annihilated if you ran into *Excalibur* by yourself, Slavkov. That doesn't gain us anything."

Well, if she was being honest, it would shut him up. Man had an impossible amount of personal money in the bank, but all that had done was to turn him into a petulant child, constantly whining when the wine was served a few degrees too warm for his exquisite palate. Or some bullshit.

Valko Slavkov, near as she could tell, had never once in his life gotten his hands dirty. He had people for that. At least he was paying well for *Kymni Gauntlet*'s services today.

"Captain Velichkov," Cunningham broke in before Slavkov could get going again. "What about sending half the force as a fleet? With the other half ready to support as quickly as a signal could be sent? What is the gap we're estimating?"

"Given that we can't find any scan evidence of them after several relatively short jumps, you have two options," Katya replied. "One: they bolted and are currently light-hours away. Given that there was a force on the ground supposedly including Navarre and Dragoon Sykora, I don't see them abandoning their comrades. They may be trying to wait us out, underestimating the project budget to keep this force in place."

"And two?" Cunningham asked.

At least he was polite. Not that she'd ever want to go to work for Walvisbaai, but they did run a more professional shop than H & W. Or Slavkov was just that big of an asshole.

"Two, that last jump put them into a shadow somewhere, as seen from *Ophiuchi* orbit," Katya nodded. "As I said, perhaps forty such places to scan and confirm, given the number of large moons and navigational hazards around *Drako III*. Additionally, we don't have any sort of scout available, so we'd have to get pretty close to *Excalibur* to identify it. That means a large number of ships supporting one another."

"And leaving *Ophiuchi* orbit potentially unguarded in the process," he nodded back. "*Blackstone* can provide a bombardment platform that will force even a Galleon to withdraw, so let us look at a division of forces that can handle patrol duties while the ground forces work, shall we?"

Yeah, she could see why Walvisbaai was generally one of the biggest clans, if folks like Kliment Cunningham were in charge. Man didn't let his emotions get in the way of the job. Unlike that fat slob still complaining that someone had stolen his land yacht and blown it up.

Katya didn't approve of what Sokolov and Navarre had done, but she was willing to admit that it had been as professional an operation as any she'd seen in forty years of piracy.

Kymni Gauntlet had her work cut out.

PART III

Zakhar studied the group. Piet and Mary-Elizabeth, plus Bethany and Suvi. Missing Afia and the others, but they were here in spirit. He just had to find a way to get back to the planet to retrieve them without getting his ass shot off in the process.

He had no doubts that Djamila was up to the task of keeping everyone alive on the surface until he got there.

"Yeoman, bring everybody up to speed," he ordered, sipping a mug of coffee and listening with fresh ears as she detailed things, answering questions from the others.

"From there, we dropped low into the shadow of *Drako III* itself, as seen from *Ophiuchi*," Suvi finished up after several minutes. "We are low enough that we cannot be seen easily at present. Radio silent on all frequencies. At some point I expect them to come looking for us."

Piet, surprisingly, spoke first. Zakhar had expected Mary-Elizabeth to be all blood and glory. She was his Gunnery Centurion for a reason.

"How do we go about picking them off?" he asked

simply. "One by one, without getting ourselves shattered in the process."

Zakhar had been thinking about nothing else for the last twenty minutes.

"If they spread out to patrol, we could pounce," he pondered. "I doubt that we could kill anyone before they fled or called for help, but we could damage them sufficiently to force a withdrawal. They don't have any repair facilities that they could call on around here. Yeoman, did they bring anything like a salvage cruiser with them?"

"Negative, Captain," Suvi replied. "All warships of one flavor or another. How long will they stay on station?"

And that was the rub. How much investment did a fleet like this represent, taken away from whatever smuggling, raiding, or other piracy they might be normally engaged in? What was this operation doing to reduce piracy in this sector for the quarter?

He smiled at that. It was all business.

"Bethany," he turned to the woman, "what's the overall capital outlay we're likely looking at here?"

Took her a second. Mostly translating that into something she could internalize as a question. Extremely sharp woman. Smart, too. He'd had his doubts originally, hiring a Ship's Librarian. A few ugly arguments with Javier behind closed doors.

Zakhar found that he was glad he'd lost that argument as she turned to Suvi and started a series of questions so esoteric that he hardly followed the language those two spoke.

Bethany listened, did some more math in her head, and quoted him a figure that had Piet whistle quietly.

"That much?" Mary-Elizabeth demanded.

"Someone had to hire all those ships," Zakhar reminded

them. "And do so from all four of the biggest clans, all of whom loathe one another with a deep and abiding hatred. And mistrust, because they are the competition. Any one of those ships they might lose is a massive capital loss. Everyone not doing things today would normally reflect on someone's quarterly reports."

"Who hates you or Javier enough to spend that kind of money?" Bethany asked.

Zakhar joined the others in a quiet laugh.

"I can get you a list as long as your arm," he said. "However, most of them don't have access to that level of resources that they could assemble something like this. And it wasn't the *Concord*, working through spies or something, because they would have dropped a sledgehammer of a fleet on this system if they had a chance to cripple all four clans at once."

"That only really leaves one person, then," Piet noted.

Zakhar nodded. Grinned.

"I wondered when he'd finally get off his ass," Zakhar replied. "Looks like he managed it."

"Who are we talking about?" Bethany asked in that curious, information-storing, librarian voice.

"Slavkov," Mary-Elizabeth said.

"Ah, the Land Leviathan," Bethany nodded. "Does he really have that kind of money?"

"He does," Suvi offered. "Here."

She projected a series of charts and notes, so obviously the woman had been tracking the man in the background. Probably expecting something like this eventually.

He saw Javier's hand in that, too.

Never turn your back on an enemy, no matter how far away from him you might get.

Bethany whistled this time.

"What does it get us, knowing who might be behind it?" she asked after a moment.

"Narrows down his goals," Zakhar replied. "Eliminates ambiguity."

"Because he wants all of you dead, and not just in prison?" she pressed.

"Oh, I'm sure there are a handful of us he'd like to torture to death personally," Piet acknowledged, then turned to Zakhar. "Make sure we aren't taken alive, boss."

"Agreed," Zakhar said. "I have put Suvi on War-status-1 at present. Suvi, make sure that they don't take us alive, those officers who were present at *Nidavellir*. I don't know if his wrath would extend to Bethany, since she joined us later."

"Not taken alive?" Bethany probed. "What does that imply?"

"It means that I might blow myself up if it came to that," Suvi assured her. "Without prior authorization from anyone, because Zakhar has put me at War-status-1. Technically, I don't have to listen to orders from any of you at that point, until someone inserts the proper authorization codes to bring me back down to something closer to sane and reasonable."

"If I didn't trust you, Suvi, we wouldn't be here," Zakhar reminded her. "Write that on a note and tape it to the side of a monitor to remind you."

"Done," she nodded. "What do we do if this really is Slavkov?"

"Bring me up a list of ships and flag them," Zakhar ordered. "Color code by clan. I'm looking for H & W Heavy Industries. They were the ones that punk Valko was most closely associated with, back in the day. He originally hired Walvisbaai to try to cover his tracks. That, and provoke a war between them and Jarre. Almost worked, too, except that we had two wild cards nobody was prepared for."

"What?" Bethany asked.

"*Hammerfield*," Zakhar gestured to the room. "And the Science Officer."

They all nodded. Javier had saved all their butts more times than anyone felt comfortable admitting, but had done so by risking his own.

"Here are your target vessels," Suvi said. "Looks like this squadron of Raider-scale boats are the most likely targets."

Zakhar studied them. *Ice Eagle* and *Fire Wyvern*, plus *Obsidian Hawk* flying the flagship colors for H & W.

"You think he's dumb enough to actually take the field?" Mary-Elizabeth asked in a voice that could best be described as *hungry*.

"I think he might be angry enough," Zakhar corrected. "This pirate fleet is a lot of money, spent on nothing but revenge. Would you trust that pirates took that kind of cash to come back with a report? Remember, Bethany has calculated a rough daily outlay, just to hire this tonnage. Speculation on my part, but grounded."

"And I concur that nobody else hates us enough to hire four clans," Piet said. "One, and it might be anybody. Four limits things closely."

"So how do we take advantage of that?" Bethany asked.

"Suvi, mark *Obsidian Hawk* as a technical number two priority target," Zakhar said formally.

"Aye, sir."

"What's that?" Bethany pressed.

"I'll shoot at anyone who gets close," Suvi replied. "However, given three vessels, I will always try to take shots at

Obsidian Hawk, possibly ignoring someone closer depending on what they are doing."

"Risky," Mary-Elizabeth noted.

"Even if we escape today, nothing stops that man from coming after us again later," Piet acknowledged. "We can run hard back to *Altai* with them chasing. Would he try something like this after we got home?"

Zakhar smiled that everyone considered *Altai* home these days. The only home most of them had known in decades.

"Considering that the Khatum's fleet rivals the *Concord* for mass and sophistication, I'm less concerned," Zakhar nodded. "More likely he has to hire assassins at that point instead."

"Against people Farouz Jashari has trained?" Mary-Elizabeth laughed and laughed and laughed.

Zakhar shared her sentiment. Another one in a select league that included Djamila. Some of the most dangerous hand-to-hand combatants in the galaxy.

"So we're on the defensive for now?" Bethany asked the group, looking around.

"Only until they start looking for us," Zakhar smiled at the woman. "That's when the dance truly begins."

"*Svalbard*, all over again," Piet offered.

"Exactly," Zakhar agreed. "And since we don't know how long until we have to do something, everyone rotate watch shifts and stay close to the bridge, in case Suvi has questions or needs help."

Not that she did, but Zakhar understood that his favorite Yeoman was a little nervous at being given *carte blanche* to work. And an upgraded First-Rate Galleon to do it with.

"Let's go rescue our people," he ordered.

PART IV

Djamila studied the foliage. The team was utterly radio silent right now, with everything that could transmit stored in bags specifically insulated to hide them. The guns could be detected, but if you were close enough to do that, you were close enough to see them, unless everyone was well-hidden.

At which point the boys would open fire with everything they had and introduce amateurs to what *superior firepower* really tasted like.

The girls had been swapping off lead position, since pathfinding at speed took a lot of emotional energy. Hajna was on point at the moment, but they'd taken another short break.

Easy to cover a lot of ground if you went hard for a time, soft for a time, then stopped dead for a few minutes. Javier and Afia weren't ready to run a marathon, let alone the sort of ultramarathon Djamila might have undertaken in this situation, were this a solo excursion.

"Current straight-line distance to base?" Djamila asked.

Sascha squinted at an invisible distance.

"Eleven and a half kilometers," she offered. "Possibly closer to twelve, depending on that one stream we crossed then followed. Couple of switchbacks in there got a little hinky."

Djamila nodded. Outside of the immediate range that trouble would be able to get to them on the ground. That meant that it was time to start watching the skies for someone scanning the ground with equipment that might see them as something other than a herd of elk moving about.

And there were large ungulates in here, but the team was making quite a bit of noise moving around, partly to scare them off. Anything like a bear appearing and folks would simply open fire, because it might be a young male trying to establish territory, and thus aggressive.

Or it might be a mother with cubs, in which case it would likely turn homicidal in a hurry.

Better to chase them off ahead of time. She could always send the girls off to kill a deer to eat if they got hungry in a week, but they had food packs sufficient for today.

"Tom, I need a skywatch while we're still," she ordered, watching the boys immediately shift around duties as Tom found a bit of a clearing and pointed a handscanner up.

"How far is safe enough to build a camp of some sort?" Javier asked, so at least he understood that they had to get deep quickly.

"Ten was my inner minimum," Djamila replied. "Twenty would be possibly an outer, but the terrain is heavy enough that I doubt any ground troops can get to us quickly."

"Unless someone inserts them via shuttle," he nodded. "We're fresh, so we can push today. I presume you'll want to circle back at some point and cause them grief?"

"Were this simply an assassination attempt on the ground, we'd have outrun them and vectored Del down for extraction," she told him. "Since they brought a fleet to attack *Excalibur*, I need to presume that they are planning to use us as the trap to keep Zakhar and Suvi close. That means we have to stay out of custody. At the same time, someone needs to pay a price for bothering me on my vacation."

His grin was wry, but serious. It had also been Javier's vacation. Possibly Afia's, too. The others had been looking forward to some heavy-duty wilderness training. Just not with this level of verisimilitude to it.

"Patrols by the twenty, fifty, or hundred coming after us?" Afia asked.

Djamila had been doing that exact math for the last hour.

"Twenty we could possibly annihilate so quickly that they couldn't call for help," she told the young combat engineer. "One hundred puts a significant fraction of their overall force in one place, so I doubt that they would do that until they've nailed down our location. Fifty feels like a hammer big enough to be a threat."

"I'm picking up long-range scans on my passive," Tom called. "Four shuttles in the air, scanning the ground pretty hard from about three thousand meters elevation. Two of them are vectored roughly this direction, with the other two lateral to our axis of movement. I presume they had scouts that told them which way we fled?"

"Valid assessment," Galal chimed in. "Do we leave lethal ambush munitions in place? Sounds like they'll get here eventually."

"Other than we left the main trail at the creek," Hajna reminded them. "If they follow the game trail, we're two kilometers north and moving away at a slant. Might even be time to rotate inward and slip back behind their zone of investigation."

"Negative on explosives," Djamila decided. "We lack the electronics to limit detonation to humans setting them off. Plus, there are a lot of creatures pounding this game trail flat that would probably set them off early. Hajna, do we have a way to slip back at this point?"

She watched the two Pathfinders consult with low murmurs, hand waving, and nods.

"This slope is a bit rough with downed trees and heavy brush," Hajna finally said, pointing. "If we make a bit of noise, we should scare off anything small as we scale it. I would expect either some sort of trail running just below the crest, or a path we might follow. Our stream or a tributary should run in the next valley, but I don't remember these two connecting anywhere close."

"Y'all didn't actually bring maps, did you?" Afia asked sarcastically.

Djamila shrugged.

"That rather defeats the purpose of the original exercise," she reminded the woman. "Plus, we could always activate electronics to triangulate our exact location if necessary."

"Some of us don't do crazy shit for fun, you know," Afia grinned.

Pixie Kodiac. That was her nickname. It fit. Tiny of body. Immense spirit.

Djamila watched her swing her backpack around and pull out a bundle of paper.

"Ordinance survey hiking map," Afia grinned as she handed it up to Djamila. "One decimeter to the kilometer, because I never intended to get more than about five or ten kilometers from home."

Djamila laughed and handed it to her Pathfinders. They were among the very best, but this had stopped being a training exercise two hours ago and turned into a live operation.

They would need every edge they could get.

Djamila owed somebody for ruining her vacation.

PART V

Suvi hadn't ever tried this stunt before, but she used to be a Probe-Cutter intended for long-range survey work. Had even gotten pretty damned good at it over the years, working with Javier.

Patience was the key. How many times had he explained that to her as they'd worked?

Sit off at the edge of the system, drinking in the faint solar wind and looking for starlight to reflect off things. Then keep watch as they moved, so you could categorize them as planets, comets, asteroids, or maybe people running around. Usually hiding, since Javier had been assigned places that were SUPPOSED to be empty.

Lots of folks out there just didn't like telling folks where to find them. Religious minorities escaping prosecution from someone. Miners that didn't want anyone finding their special place.

People who just wanted to be left alone.

Today, she'd dropped down a bit into the atmosphere of *Drako III* itself. Not far. Not even a threat to her hull. Just low enough that clouds were only a few hundred kilometers below her and gravity was high enough that she had to actually pay attention. No storms around here, but if she stayed put for more than a week, one of those blue eyes could come into view north of her.

Mouse in the cupboard time. And trying a trick. Or rather, proving if it worked.

Every other ship in local space was broadcasting a signal. Usually, it included a location marker, a three-dimensional plot drawn off a zero point over the north pole of *Drako III* itself. Lots of moons running around, plus the faint rings that used to be a pair of moons that had hit each other and gone boom some half a million years ago.

Suvi was so low that she couldn't see hardly anybody. And a lot of folks had scattered when the pirates showed up, so things were quiet.

However, there were a lot of moons around her. And a layer of rings that made a pretty good sounding board.

Surveyor Suvi had put on her cap with the long green bill and started looking for radio reflections off all those rocks. Then washing out noise and echoes. *Blue Amsterdam* was still below the horizon, moving in a complicated dance that orbited a little faster than *Ophiuchi*, but not enough to matter in the next week. *Mauta* was above and behind her, but pretty far out. As long as she stayed quiet, nobody should have a reason to point a scanner at her and ask what she was about.

Time to listen. Helped that the bad guys didn't really like each other, so they didn't talk much. Only those four flagships tended to broadcast powerful signals. And all of them were down orbiting *Ophiuchi* while they tried to figure out what they were going to do next.

How many would start patrolling local space looking for her? That was the twelve-drachma question. And would they do it individually, or in big groups?

She'd only have true surprise once. After that, she would be a ghost haunting an old manor house, with folks alert and staying up all night watching.

Of course, she could use that to her advantage, too. But Zakhar and the others had been pretty certain that the pirates needed to make the first move here.

Then she could pretend to be a great big kitty, pouncing on her first mouse.

Suvi couldn't wait.

THE SHADOWS

PART I

Katya kept her grumbles inside as she watched the others on the screen. And a polite, neutral smile on her face. She might have warned them that gathering up four major pirate clans and having each put in equal forces for this job would be a dumb idea. Nobody had listened. Or rather, they'd listened to Slavkov's coin jingle and lost their flipping minds.

At least she wasn't in charge of anything more than Jarre Foundation forces, and every single one of them would listen to her. Answer to her, because that was her job. Slavkov obviously had no experience at starship command, to say nothing of squadron operations.

And today, they had a full fleet, even if this meeting was just the top people. Her. Slavkov. Cunningham. Geno Goranov off *Blackstone*. Tsvetanka Ivankova, captain of *Yorrick*. *Obsidian Hawk* didn't even rate their own captain attending this meeting, but again, she wasn't surprised.

"You must find them!" Slavkov snapped, circling back to the same lecture like a one-trick pony.

A short, bald, fat, annoying, one-trick pony.

Katya figured that she'd really had enough of the man at this point. When she got home, there would definitely be a note to the bosses to not get involved with this jackass again.

That, or to triple the rates charged, from what they'd already raised things to in order to get there. He had the funds, as far as anyone knew. Let him buy his own damned fleet to do this.

"Admiral Cunningham, I propose that *Kymni Gauntlet* and *Yorrick* lead a squadron out to start our first patrol," Katya managed to say in the moment when Slavkov stopped for a breath. "That puts a serious amount of offensive firepower in place, since *Yorrick* is so heavily tilted towards Ion Pulsars. Especially for being on a frigate-scale hull. Sokolov might not understand how dangerous Captain Ivankova is until it's too late."

Ivankova perked up at that. Probably looking for an insult she could take umbrage at. Woman was like that.

Young. Well, two decades younger than Katya. Late thirties. Brown hair that might still be that color naturally. Katya had long since let hers come in gray. Less hassle. And kept hers short, where Ivankova's was long and wavy.

Hazel eyes on a hard, triangular face that was probably more attractive when she wasn't scowling at everyone. Like now.

Woman had a voice like a rusty ball of steel wool.

"*Kymni Gauntlet* flying on my wing?" Ivankova demanded quietly.

"Something like that," Katya replied. "Except that we probably need *Yorrick* on mine, like an escort. Otherwise, they might figure out how lethal you are before you can nail them. Throw in *Hummingbird* as an escort, plus *Epsilon*

Cavendish for a Raider, and we should be able to hold our own long enough for everyone else to pile on."

"That seems to be a bit light for a patrol, Captain Velichkov," Cunningham finally spoke up. "Are you certain?"

"Bait," Katya offered. "If we're too much to handle, they won't try anything. If evenly matched, they might still hold off. A force this small shouldn't be an obvious threat to *Excalibur*, so they'll jump in and start blasting. *Yorrick*'s Ion Pulsars should do a lot to neutralize them in that case, evening the odds. Assuming we can count on everyone else jumping on thirty seconds notice, Sokolov is in a box. If he jumps, we should be able to calculate pretty accurately where he goes and pursue. If we can keep sniping, eventually we hurt them enough to matter. Not like they can sail into a repair yard around here or anything."

"Nor can we, Captain," Admiral Cunningham reminded her.

"All the more reason to hit hard and fast, sir," she countered.

Cunningham, she respected. Man had come up from the pirate side of things, instead of ground troops or accountants. He knew ships.

They hadn't crossed swords more than a few times in the old days, and nothing in close to two decades now, since he'd been promoted to the administrative side of their clan.

And she was pretty sure he didn't have any old grudges against her. Not that she trusted any of those people as far as she could throw them, but this should be a pretty clean operation.

Now they just had to locate Zakhar Sokolov.

And kill him.

PART II

Javier would never admit it, but nightfall had only barely managed to arrive before his legs had given out. He was getting too old for this shit.

Once he got home, either he needed Behnam to build him a warship so powerful that nobody bothered him again, or maybe he'd just have to admit that it was time to become a homebody.

Maybe turn into an academic with more seriousness.

That, or build one of Suvi's resort designs and turn himself into an innkeeper. That might actually be fun. Sail around in a battleship that just happened to look like a resort. And all the staff just happened to be trained killers certified by the Dragoon and Farouz.

Heh.

Right now, his butt hurt. Legs were doing okay, but that was all the yoga. Kept the body flexible. He had not climbed this many hills in a long, damned time. Starships and stations were flat.

Javier could see Djamila ripping out part of one of the

cargo bays to put in some stupid staircase that spanned like five decks or something, just for the butt work.

He would not, however, ever mention that out loud where she might hear it, if it hadn't occurred to her

"Are we there yet?" Afia asked in her best six-year-old whine, eliciting laughs.

Not far above, a stream was running. In kind of a bowl where a hill wrapped around. Couple of trees had fallen in such a way as to provide a wide Vee that they could put a tarp over and have a shelter big enough for the whole group. Not that everyone would rest, but he didn't have to stand a watch rotation with the Gun Bunnies around. Benefits of being an officer, and all that.

"This is where we will sleep tonight," Djamila announced.

Javier watched the eight explode into motion, six men clearing space and the two babes heading down with collapsed water bottles they would fill to top everyone off.

Javier planted his butt on a handy log and blew out a heavy breath. Considered one of his beers. Went ahead and cracked it. Got one sip before Afia was leaning on his arm making puppy-dog eyes at him. She took a long drink when he handed it to her, then handed it back and sighed.

"Always an adventure," she muttered darkly enough that he snorted at her.

"You'd be bored with a normal job," Javier reminded her.

"Not arguing," she nodded. "Rather not be chased through the damned woods like an elk though."

"Only for now," Javier replied, marveling at how quickly the space was being cleared, in spite of how long he'd known these men.

Machetes and folding shovels made quick work of it.

Iqbal and Heydar had the first tarp unfolded and slung before Javier finished his beer. He carefully held it as he slipped down and got inside. They'd chopped a branch or something as a central tentpole, so he could stand up in here, though Djamila would have to hunch.

Still, nine of them under cover took less than fifteen minutes. And it was cozy. Dry, too, because the clouds had started rolling in in late afternoon and the temperature had dropped enough to presage rain.

If not something worse.

"What's snow do to your plans?" he asked the big Dragoon as she squatted near the opening.

"Little," Djamila replied. "The trees are heavy enough that you'd only get accumulation in clearings for the most part. And the season is late enough that graupel is more likely. Given the average temperature, that would melt off quickly enough not to matter, save for the people caught out in it."

Javier nodded. She'd been planning to haul her team out into this mess and live off the land for two weeks. Only because of those berks in orbit were he and Afia joining them.

"Do we end up splitting into two groups?" Afia asked, leaned against his arm like she was going to steal all his heat. She was like that.

"I have considered it," the Dragoon nodded. "Leave you two in place here or someplace reasonably secured as a base, while the rest of us test the perimeter defenses of the attackers. We can certainly cross terrain faster and cleaner without you along."

"Might not be the worst idea," Javier offered. "You could have one of the ladies come back for us occasionally, just so we don't have to try to strangle a deer or something, but we've got food for a week, assuming the creek is adequate for hydration."

"We'll sleep on it tonight and make plans in the morning," Djamila replied. "Our foes will be aggressive in patrolling today and tonight. By tomorrow, I expect them to begin to shift to a base and patrol mindset that goes defensive overall. And Zakhar will need time to deal with the fleet in orbit."

Javier started to say something, then thought back to some of the things he'd seen that man do, even when they were aboard a Strike Corvette like *Storm Gauntlet*. Today, he had a First-Rate Galleon that had been upgraded a notch or two. And Suvi.

"So we just monitor for them to call?" Afia asked.

"With appropriate code words indicating safety on their part, yes," Djamila replied.

"What do we do if the bad guys win up there?" Afia pressed.

"Either hide down here for a long time, disappearing into the brush, or walk long ways to some town and try to get ourselves smuggled off planet without the pirates finding us," the Dragoon described seriously.

Javier couldn't argue with that.

It wasn't like she was wrong.

PART III

Zakhar had run Piet and Mary-Elizabeth through a watch, hard napping himself after a heavy meal to refuel and reset his internal clock. He didn't know if the clans were running on local time, but the resort where Djamila had been was in the middle of the night right now. Fifteen hours after the original ambush and just enough time for everyone to settle in and start the next phase of their operation.

At least mentally.

Time to relax and maybe do some paperwork. Have a meal. Maybe a glass of wine with it. Or three.

Lose track of the purpose for being here, because whoever had launched this assault had to have been up for a while before they appeared, just in the process of organizing. They had to sleep at some point.

"Yeoman, show me your latest plot of all vessels in local system orbit," he announced, apparently catching Suvi off-guard because she actually paused to blink at him in surprise.

And he knew how quickly she thought with the latest updates to her hardware.

His screens all shifted around, showing *Drako III* centered and a pie-slice of heavens above them marked crisply. Others were shown with various levels of confidence that seemed much higher than he was expecting. Except that the young lady had been a survey scout. And was more than a century old at this point.

Plus, he'd taught her a few tricks even Javier hadn't thought of.

"These numbers seem questionable," he pointed at the screen.

"Navigational data as broadcast by all vessels includes triangulation plots from *Blue Amsterdam*, sir," she snapped crisply.

"This group of pirates appears to be moving out to patrol the local vicinity," Zakhar noted. "Smaller than I expected that squadron to be."

"Baiting us into an attack, sir?" Suvi asked.

"Assuredly, Yeoman," Zakhar nodded. "Add the probability that *Yorrick* is on a par with *Kymni Gauntlet* for lethality, in spite of its size."

She brought up a set of blueprints and ship specs for *Kymni Gauntlet*, rotating them.

"Where did you find those?" he asked, surprised.

"*Storm Gauntlet* had them, sir," she replied. "When you dumped your entire datacore into *Hammerfield*, I was able to access your old logs and records from when you were still employed by the Jarre Foundation. You sailed into harbor with them twice, and stored those logs."

Zakhar rocked back a little in surprise. That had been eight years ago? Something like that. He'd honestly forgotten, but they hadn't actually interacted with the Foundation's flagship. Merely sailed by to deliver stolen cargo.

"Any of the other vessels you recognize?" he asked, intrigued.

"Negative, sir," Suvi sounded disappointed. "*Yorrick* is a frigate by displacement. *Epsilon Cavendish* is a Raider. *Hummingbird* appears to be some sort of Escort."

"And that, young lady, is a trap," Zakhar nodded. "They want us to jump in and start blasting, confident that we can overwhelm them before they get away. Obviously, they are up to something and we probably won't know what until *Yorrick* does whatever they do."

"I could take *Kymni Gauntlet*," she replied. "Even with a Raider and an Escort handy. What radically changes the balance of engagement when you add *Yorrick*?"

"I have no idea," Zakhar replied. "Any number of guesses, but they are only that. You start a file and list ideas that would make *Yorrick* the firepower equivalent of *Kymni Gauntlet*. I'm more interested in *Blackstone*. Mostly because I have never seen a vessel like that before."

She flipped screens around and the new vessel was displayed, rotating in three dimensions.

Long and skinny. Almost perfectly rectangular through most of the body. Squared off corners top and bottom, too, when you could pretty much build your ships into any shape you wanted. And not a freighter, where you did build them cubic to maximize internal cargo space.

And perfectly flat across the top. No, wait, it wasn't.

"Yeoman, pause the display and give me the best image you have that shows the top of *Blackstone*," he ordered sharply.

The screen blinked and he was looking at a tiled floor. Every tile the same color, but the entire length of the vessel was like a cobblestone road, save for paired turrets fore and aft at the extreme ends.

Zakhar closed his eyes and let the image wash over him.

"Yeoman, zoom in on the forward quarter of the vessel and use your best guess to clean up the image," he said quietly.

Didn't take long. Crop and zoom until fuzzy, then the fuzziness started to resolve.

"How's that?" she asked after about four seconds of work.

"Those are launch bays," he said.

"Sir?"

"Vertically launched torpedoes, stacked individually in tubes rather than coming off a rotating magazine rack," Zakhar said. "You can pack them closer. More importantly, you can launch a whole bunch of them at once, rather than cycling them out one at a time."

"Based on extrapolation, I estimate there to be twelve launchers to a single row, and slightly more than one hundred rows, Captain," Suvi acknowledged. "More than twelve hundred torpedoes that they could launch, presumably all at once, but I would assume the need to salvo them in smaller groups to prevent exhaust from damaging subsequent launches and to provide clear flight paths for the torpedoes as they begin tracking on their targets."

"I'd zig-zag down the spine," Zakhar mused. "Bay 1-1, 2-12, 3-2, 4-11, etc., assuming that I wanted to fire one hundred torpedoes at someone. At once."

"There is nothing I could do to stop that many inbound missiles at short range, sir," Suvi admitted after just enough of a pause that he knew she'd spent a significant amount of personal time devising and testing various scenarios.

"Agreed," Zakhar replied.

Then he spotted something with the way the ship itself was laid out and smiled.

"Sir?" Suvi asked warily.

"Bad *feng shui*, Yeoman," he replied. "Here's how we'll take advantage of it."

PART IV

Katya had fortified herself with tea. And a biobreak. And food.

She knew Zakhar Sokolov from the old days, when he'd flown a small combat vessel for the Jarre Foundation. Man had never wanted to be promoted to one of the big enforcers, like *Kymni Gauntlet*, but he'd spent twenty years as an officer with the *Concord* Navy and knew his shit.

Eutropio Navarre was still a wild card, but all of that one's reputation seemed to revolve around ground operations pulled off with stunning audacity and utter precision. The ground teams *Para Bellum* had put down would have their work cut out for them.

She had to hunt a First-Rate Galleon.

"Mihail, stay sharp," she reminded her Gunnery Centurion. "I'm expecting *Excalibur* to drop out of a short jump right in our laps, already firing. Your job is to hold them off until *Yorrick* can ionize the shit out of them. Keep every spare erg of power routed to the shields for now. We can get nasty on them after they're trapped in range."

He nodded, but didn't look up from his screens. Nor did she want him to. Katya knew that she was taking a risk here, but Sokolov had been one of her captains, back in the day. He needed to be punished by Jarre. Even at those risks.

Plus, with the other three flying close escort, she figured that they could wallop the hell out of *Excalibur* pretty quickly. Lame them, or at least hold them in place long enough for the rest of the squadron to pounce. Because everyone over there was just playing possum right now, waiting for the signal to jump in and start firing.

"First checkpoint reached," Anton announced. "Scans are all clear. I have visuals on a number of vessels and can confirm shape against transponder codes. Moving on to second checkpoint."

That had been a concern. That *Excalibur* might suddenly throw up a false flag and start identifying themselves as a freighter wallowing around, pretending to be harmless. You could pull a stunt like that if you stayed out of visual range.

She was simply bait today. Tough. Mean. Deadly. But bait intended to provoke Sokolov into launching a surprise attack.

"Oh, shit!" Anton suddenly barked. "Boss, we've been had."

"WHAT?" she demanded, looking at the back of his head as he listened to some comm on an earpiece and typed furiously.

"They attacked the rest of the squadron over *Ophiuchi*, Katya," he said. "Plotting a jump to get us back, but the drives need to power up first. We're completely out of position to do anything about it."

"Hurry," she ordered quietly.

What the hell had Sokolov done?

PART V

Suvi had gone back and dug into her library for every scrap of data she could find anywhere. Helped that she'd been flying close enough to the outer edges of claimed *Concord* space that they had databases of pirate vessels to watch for. And captains.

Plus, she had Bethany. Her favorite Research Librarian had been collecting all sorts of random stuff at various stops, describing the entire process as trying to fill a bucket with an eyedropper. Lots of raw data. Not a lot of information.

Nothing critically useful, and she could easily update a lot of it as soon as she got out of this situation, but at least she had a better understanding who these yahoos were now.

Para Bellum looked like a troop transport. Djamila's problem for now, but Suvi would presume a ship heavy with Ion Cannon of some sort. You wanted to disable your target if you planned to flood it with boarding troops, rather than blow holes in things.

Similarly, *Blackstone* had all four of those turrets mounted on the top deck. Made perfect sense, if you fought by either pointing your bow at a ship or rotating to give them the entire top broadside without the torpedoes needing to maneuver much before accelerating.

Kinda less useful if somebody bipped out directly underneath you.

So she'd paused and spent nearly twenty minutes of real-time doing the math. Lots of math. Complicated stuff, when you had to derive gravitational variants for this many moons and rocks flying around, on top of the gas giant that messed with everything by dimpling space/time pretty hard.

Still, she thought she had it. Didn't help, doing everything blind, but helpfully everyone was still broadcasting their locations and vectors, and *Blackstone* had parked itself in a geosynchronous orbit directly above Javier's resort. Right in the middle of the pirate fleet defending *Ophiuchi* from anyone who thought that they should have an opinion.

Suvi had opinions, but most of them weren't repeatable in polite company. Fortunately, those pirates didn't qualify.

She looked around her bridge. Noted that Zakhar had ordered Mary-Elizabeth and Piet to go to sleep, taking something if they had to, in order to keep them sharp later. Kibwe Bousaid was in his station, mostly just checking out various feeds, since he wouldn't need to talk to anyone. Still, his presence brought her warmth. Tobias Gibney was handling Science Officer duties, but again, nothing to really do except be there for what was coming.

Later, Kibwe and Tobias would have data to work with, but even Zakhar had purposefully put his hands in his laps as a statement. All of the **everything** he had planned and ordered was going to happen so rapidly that even taking the time to explain it to an organic and get a response back was too long.

She was just happy that ships like her were so damned expensive to build and maintain. None of the pirates had anything *Sentient*. Hell, around here, only the *Concord* did, and those tended to be Warmasters, with all of her old Probe-Cutter cousins completely dismantled and largely forgotten these days.

Like she'd have been if Dad hadn't rescued her.

He needed her today, but Zakhar needed her more.

"Captain, I am ready to execute," Suvi announced to her bridge crew.

Zakhar nodded, face deadly serious for a long moment before he broke into a smile.

"Yeoman, all ahead crazy."

Yes. All ahead crazy.

Suvi jumped.

PART VI

Suvi stepped between points in space/time. And landed within about four percent of her target, which was honestly better than she had been expecting, even over this short of a jump.

Drako III was just a flipping mess of a mini-system, with all those damned planet-sized moons and the rings messing with things.

She'd take every gram of luck she could.

And this exact moment was why she was glad there weren't any of her cousins nearby. Nobody who could react as quickly as she could. Helped that all the ships had stayed static for the last four hours. She had exact coordinates and didn't have to pause and scan nearby space in order to locate and identify her target.

Blackstone was exactly where he'd been before. Camped in orbit like he was watching the ground, except that she knew they'd be watching nearby space for someone to pull a stunt as crazy as this.

Except that a human would have needed about a year to

do the necessary math. And anybody but Javier and Zakhar would have intentionally come out high. Above the squadron, where you had more space to maneuver. And less risks of silly buggers happening when you jumped back out later.

Because there was no way in hell she was going to try to **sail** out of this mess in realspace. That was an invitation for EVERYONE to want to fill up her dance card.

Nope. Today she'd put on the pink polar bear furs and the flying ace cap. Goggles down, even. Red Baron music jamming in the background, because it was going to be that kind of scene.

Blink. *Blackstone* above and slightly ahead. Already centered on every turret that she could bring to bear on a target that close. And she was too close, really, but she wanted everything hitting as hard as possible. Inverse tenth power loss over distance still added up.

And she needed *Blackstone* hurt. Way hurt. If there was any sort of way to copy herself into their systems and order it to fire every single torpedo at once into *Drako III*, she'd have done it.

Alas.

Suvi cut loose with the Pulse Cannons. And the Pulsars. And the Ion Cannons, just for the hell of it. She'd locked down internal bulkheads hours ago, which kept folks to their normal decks, except when the wardroom people needed to feed folks. Chay and Burdine had understood and closed the Bistro for the next couple of days. Or at least until everything was sorted out outside the hull.

Blackstone had his shields up. A man would have to be a fool not to. It slowed her down. Some. Not lots, because she'd gone shark on them, emerging from the dark depths to take a bite of someone's leg. Arm. Whatever.

Y'all are sea lions that need to be buffet, bubba.

Every generator was online. Andreea Dalca didn't like to talk to people much, but got along fine with Suvi. And had actually smiled when Suvi had asked her to tune everything for a red-line moment.

And they were at red. Every system was screaming as it overheated and she couldn't bleed excess energy into nearby space fast enough. Didn't even bother with torpedoes, because those would take nearly a minute to cross the intervening space from a dead stop.

Nope, light-speed trouble. Booms and bangs and zaps.

With soundtrack, natch-yurallie.

First-Rate Galleon against a flying manticore. Or whatever the hell they called that thing. Cruiser size. Shit for beams. A stupidly impossible number of torpedoes if Zakhar was right.

And he probably was. Zakhar was like that.

Scanners finally caught up with her, wavefront bouncing off everything nearby and starting to provide more detail of the things she was already firing at. She'd go back later and actually look at all the data logs, but *Blackstone* needed her undivided attention for the next seventeen tenths of a second. It was enough to know that she was sitting almost in the middle of the posse, with several small ships much higher in orbit and only *Para Bellum* lower.

Not exactly a blind spot, but y'all been looking up, instead of down. A smart captain would have known better, but there's only one Zakhar Sokolov.

Suvi watched her clock timer counting down. And the generators recharging the JumpDrives as fast as they could.

Most ships couldn't do this. They required ten or maybe sixty seconds to generate that much power. Especially if they were firing everything that could fire.

Well, not everything. She could have lined up a couple of the other ships and tattooed them from this distance, but that might have overheated everything too far. Or held her in place too long.

Nope. Hit. And Run.

Four tenths of a second left. Scanners finally showing where she'd been bashing the hell out of *Blackstone*'s keel. Or whatever you called it on a ship that very obviously had a top and a bottom, and the bottom didn't have guns to shoot back at her.

And nobody else was all that close, save *Para Bellum*.

Whoopsie. Probably won't make that mistake again, will you? Or are you that dumb? Hey, a girl can hope.

One tenth. Suvi cut the guns and routed that extra bit of juice into the JumpDrives, then triggered them.

Up, up, and away.

FIRST BLOOD

PART I

Zakhar had tried to follow everything, but understood that organic computers like him simply lacked the bandwidth to process that much data that quickly. Where humans excelled was in pulling together a crazy-wide spread of things and synthesizing them into a coherent whole.

Suvi, for all her raw intelligence and processing power, didn't make fantastic leaps of intuition worth a damn. That was why she needed a crew. And him.

Still, he felt both jumps, understanding that she'd done it all herself, after a brief explanation that merely went over the salient points.

They dropped into realspace for about ten seconds, but she never looked up from her screens, so he didn't bother interrupting her. Sure, she had the extra processing power to split off an avatar and talk, but he'd let her settle back safely.

A third jump and the stars blinked funky, then *Drako III* filled the sky like it had all of about thirty seconds ago.

He waited.

"Think we escaped," Suvi finally announced, looking up and grinning. "*Blackstone* is gonna be a little pissed, though."

"Oh?" Zakhar asked, hands remaining in his lap until he was certain that things were safe.

Sentient warship. He was one of the few folks in the galaxy who understood everything that such a name implied, because only the *Concord* still flew them. Everybody else had gone back to humans as pilots for now, because of the tremendous expense and occasional risk involved with automating things to that degree.

Like *Hammerfield*.

His screens rearranged themselves, showing the vessel *Blackstone* in a diorama view, as well as from the underside and port flank as Suvi had hammered the living shit out of it from short range.

As he watched, dark spots appeared fore and aft.

"You ignored the middle?" Zakhar confirmed.

"Nothing worth damaging there," Yeoman Suvi nodded. "Just racks and rows of torpedo launchers that I could really only hit individually. No, Captain, I focused everything on the two ends, expecting those to contain power and control systems. I wanted him lamed and possibly suffering the shipboard equivalent of a concussion. Think I might have succeeded in that."

"Show me," he ordered, finding himself leaning forward to study as the images grew.

Not a lot of scans of the vessel initially, because she hadn't attempted anything during the first ambush when she'd been smart enough to flee. More data showing up with degrees of certainty.

Helped that she currently contained almost the complete

specs of the *Concord* Navy. That was a lot of ships. She could extrapolate reasonably well.

Bridge should be about here, her images indicated. Just about the exact center of that nub welded on to the front of what was really just a lot of shipping containers. And she'd put everything she had into that tiny area. That and the engines aft. Not the engine room itself, but the actual machines.

As they'd discussed, nowhere handy to pull into a drydock to fix anything that got broken today. Generators, but not all that many, because torpedoes only needed enough juice to open the bay door and trigger the launch circuits. JumpDrives and impellers for realspace, but again, not all that many relative to the size.

This was not the ship that chased someone down like a cheetah. It came out of jump on top of you and either you surrendered or they overloaded you with missiles and you died.

He could have used that sort of silliness at *Nidavellir*, but he and Suvi had done pretty well. Helped, having a Land Leviathan to throw at the bad guys.

As he watched, she added more and more damage markers, presumably reviewing all of her scanner logs and processing things into a reasonable facsimile.

"I'm reading from this that you did a significant amount of damage to the bow section, Yeoman," he finally said.

"That's my assessment, Captain," she replied. "And it was my intent. Aft damage might have caused the vessel to fall out of orbit without someone that could drag it to a safer orbit, and the pirates left all of their salvage vessels at home."

"Do we presume they learn a valuable lesson from this

exercise, or that they will be vulnerable a second time?" he asked.

"Would you fall for it again, sir?" she laughed.

"No, I suppose not," Zakhar agreed. "Keep a watch on the patrol force to see if they pull back or press on. That will give me a better understanding of their commander."

"Do we not presume Yekaterina Velichkov?" Suvi asked.

"We do not," he replied. "At least not until we know Katya is or isn't aboard. She might be, but she might have also retired from the clan and left us facing someone else with different habits and tendencies."

"Gotcha."

Zakhar paused and considered a small screen off to one side. Showing all of nearby orbital space with several hundred dots, though far fewer than there had been a day ago.

Nobody smart stayed put with pirates around. And local police forces weren't suicidal, so either they were staying on the ground at *Ophiuchi*, or holding near their armed stations in orbit.

Not that he could expect them to help. Not against that level of firepower.

At least they would probably stay out of the way, at least as long as any battles happened away from innocent civilians.

"Yeoman, I expect them to have to reorganize and revamp their original plans, now that they know we are willing to go on the offensive if they let us," Zakhar said. "Maintain a heightened watch for the next several hours, ready to jump away randomly if anyone does locate us, but otherwise let the crew handle any new maintenance issues that have arisen. It will be day for Djamila in a few hours, and I think the clans we're facing need time to argue with one another and maybe get a little spooked."

"Understood, Captain," she nodded. "How soon until we try some new trick?"

"That depends on how smart they are," Zakhar said.

He kept his eyes on the dot that represented *Kymni Gauntlet*. Probably the most dangerous ship in that fleet, now that *Blackstone* might be hobbled.

How would they react?

Katya had been on duty, hair-trigger-sharp to launch and fire everything as soon as *Excalibur* made a mistake. After hearing the radio from Cunningham and Slavkov, she could see where she'd underestimated Sokolov.

Badly.

"Gunner, anything nearby?" she called.

"Negative, Kat," Mihail replied. "They could have just as easily done that to us, but we're packed close enough together that we'd have been able to open fire. Especially at that kind of range."

"Pretty sure Sokolov knew that," Katya acknowledged. "Anton, maintain current heading, but shift your course some random amount and transmit that to the others. If *Excalibur* is about to repeat that performance, I'd like them to miss."

"How did they find *Blackstone*?" Mihail asked.

She had to stop and consider that for a long moment.

"We're all broadcasting our locations and flight vectors

automatically," she said, growling at herself. "He's out there somewhere listening."

"How?" Anton replied. "And do we turn them off?"

Katya considered it. They were all pirates, so it wasn't like they followed most of those laws anyway, even if they had been trying to not antagonize the locals. *Drako III* wasn't affiliated with the *Concord*, but they were trade partners. Not any *Concord* warships in harbor right now, which was why they'd picked the place.

That, and nobody here really *liked* the *Concord*. Merely tolerated them most of the time.

That might have changed with a sudden pirate invasion.

"Leave them on for now," Katya decided. "We can shut them off later if we need to, but I'd rather not antagonize the locals more than I have to. If he's reading it, he's close, so start thinking about how he might listen to our signals if we can't immediately see him."

"Kat, I have an inbound signal from *Obsidian Hawk*," Mihail called. "Sounds pissed. Or frightened. About a two-second lag."

"Probably both," she agreed. "Patch it to my station."

Slavkov appeared. And he'd gotten an entire shade of paler than he had been. She put that down to sudden panic that Sokolov might have gone after him instead of *Blackstone*. That would have certainly had an impact on the fleet, but she wasn't sure what.

Wasn't sure if she wanted to find out, either.

"Sir?" she asked, keeping her voice calm and neutral.

He might be an asshole, but he was worth a lot of money and had already shown himself willing to spend it to go after someone that had wronged him. She didn't want to be next on the man's list.

"WHERE IS HE?" Slavkov demanded.

"We're searching now, sir," she said, gritting her teeth at being second-guessed by a pipsqueak punk who'd never been in a space battle before. "I have my team working to eliminate possibilities. Eventually, he has to either flee completely or fight up when we box him in."

She left it at that. Slavkov hadn't volunteered to sail out into risk and danger looking for *Excalibur*. That was her gig. And her responsibility, because at the end of the day Sokolov had been Jarre Foundation before he'd quit and moved to *Altai*, if the rumors were to be believed.

She watched Slavkov master his temper. Probably somebody off screen motioning. Or whispering into an earpiece he was wearing. Reminding him that if they all just sat in orbit, either *Excalibur* eventually got away, or entropy set in.

Stalemate was an expensive proposition around here, and favored Sokolov.

At least as long as his people on the ground could stay free.

"Have we heard from the ground forces?" she asked, stepping on his words with the lag.

He stopped and cocked his head. Definitely listening to someone.

"They have established a base on the ground and continue to patrol, seeking our fugitives," he said, sing-song parroting of what someone else said.

"Then we need to continue our patrol here, and force him to act," Katya noted. "What is the status of *Blackstone*?"

She was too far away for anything to be resolvable. Still, from the traffic they'd picked up, it had been bad.

"*Blackstone* has been badly damaged," Slavkov growled. "Admiral Cunningham was injured and is currently in surgery. They won't know for several hours if he is expected to survive."

Katya winced. He'd had to have been in the safest part of that ship, and had still been hurt badly. Worse, that probably meant that Slavkov would take over issuing orders. A man who wore his petulance on his sleeve.

And his ignorance.

Still, it was his money on the line. The rest of them had already put their lives up, but they did that every day as a pirate.

"What are your orders, Admiral?" she asked, putting him on the spot.

Mostly, because she doubted that the senior captions from other clans would necessarily promote her to take that flag with Cunningham out. Too much rivalry and bad blood going back too many decades.

Plus, if Valko Slavkov was issuing orders, she could always fall back on that when questioned by her own Board of Directors later. And she would face some sort of inquiry, assuming she didn't walk into that boardroom with Sokolov's head on a stake.

Metaphorically or otherwise.

Someone with half a brain was advising Slavkov. She watched him shut his mouth and listen for a long moment, then nod.

"You will continue your patrol, exercising care and prepared to call for the rest of the fleet immediately," he ordered her. "When you locate *Excalibur*, we will all move to pounce on the ship and destroy it, though I am given to understand that *Blackstone* will likely be unable to assist. It and *Para Bellum* will remain in orbit, where the two of them can provide a bulwark that prevents Sokolov from jumping in and rescuing his ground forces. Questions?"

"Negative, sir," she said. "We'll keep hunting here."

She cut the line and typed a message to *Yorrick* on a laser-connected network linking the patrol ships.

Blackstone out of action. Slavkov wants us to continue. Heading to checkpoint seven next.

She transmitted and leaned back to grimace at the whole situation.

Somebody had fucked up. Badly. Either someone in the clans had warned Sokolov at the last minute, or the man was better than her records indicated. Certainly, the ship was something exceptional.

Katya had never fought a *Sentient* warship before, so she'd come in with no expectations. And still been wrong. The thing was fast to react. And smarter than any she had ever even read about, to be able to do some of the things it had in the short windows when her people had been vulnerable.

"Orders, Kat?" Anton asked.

"Checkpoint Seven, but take your time," she replied. "Mihail, shoot first. Maybe don't bother asking questions later. Go for the kill on anything that gets close, even before identifying it. At this point, we assume *Excalibur* at first motion."

"Aye."

She watched her Gunner hunch forward and focus on his boards and his gun teams.

Who was the hunter here, and who was the hunted?

PART III

The sun was close to rising. Djamila had meditated instead of sleeping. Old habit developed when she'd been an Assault Marine, and she could easily go for three or four days on catnaps and power breaks. Plus a few pills she kept in her medkit for exactly that reason.

The other eight had rotated watch assignments in pairs, although she doubted that any of them slept either. Well-trained troops, used to field deprivation.

They needed to hit the pirates tomorrow. Not at first light, when they might be expecting it, but closer to midday, when folks would have settled into some semblance of base operations. That false sense of security you got when nobody was firing at you.

Not yet, anyway.

Four shuttles in the air. Presumably they would sweep out with troops aboard to hotdrop on a detected target any moment now. If she could get inside their patrol radius, they might come running when she attacked the base. So many options, but it also presented problems.

Djamila reached out a foot and tapped Javier with a toe. He stirred and opened his eyes without moving.

"You and Afia will remain here," Djamila announced. "We will be spending a little time this morning hiding you better."

He sat up and rubbed his face once. The whiskers were all coming in white these days, same as much of her hair.

Age, catching up with all of them, but it beat the alternative.

"How soon until we have to flee into the deeper brush or face being captured?" he asked, skipping over all the middle bits.

Javier and Afia weren't emotionally or physically prepared for what she had to do next, as much as she loved both of them.

"Four days," she decided. "If we haven't made it back by then, chances are we are all dead or captured ourselves."

He nodded.

"Got water," he replied. "Assume that you'll leave the big jug here. Have a field expedient outhouse we can use. And guns. And food. Stay mostly under the tarp and hope no critters sneak in at night?"

"I'll build you a door you can slide into place," Galal murmured. "Have the necessary cord and there are enough branches at hand to do a weave. Mice might be a problem, but snakes are uncommon in this climate."

Javier turned to the man. The Gun Bunny, as he called all of them, though it had become much more a term of respect and endearment than it once had been.

"How much of your gear will you leave?" Afia asked, awake now and bright-eyed.

"We'll carry most of it forward and stage it," Sascha offered. "I have a couple of locations in mind that should work. And it keeps us from leading them back to you later."

"If we're radio silent, how do we know when Zakhar wins?" Javier asked.

"You assume so?" Djamila asked. Not surprised at the sentiment. Maybe at the certainty in his voice.

"He has Suvi and a crew of killers," Javier nodded. "If all the pirates have come for our souls, I expect him to run up a dinner tab that they can choke on. At some point, we have to power up radios."

"Or have Del fly a pattern," Hajna said. "The four shuttles look nothing like his, so presumably you'd be able to identify him from the ground and call for evac. Especially if we're already successful and too lazy to walk out to get you."

Javier fixed her with a cold eye, but Djamila could see the grin on her face.

A team. A family. Nobody left behind, except that Javier and Afia needed to remain here at base while her team did the sorts of things she demanded of them.

The excellence that was the very minimum necessary to belong to the Gun Bunnies in the first place. Idly, she wondered how many of them might retire when they all got back to *Altai*. She and Zakhar had certainly discussed it, but that was a thing for another tomorrow.

Altai's army could probably use nine new expert instructors, if nothing else. Farouk would appreciate their experience. As would Behnam.

First, they had to get home safely.

All of them.

Javier nodded and shifted into a squat.

"Let's do this, then," he said, moving to where the tarp provided a door of sorts.

At pace, she needed two hours to get into position to launch her attack.

There was enough time to break bread as a unit.

Before she went to smash heads together.

PART IV

Piet had stayed in his own station as Pilot when Zakhar retired to get some sleep. And both he and Suvi had provided a solid briefing on what they'd done overnight.

Utterly rude. Perfectly in character, going back many years to *Storm Gauntlet*.

Before Javier had upended all their lives.

"Suvi, any change?" he asked without looking up from what he'd been doing.

"Negative, Piet," she replied. "They are following a reasonable minimum-distance patrol pattern designed to locate us, but I picked my current hiding place based on that. Unless they change suddenly, we have forty hours before they come over my horizon."

"And they are still broadcasting location signals?" he asked her.

"Affirmative."

"Are they lying?" Piet asked.

He looked up and winked when her image goggled at him. Brilliant woman. Pretty sneaky. Had never really been a smuggler. It taught you a whole different way of looking at signals intelligence.

"How do I tell?" she finally asked.

"I assume you are catching reflected radio signals off solid body surfaces, yes?" he pressed.

"Correct," Suvi said. "Got a lot of moons, plus those rings do a great job."

"So compare the light-speed wave signal with their reported location," he nodded. "If that starts to diverge, we know they are broadcasting a false signal. Also, point an ear at *Blue Amsterdam* and see if the authorities over there complain. There's nothing they can do about it, but they might challenge the pirates to behave."

"Oh, I like that," she said. "Done. Currently, sounds like they are at least within fifteen percent of where they claim to be."

"Solid enough for now," Piet said. "You planning on attacking anyone in the next hour or so?"

"Negative, Piet," she replied. "Zakhar wanted them to stew for a while, working themselves into something of a lather and jumping at shadows first."

"Wise," he nodded. "Let me know if you need me to do anything."

"Will do," she said. "What are you working on?"

"New symphony," he said. "Felt like this whole thing was a major event, so I put the other one aside for now. Too much a love ballad for this situation, so we're aiming for a bit more *Götterdämmerung* here."

"You think this is the Twilight of the Gods themselves?" Suvi asked.

Something in her voice caused him to look up, so Piet paused to frame the words in his mind before speaking them.

"Someone caused all four major pirate clans in this region of the galaxy to band together, Suvi," he explained. "To come together as a fleet and attack us. While this might not look like Valhalla, I can't help but see them as frost and fire giants charging across Bifrost, led by Hrym and Surtur."

"Nobody important survived that battle, you know," she pointed out. "All the major gods were killed, leaving only a handful of lesser, mostly kids."

"Plus a pair of humans hiding in the tree when the world drowned," he nodded, smiling grimly. "The visual comparisons, then, have an eerie resonance that demanded a double helping of brass to really give it the mass I needed. Two full orchestras, if you will. Possibly arrayed facing each other and blasting notes at each other like a real war."

"Gotcha," she said. "How do we win?"

"Stay away from wolves and sea dragons," he suggested, grinning at her. "What do we have to mimic Gungnir and Mjolnir?"

Her pause was long enough to be for his benefit as she looked up various things. Possibly going back and rereading all her books on the topic, since the Prose Etta and a few others had survived this many millennia.

"Lightning bolts and a great big fucking hammer," she replied. "Huh. Not sure how to compare them, since I'm likely not throwing torpedoes at someone."

"If they jump in, they will need time to recharge drives," Piet mused. "I suspect that we should look to use up our torpedoes in this engagement, rather than save them for some hypothetical tomorrow. Plus, we can always look to buy more later. Zakhar has friends and contacts through a wide stretch of space here."

She nodded pensively on the screen and he went back to

listening to the music in his head. There were melodies that he would layer deeply through the entire work, bringing it all to a massive crescendo, before winding down the final movement in victory.

Hopefully, the bad guys would be just as accommodating in real life.

PART V

Javier found himself alone with Afia, everyone else having left to go sow the seeds of chaos o'er yonder. Thought about fooling around some, if only because they had privacy right now and had been planning on that before all hell broke loose, but there would be time later.

Especially if the Dragoon was about to go commit art on some people.

He moved to a log and planted his butt on a comfortable spot and thought about his other beer. It would be warm by now, so he immediately got up and went back into the dugout.

"Will you make up your mind?" Afia asked from nearby.

"Walk with me," he said, grabbing the beer and checking the pistol on his thigh.

He wouldn't be without a weapon again, as long as he was on this planet, he knew. Maybe any planet until he got back to *Altai*, if Djamila put her foot down.

And she probably would.

He grabbed his last beer and started downhill to the stream, Afia a few steps behind him.

"Oh, gotcha," she said as he found a spot to stash it in the cold water.

Only a few degrees above freezing here, not far from a glacier in the cool uplands. Great to keep your beer chilled, as long as no greedy beavers came along for it.

He found a different log and settled, watching the distant sky lighten. Too many trees to actually get direct sunlight here. Sascha had chosen this spot for that reason. No clearing handy for enemy troops to land.

They'd have to rappel out of a shuttle or use powered chutes to get here, giving him and Afia hopefully enough warning to do something.

Javier doubted that they had the trailcraft to evade experts, but they might be able to hurt a few.

"Whatchathinking?" she asked as she settled beside him, then leaned on his arm.

"How much trouble we're in here," he replied honestly. "I had thought that Walvisbaai would have gotten over themselves, but obviously I guessed wrong there."

"You insulted them, Javier," she reminded him. "Got up in their faces and slapped them twice with open palms to really make it loud and ugly in front of the whole damned sector. Of course they were going to remember it. I can't figure the other three, though. Jarre might not have liked us leaving, but to send a fleet after us?"

"I'm presuming at this point that Walvisbaai made common cause with the other half of that affair," Javier chuckled. "No, strike that. Probably that punk Slavkov hired everyone else. He's got the wealth to do it. That brings in H

& W Heavy Industries. If he doesn't own H & W, he owns the people that do."

"And you did blow up his yacht," she grinned.

"Technically, you did that," he grinned back. "Threw it at a Walvisbaai orbital platform and everything, though I'm sure they're mostly pissed at me and Zakhar. Not enough to let the rest of you go, mind you, but we're going to be high on his list."

"How do we get away?" she asked.

They were facing the mid-morning sun, more or less. Enough that things were growing warmer around them. Small critters had already scampered to cover for the day, while bigger ones were coming out to graze. Hopefully he didn't have to deal with anything but deer today.

"Right now, we gotta survive, kid," he told her.

He could call her that. She wasn't quite thirty yet, and he'd turned forty-four last time around.

They were all getting older. Hopefully, he'd be like a fine wine instead of a block of cheese.

"Not a lot we can do to survive here except hide," she countered. "Unless you had something else in mind?"

Her grin spoke volumes.

"Later, when they're distracted by Djamila," he nodded. "Thinking about the larger context. About pirates."

"Bad folk," she turned sober. Still leaned against him, though. "Gonna have to destroy them to make them leave us alone?"

He paused and considered her words. Chewed on them like a bulldog with a good bone.

She leaned away far enough to study his profile.

"You have an idea," she said quietly.

"The affair at *Shangdu* was probably where it all started," he replied. "They hired Navarre. A smart person in those days would expect a mass casualty incident. Pissed somebody off when they got a social assassination instead. So they set us up at *Svalbard*. And nearly killed us all."

"Pissing you and Zakhar off in the process to the point that we got to meet Suvi for the first time," Afia said. "Before going after Slavkov."

"They started it," Javier stated. "And keep escalating things, every time I'm willing to call it good."

"Every time you've won a round," she laughed throatily. "You're dealing with men defined by their egos, Javier. Of course they can't let you win a round and quit."

"You understand what that implies, don't you?" he turned to look directly at her.

Her face got hard and cold. He could see what she'd look like when she turned sixty. Still cute and impressive, but carved in a burnished, golden bronze etched with decades of experience.

"You're going to go junkyard dog on them," she replied slowly. "You and Zakhar."

"Only way to get them to listen, it seems," he agreed.

"Javier, that's four full pirate clans you're talking about destroying," she implored. "Are you even more nuts than usual?"

"I don't think you've ever really seen me angry, Afia," he told her calmly. "Pissed. Rude. Lots of other things. Not angry."

"*Sing for me, oh muse, a song of the rage of Achilles,*" she quoted at him quietly.

Javier nodded.

He wondered where she had encountered *The Iliad*. Standard part of the *Bryce Academy* curriculum, intended to turn out well-rounded officers who knew which fork to use at dinner. And it was almost nine thousand years since the war for Troy, back on Ancient Earth.

He assumed Bethany had a copy in her library, but hadn't checked.

Hadn't cared that much, since he really wasn't a reader, except when new plant catalogs came in the mail.

But Afia was right. One hundred percent accurate.

He would need to tap into the rage of Achilles on this one.

One idle part of his mind wondered how history might view what he was about to start here. Assuming he survived.

What would be his place in the pantheon of ancient figures?

Of course, Suvi would likely outlive all of them. She was already one hundred and thirty-some years old, and could live a long and hearty life if she kept getting poured into newer ships on a regular basis.

Long after he was gone, she would be his immortality. Fitting, as his only known daughter.

Known, at least.

"When we get out of here, we're going to have to do something about piracy," he pronounced firmly.

"Like we did to Zhenya Kovalev and her people at *Syntha*?" Afia asked.

"That's a shoving match in a sandbox compared to what I have in mind," he replied. "Tack three zeros on the back."

"Three?" she gasped.

"You think they will really nod and shrug if we get out of this one?" he asked her. "Wave friendly as we sail away to *Altai*? No. They'll keep coming. Keep sending trouble. Then hiring assassins to go after a group of probably about a dozen of us. Your name will be on that list if they know anything."

"How do we stop them?" she pressed, eyes big but focused.

"We destroy them," he said simply. "Root and branch. Burn their cities, then knock the walls down according to the ancient formula that saw no two bricks stacked atop one another before salting the earth itself."

She swallowed, lips pressed tight enough to turn white.

"How?" she finally asked.

"We are close to the *Concord*," he said. "Several of us have contacts there."

"And all of you are pretty much exiles at this point, from what I understand," she challenged. "Wanted criminals with prices on your heads."

"I have something they will want," he countered. "Maybe enough to deal."

"All the data you stole from Jabril Qadir at *Sovereign Nakhimov*," she replied. "Thought you were already planning to tell them what had happened."

"We did," he said. "Sent them a note with enough file names to get their attention, figuring that it would take even their bureaucracy a while to process all that and actually respond. We'd have likely been well on our way to *Altai* before they could chase us."

"And now?"

"Now, I feel the need to sail someplace where I can talk to them directly," Javier smiled grimly. "Offer our services and knowledge against some help from them."

"To do what?" she asked.

"To destroy H & W Heavy Industries," he replied. "And

Walvisbaai Industrial. And The Belfast Group Holding Company."

He paused.

"And the Jarre Foundation."

Her eyes were about as big as he could ever remember them getting.

"Everyone?" she pressed.

"If I leave any of them to survive and breed, it will be like rats," he said. "They'll slink away and rebuild."

"That rebuild will likely take decades," she noted. "Possibly generations."

"You want to still be looking over your shoulder when you're Zakhar's age, kid?" he challenged her. "Rest of your life waking up each morning wondering if today is the day some assassin pulls it off? I don't. Even with Behnam and her people protecting me, someone only has to get lucky once."

"So you intend to go fully and completely to war with every pirate clan in this region of space?" she asked.

"And utterly annihilate them, yes," he agreed. "Might have to find a way to get the Doctors St. Kitts home separately. Maybe buy a smaller ship and hire them a crew. Or find a few of our folks who are tired of this life and can sail it for me."

"Because you're only going home with a row of heads on stakes as trophies," she nodded.

"As a warning to future generations not to mess with me," Javier completed the thought.

She shrugged, then grinned.

"I always knew we were in trouble, the day Zakhar announced that he'd hired a new Centurion as our Science Officer," she said. "Never imagined what it might turn into."

"Same, kiddo," he nodded back. "But it needs doing. Once we get out of here, we're going to have to destroy all of the pirates. Everywhere. I'm going to need the *Concord*'s help to manage that, but if we're offering to do most of the work, I don't see them complaining too much. They ought to know what we've been doing since we got to *Ugen* originally. This just ups the scale."

"Tacking three zeros on," she agreed. "I'd ask if you were nuts, but I already know the answer to that."

He laughed. It felt good to laugh, like those ancient heroes facing death and not letting it get them down.

He would win. Or drag as many of them to hell with him as he could.

He'd need the company to keep him warm when he got there.

PART VI

Sascha didn't have the long legs of Hajna or the Dragoon. Without Afia around, she was the shortest one here, and had to churn usually to keep up.

Fortunately, she was on point today. They could slow down to her pace. Hajna had the rear, keeping everyone else safe from patrols and bears, but Sascha had memorized Afia's map and had the perfect spot in mind for what was coming next.

Around them, trees. Heavy. No game trail here, because they'd slipped through the thick stuff, expecting any ground patrol to stick to the easier places.

Sascha waved everyone else to stillness as she got close to the top of the slope. Hill wasn't much of a ripple here. Not even a watershed. Mostly just a lot of downed trees fallen wherever a storm had dropped them. Made the going hard. Meant that raiders were unlikely to have gotten aggressive enough to get into this thicket.

She peeked over the top slowly, but saw only more trees across and below. Shuttles had flown out and over them, but the team was observing the *Dragoon's* idea of electronic security here, so nothing those folks could pick up easily. And if they did point a scanner toward her group, they might mistake the things on their screen for a herd of elk or one of their own patrols.

At least until Demyan or Tom put a SAM into their lifters. Then they'd have other problems to worry about.

Sascha closed her eyes and listened. The forest absorbed most sounds pretty quickly, but machinery tended to carry. Especially up hills and along the course of long valleys, like she'd slipped in on.

The resort was just over two kilometers away. Across a small tributary stream that was only ankle deep at the ford. Each of the main hiking trails coming this direction got no closer than four hundred meters to this spot.

Safe. For now. At least as safe as a live-fire exercise could get.

Or a small-forces assault against an enemy given one day to entrench.

Somehow, she doubted that they'd gotten all that serious. Sascha was dubious that most pirates who had gotten that level of ground-forces training took it all that seriously, where the very first thing you did when you stopped moving was to dig a hole big enough to hide in.

But the Dragoon would likely cure them of such laziness. The survivors, anyway.

Sascha simply watched the valley for a bit, thinking about how she would establish an electronic perimeter with this much wilderness, and what form it would take. She turned and looked back at the shadows behind her.

"Galal, need your mind," she called quietly, waiting for

him to slither up close. "Where would you put your scanners?"

She pointed, then sat still as he took a bit to absorb it all.

"Close in to the camp," he said after three minutes. "They will have pushed out on the trails and put cameras with radios there, tasking someone with reacting to every false positive that wildlife throws up, but not gone deep into the trees themselves. You'd hear more noise from people moving around if they were better at this."

"Agreed," Sascha said. "You walk on my flank and keep your eyes up for sensors as we approach."

Sascha turned to the Dragoon and nodded. The team rose and fell into single file.

The game was afoot.

PART VII

Djamila understood that they had a priceless, and unique, opportunity here, watching the newly built camp from a slight elevation. Enemy forces just slack enough to have done the most half-assed job possible in setting up their defenses. She'd have fired and blackballed anybody who called that work acceptable, but it worked in her favor today.

They'd taken the resort, but the commander over there hadn't allowed his forces to scatter themselves too badly. Or get that lazy. Probably would have happened in another four days, but she intended to put the fear of God Herself into these punks over lunch.

Instead, several tents and popup buildings in the parking lot and landing field, spilling over onto the access road and a small clearing across the way that had the rawness of having been done with explosives.

Djamila had wondered what they'd been blowing up. Looked like using detonating cord to drop trees in a hurry. There was one pillbox over there that looked valuable. Well built, using those dropped trees and adding in dirt as insulation. It would stop anything handheld in the time she had to work against it, unless she tasked someone with a likely suicide mission to penetrate and place explosives.

Fortunately, she had better options, because she intended one gratuitous strike today to use up most of her heavy resources, with a few things cached out in the woods for later. Big stuff would only slow her down in fleeing anyway, so they might as well unleash it all at once.

She lowered herself slowly behind a downed tree and gestured the others to listen. Tom and Demyan were watching the sky, but sound would carry long before any of those shuttles returned.

"One command post, long ways across," she said, sketching in the cleared dirt with a knife she drew. "Landing field here, currently empty but they have supplies stacked there. Galal, we'll close to a range that you can hit that area with grenades from your launcher. Demyan, can you hit a command post with a Surface to Air Missile, given clearance?"

"Probably, Dragoon," he said. "I'll need a perfectly clear shot, though, because I'll have to arm the missile in the tube so that it detonates on any significant impact. Branches would matter."

"Go ahead and start that process," she ordered. "Disrupting command and control capabilities will degrade enemy forces significantly. Remember, these are pirate mercenary troops, not patriots. Tough, but generally brittle in my experience. Tom, you will maintain air defense overwatch."

Tom nodded, then sharply held up a finger, turning and pointing to the south as he suddenly raised his launcher to his shoulder and glanced back to the others to get out of the backblast zone.

Then she heard it. The whine of shuttle thrusters vectoring in as at least one of them returned to base. Pretty much on schedule, as she had been expecting morning and afternoon patrols, with a meal in the middle. Already, soldiers below were making their way to what she interpreted as a mess tent from the smoke and activity.

Pity she didn't have anything that she could have dropped on that tent when it was full of pirates. Grenades would do some damage, but she was expecting that there were some four hundred men and women down there, after just a quick counting tents for sleeping. A full battalion of troops.

"Do I engage?" Tom asked.

"Negative," Djamila replied. "Let them come in to land. Engage if they start dropping troops on us. Otherwise, let them disembark and prepare to hit the second one coming in to reinforce the base when we attack. Galal, you and Hajna take point and get us to a place where you can initiate. Sascha and Demyan, move to where you have a clear horizontal shot. Galal will signal the attack. Everyone pour fire into supplies and equipment priority over personnel. We can't starve them out, but we can disable and hobble them with this attack. On the recall signal, make your way out and rendezvous at point four. Questions?"

"What about officers?" Iqbal asked.

"Force decapitation is beneficial if you have a shot, but don't waste time," she replied. "Demyan will be going after Command and Control."

Nods.

Galal looked around his options, and began to move.

Djamila would be on his forward flank when all hell broke loose, raining fire down on these assholes who had ruined her vacation.

TROUBLE

PART I

Benedict heard the second shuttle returning from a morning sweep that had turned up nothing. Not that he was entirely surprised. Sykora had managed to get away from him into heavy woods and forested terrain. She would be like a tick to dislodge.

The sweeps had been in case someone made a mistake that showed up on a scanner. A comm turned on. Someone crossing open terrain. Light reflecting off metal such that it drew a second look. Hell, even someone deciding to shoot at one of the shuttles. He doubted that Sykora had anything that could bring down one of his craft, but she might lose her cool and fire.

And, truth be told, he had assumed that he was going to lose one of the shuttled before this operation was completed. Things like that happened when you went up against the very best. And she had been, once upon a time.

Never assume your enemy is unkillable, but also remember that they are going to be smart, trained, and desperate.

Losing a half company of troops with a shuttle would be the price for nailing down her location so he could drop the rest of the force and box her in. At that point, the choice would be hers.

Benedict checked the local time and decided that morale would be improved if he took an early lunch with the troopers getting ready to head out for the afternoon sweep. He exited his command bunker and started across the way to the main mess tent. Folks had been staging through for an hour already, and the hundred and sixty or so soldiers returning would be next in line. He could linger and talk to both teams.

Be seen. Let them know that he wasn't over in the cabana sipping rum drinks with ice while they slept in the mud.

A whistle cutting the sky hurled Benedict to the ground before his mind even identified what it was. Just a shrill sound, but he was face down in the dirt with his hands and arms over his head.

Some things get pounded into you in boot camp and never leave, regardless of the decades since.

Then all hell broke loose and he was deaf. And buffeted by overpressure. The sky turned red for a moment and he was rolled over twice before his head cleared.

Then more explosions. Mostly ahead of him, but a few on other sides. Beam fire as everyone opened up, but he couldn't see any target.

Then the landing field lit up so bright that Benedict was seeing stars as he dove right back down behind a box of something that had happened to be close. He didn't know what it was, but his unconscious mind had made for it when combat broke out.

Smoke. Everywhere. That dark, acrid scent that told him

someone had blown up the fuel depot. And set a lot of supplies on fire at the same time, because they'd been unloaded from the shuttles, but not moved very far.

Why would they need to, if they were only going to be present for a few days, most of that out in the trees hunting the Dragoon from *Excalibur* and her people?

Except that she was hunting him. That much was obvious.

Most of the fire seemed to be coming from the hills nearby, though his people were acting like juvenile delinquents and shooting every which way.

Benedict looked back and realized that he'd been about four seconds from standing in the middle of his command post when someone blew it up. Four seconds later on going to lunch, and he'd be smoked meat. Maybe dead.

It wasn't clear how bad the damage was, but someone had put a missile inside those tree trunk walls, so the explosion had had nowhere to go but up. He was glad he hadn't had time to have them put a roof up, letting a simple tarp keep rain and sun off.

That might mean the difference between a lot of concussions and broken bones, versus everyone that had been in there being dead about now.

The sound of fire started tapering off. Or the explosions did. Hard to say.

Benedict finally got hold of himself and located his comm.

"Force Dragoon Naoumov to Group Leaders," he said urgently. "Check in. Where is the attack coming from?"

He couldn't tell.

"This is Group Leader Walkell," Kathra replied quickly.

"It seems to be from your northwest, according to our scans. Moving in to investigate now."

Before he could reply, Benedict heard that scream whistle a second time and threw himself flat, but on his back where he could see the sky.

A missile contrail, indeed from the northwest corner of his base. It rose on a pillar of flaming smoke almost too fast to follow, then slammed into the underside of Walkell's shuttle like a hammer.

Impact.

The shuttle wobbled onto its right wing and started to fall out of the sky, not quite turning turtle but rotating in a flat spin that ended with a terrible crash as it slammed into trees.

Benedict didn't know if hitting trees before ground would be better or worse, but he could see a hole torn in the forest over there.

Then silence fell, like that had been the signal to end all hostilities.

Certainly, it had shocked the hell out of him, and he had more experience in ground warfare than most of his troops. They were pirates. Take a ship in orbit or deep space. Not dig in and hide from people shooting back.

He could see that changing this afternoon.

Once he knew how many people had survived his mistakes.

PART II

Djamila trailed the others in withdrawing. Sascha and Hajna were possibly better Pathfinders, but not by much and she wanted to make sure that all of her people got out safe.

The chaos and destruction they had rained down on the pirates still had her smiling. Someone had certainly just failed a mid-term exam on applied defensive tactics. She wanted to know if they could learn from it, or would end up panicking, and running for their lives.

They might escape her wrath. For now. There was still Zakhar and Suvi up there, and Djamila had no doubts that they were aiming for the same sorts of response.

She paused at the lip of that last valley with a view, sliding behind a tree before turning to look back. Black smoke from the landing field, where fuel barrels continued to burn and occasionally detonate. More from the trees where Tom had dropped one of the shuttles with a perfect hit.

Djamila would assume about half of those troops would be out of action for a few days or longer, with the other half ready to return to duty after a meal and a nap. Assuming four hundred or so invaders, she'd have put forty or fifty on any shuttle, so a score were off the game board.

Plus however many they'd gotten in that first attack. Pity that they'd missed the force commander at the last moment. Or one of their lieutenants had managed to step in and take command quickly. She'd been hoping for another ten or fifteen minutes of panicked volleys into the trees that accomplished nothing but wasting ammunition and rattling troops.

Still, someone had a lot less fuel and food than they had planned for initially. Right about now, a sniper rifle would have been a lovely addition to her gear, but they had been expecting heavy forest, where your best sight lines to shoot were under one hundred meters. Plus, that much metal would probably show up on a scanner tuned correctly.

Assuming someone wanted to get close when she'd proven to have surface-to-air missiles. Two gone. Two remaining at the cache, but they didn't know that.

Their commander would have to walk more carefully now. Slower patrols spooking at trees and deer.

As intended.

There was almost no way she could win against that many enemy troops, but Djamila planned to make them pay a heavy cost.

And she was just getting started.

PART III

Zakhar had awakened refreshed, though a bit sad to be alone in his bed. After years of solitude, Djamila had turned him into a new man. Now, she needed him to rescue her and the others from all these damned pirates.

He showered and shaved his skull. He'd grown in a full beard recently, so he trimmed it with the sort of precision that might have been lacking over the last few months.

Hell, he'd considered shaving it, too, but decided that his head was too round and didn't feel like letting the ring above his ears grow back in.

Too easy to end up looking like an accountant.

From the closet, he'd gone to the back and dug out moss green. Used to be, that had been all he wore, a pale imitation of twenty years in a slightly darker forest green of a *Concord* Navy officer's day uniform. Javier and Djamila had gotten him into other colors, as alien as that had felt at first.

Less so today, but he was making a statement, standing before the wall mirror and taking it all in.

Sixty years old. Twenty as a punk. Twenty as an officer. Twenty as a pirate. What would the next twenty be?

Zakhar didn't know, but had a feeling that it started today. Here.

Now.

"Yeoman, what is your status?" he called to the room, knowing that Suvi was everywhere around him, monitoring every chamber on her ship but generally letting people maintain the illusion of privacy.

"Mary-Elizabeth has the conn, Captain," Suvi said as she appeared in the monitor by the main hatch. "Enemy forces are attempting subtlety, but Piet offered a whole new raft of sneaky ideas that I have been researching and implementing. Countdown still estimates twenty-nine hours before any enemy vessel moves to a position whereby we could be easily detected."

"Does that include someone randomly jumping around the edge of the *Drako III* system and scanning inwards?" he asked.

"Affirmative, sir," she replied. "I'm deep enough in the clouds of the main giant that they would have to point a scan directly at me, at which point I will have sufficient warning to react."

"Any news from the ground?"

"Apparently, someone let a fox loose in the henhouse when the dog was sleeping, Captain," Suvi grinned.

"She's like that," he smiled, thinking about his Amazon warrior goddess, armed and angry on the surface of a planet with enough cover to be used offensively. "Maintain watch to see if she inflicts enough damage or casualties to alter their arc of engagement."

"What are you expecting, sir?" Suvi asked.

"A smart pirate brought enough people to hold," Zakhar replied, stepping closer to make the conversation personal. "I doubt that Djamila can destroy them, but she might pin them down and inflict enough damage to cause the folks in orbit to rethink and alter their plans. If so, we might be able to react and do something about that."

"*Para Bellum* is the troop transport," she nodded. "It and *Blackstone* have been maintaining a close patrol pattern, still surrounded by the others in low orbit above *Ophiuchi*. They have learned enough that I don't think I can pull another hit and run without significant risk."

"As to be expected, Yeoman," he replied. "We hurt them the first time, and they will be more careful later. Where is *Kymni Gauntlet* at this moment?"

"They have a patrol pattern worked out to travel to as many locations as possible looking for us," Suvi replied. "Based on what they have done so far, I have been able to fill in the remainder with reasonable confidence, but Piet warned me that they might randomly jump anywhere at any moment, trying to outguess us on the topic."

"Wise man, Piet Alferdinck," Zakhar noted. "He'd have replaced me in command of *Storm Gauntlet*. Probably by now, had we not met you and the goofball."

She grinned. It had been a hell of a meeting, though she'd only gotten the stories from everyone involved, hiding in her various remotes for the longest time before taking command of *Hammerfield*. None of the original chickens were still around, but they had expanded the flock some and maintained a small farm aboard to go with Javier's original botanical research station.

On the surface, they almost looked like a legitimate operation. And would have been, all things considered. A diplomatic courier carrying an ambassador and trade mission from *Altai* to the rest of the galaxy.

Not counting a lot of angry ex-pirates. Supposedly ex-pirates.

"Is Bethany awake?" he asked abruptly.

"Forward wardroom," Suvi replied. "Just about to sit down with a tray of food."

"Let her know I'll be joining her," Zakhar said. "Have some questions for the woman."

"Done."

Zakhar nodded and started towards the main hatch.

This was much bigger than merely an extension of the war of the pirate clans that he and Javier had started. Or thought they had finished.

Those next twenty years beckoned as he exited his cabin.

PART IV

Bethany had gotten Suvi's chirp, so she was in no hurry to eat. Not that she had much in front of her, but that was the stress of the situation. Some fresh eggs, because her name had come up on the rotation and you didn't skip your shot at fresh eggs. Some sausage. A slice of toast. A mug of tea.

Zakhar joined her quickly, seated directly across at a four-top table in the corner she had selected for the illusion of privacy. Anyone listening could still follow the conversation, but weren't in the middle of it unless they spoke up.

Some might, depending, but she doubted it.

And Rainier and Emma had started to join her before Suvi's message. They were across the way watching now.

Bethany was always surprised that so many people worried about her. Watched over her. Protected her.

Too many years as a research librarian in an era of declining budgets and disappearing job billets.

And now she was a pirate. For whatever good it might do her.

Zakhar sat, food tray placed just so.

He wore green today. She took her cues from that.

Captain Sokolov looked deadly serious.

She ate, waiting for him to speak. He ended up eating first as well, so Bethany suspected that this was just the first chunk of what might be a much longer conversation.

"We are surrounded by enemies that are only yours by association," he spoke abruptly as she sipped her tea. "For about half of the crew, that describes the situation outside the hull."

Bethany nodded. He hadn't asked her a question.

"For that other half, it might be all the chickens finally coming in to roost," he continued. "I have been giving thought to what that implies, and how we handle the situation."

"There are no *Concord* vessels present," she noted when he paused to sip some coffee. "Local forces are desperately inadequate to attempt any sort of force superiority."

"And we cannot help them with that," he agreed. "Even a First-Rate Galleon does not tip those scales sufficiently. However, you are not, as far as I know, wanted by the *Concord* for anything but guilt by association."

That took her a moment to translate, then she nodded. None of the things that they had done since she joined the crew were all that bad. Beneficial, even, considering what they had seen and done.

And the pirates they had destroyed in a few places.

"Sir," she replied as a placeholder, eyeing him like the superior officer he was.

One of the few that she had ever respected.

"At *Sovereign Nakhimov*, we came into possession of the results of a significant intelligence operation," he continued. "I've sent a few quiet messages to folks I trust from the old days, letting them know. However, I think we will need to leverage that information."

"Sir?"

"We're surrounded by a hostile fleet, Bethany," Zakhar told her. "Comprised of four different clans that are generally as hostile to one another as they are to the authorities. The rules of engagement have changed. We must adapt. More importantly, we must overcome. I suspect that means we must visit unto our enemies a terrible and seemingly divine retribution."

"*The War of the Pirate Clans,*" she replied. "I have a manuscript mostly completed at this point, based on interviews with all the key players."

He nodded. Only because she had promised not to publish it anywhere until the youngest members of his crew were dead had the man been willing to tell her about the things he'd done. As far as she could tell, he had taken that opportunity to go far deeper into his past than her project had technically required, but he'd told her at the time that it had been necessary for her to understand how the pirate clans had operated.

And how he had come to be Captain of this crew of misfits.

"This will be *Volume Two*, Centurion," he noted severely. "I hope that it is not necessary to write a *Volume Three*, but that depends on how successful we are here and now. And where it takes us over the next six months."

"You assume that you will not only escape from *Drako III* but emerge victorious?" she asked. "What about Javier and Djamila?"

"I assume that they will join us before we depart this

system," he answered. "And knowing Javier as well as I do, he's already come to a similar conclusion."

"You think so?" she asked.

She could hear the disbelief in her own voice as she spoke, but her career had taken a radically different tack before she'd been rescued by Javier and her old professor, Dorn Hetzel.

Zakhar, she knew, had done his twenty and retired. Javier had served about fourteen years on active duty before being medically discharged as a fuckup.

The *Concord*'s fault for putting him in an impossible situation. And not recognizing that they had broken the man. She knew that now, from speaking to everyone else on the crew.

It had taken Suvi, Afia, and folks like Ilan Yu to get the man whole enough that Behnam could finish the job. To put him in the position to recruit her in a greasy-spoon dive bar in the middle of nowhere, for the adventure of a lifetime.

Javier Aritza was back to what he could have been. Where he might have ended up had he served a simple twenty-year hitch and retired.

The galaxy had had other plans for all of them.

Zakhar rapped his ring once on the table, a thing that *Concord* officers shared when they recognized one another. Him. Her. Javier.

"I probably know the Science Officer better than anybody else," he replied. "That includes Suvi, because while she is his daughter, she doesn't have the frame of reference to see some of the things that drove him to what he became, then or now. You do, to some extent. About as much as Suvi. Almost nobody else on this vessel does."

"*Bryce Academy*," she murmured, framing it that way. "The *Concord Navy*."

"The good guys," he nodded. "At least that's what we tell ourselves. The ones that didn't participate in the Great War, but rose later to hegemony to hold the peace when it came. At least for a time. That time, I fear, has finally passed."

"The Rising Storm," she nodded back. "Dorn's latest draft puts it about twenty years from now."

Zakhar smiled grimly.

"That fits," he said quietly. "I was just thinking earlier that I had been a kid, then an officer, then a pirate, all in roughly twenty-year chunks, and that I had those next two decades facing me today. We have that gap to make our difference in the wider galaxy, Bethany, if everything will come undone after that, when I am an old man and nothing much will matter."

"Everything?" she asked.

As a librarian, such broad pronouncements tended to offend her. At the same time, she had come to understand that Javier Aritza and Zakhar Sokolov were larger-than-life figures, and would be recorded by historians as such. Her. Suvi. Others.

"Everything," the man confirmed. "What we did at *Surayya*, *Syntha*, and *Valadris* merely helped give those worlds the time to build something that might survive. We can't stop a wider war. Javier's entire mission to *Ugen* and back was to tell people it was coming, like some terrible Cassandraic oracle that most won't believe until it is too late to do anything about it. He will have tried, and that is the most any of us can say about our time. So I have these two decades to leave my mark. Our mark. That thing by which history will remember all of us."

Bethany was aghast at the words, feeling the jolt of cold adrenaline spike in her stomach, before racing up her spine.

The implications. Here was a man declaring his intent to simply take on four major pirate operations with the intention of fighting them all.

And winning.

"You wanted to see me about something specific, sir?" she asked, circling back to the chirp from Suvi to linger at her food.

"I cannot ever return to *Concord* space, Centurion," he replied, turning into some dark, foreboding war god as she watched. "That was something of the implicit deal I made with them at *Nidavellir* in order to escape afterwards. Not that it matters that much, because most of my family is here on this vessel, or on *Ophiuchi*. It does, however, restrict my options."

Bethany nodded as a placeholder.

"When we get clear of this situation, I will need to send you to someplace like *Purton*, on the nearer *Concord* border, where you will make contact with the necessary authorities to negotiate enough of a peace that we can turn our attention to conducting *Volume Two of our War of the Pirate Clans*," he told her.

Luckily, Bethany wasn't holding her tea mug, or she might have dropped it. Her jaw did fall.

Catching flies, as her father might have said.

His grimness did turn a bit humorous.

"Just like that?" she managed. "What about Javier? It's his ship, technically. His mission."

"As I said, I probably know him best," Zakhar chuckled. "If anything, the Science Officer has already gotten that far in his head, and then gone further. Until both Captain Sokolov and Captain Navarre are both dead, I doubt at this point that those four clans will rest. Ever. So we need allies. The

Khatum is already on board, but there are limits to what she can do, this far from home, just like it would be nearly impossible for the *Concord* to threaten her at that distance. We'll take what we can get, and do what we have to."

Bethany knew that she was failing to hide her shock at those words. At the scale.

She couldn't call it pomposity, though it would come off that way from any other mouth.

Or arrogance. She'd known a lot of admirals like that.

Not Zakhar. From him, it came across as a dead certainty that was all the more chilling because he firmly believed that he could take on all those pirates and destroy them, if the *Concord* helped out.

What would they do? What COULD they do, in the era when declining tax base and shrinking fleet budgets meant that fewer and fewer ships were in commission every year? When trained librarians no longer had jobs, because there were no jobs for them to hold?

When the *Concord* stopped being the regional Hegemon holding the peace?

It would all catch fire. Not tomorrow, if Dorn was right, but even he admitted to only guessing. To estimating on generational and lifetime scales, studying history all the way back to ancient Earth before starflight.

What would happen on the day the whole galaxy caught fire? Again.

"What do you need from me, Captain?" she forced herself to ask.

Unbloomed Rose, Dorn had supposedly called her. And it had fit, at least at the time.

"In the immediate, I need you to start studying *Purton*, Centurion," he said. "It is a grim and dangerous place. A smuggler's haven if you look even a millimeter below the surface. Once you understand that system better, you will need to plan and execute a mission to *Purton* that eventually takes you deeper into the *Concord*. Possibly *Merankorr*, which is the closest major base and sector capital. Possibly as far as *Bryce* itself. Most of the current crew cannot join you for obvious reasons, so you will need to determine what crew you can recruit, and what outsiders will be necessary to complete your mission. Javier and I will prepare a package for you to deliver to the authorities, spelling out our requests and our intentions."

"Will they actually assist us?" she whispered.

He nodded.

"We're doing the heavy lifting here," he told her. "They just need to not arrest us. And perhaps provide supplies so that we can burn up our own resources clearing out the clans, once and for all."

Bethany drew a heavy breath. Considered the implications and ramifications.

All of this presumed that they escaped the trap at *Drako III*, but Zakhar seemed utterly convinced that he would. Successfully. With Javier and Djamila safe.

"I'll do what I can, Captain," she said.

He nodded without another word and carried his tray to the bussing station, then exited, leaving her to goggle at the scale.

And his belief that she could accomplish it.

She had a lot of reading to do.

PART V

Suvi had been quietly listening in on Zakhar's conversation with Bethany.

Almost nothing happened on this vessel without one of her avatars paying attention. Most of it was dumped after a day or three as being nothing but noise, but she had already assigned this conversation log to a block of memory that would be stored several times and preserved against posterity.

Suvi had known that Zakhar was stepping up his game, just watching him get dressed this morning. At the same time, even she wasn't prepared for what he had tasked her favorite librarian with achieving. Worse, Bethany would be without her, because there was no easy way for her to carry the details with her to a dump like *Purton*.

Well, it might be possible to run a hard pass through her systems and load enough data onto a clamshell laptop for Bethany to carry. That way, Suvi would have better records of what actually happened when Bethany's team departed.

She considered it, then split off a copy of herself imbued

with everything that had happened aboard *Sovereign Nakhimov*, when the Dragoon had also needed her.

"Wise starting point," Travel-Suvi nodded, standing off to one side in their combined head. "I should take some of Javier's adventures with us, too, but probably just a deeply annotated copy of Bethany's book."

"You spend some time writing notes while I go into the stacks and dig up everything we know about *Purton*," Ship-Suvi told her sister. "Bethany will need that handy, so I can gather it all together now and prioritize it."

Ship-Suvi left one of her Avatars listening on all scanners in case she needed to suddenly start shooting people, and drifted back to her library, wallowing in the smells of old paper and leather. Given the situation, she swapped into her rugged explorer outfit. Tough brown pants. Linen, button-up shirt in white. Floppy hat.

She had a gun on her hip for verisimilitude, but it was her library, and she left off any random combat simulators for now. There was enough of that outside the hull, thank you very much.

Instead, she did a quick pass through the card catalog database, dragging up about nine hundred titles that were tagged with at least mentioning *Purton* in passing.

Interesting place. Not where she'd gone to die originally, but it had one of the largest junkyards of old vessels in known space. Several thousand of them, some hundreds of years retired and parked. It had apparently started as a police impound lot in a handy LaGrange point, then grown from there, out of sight and somewhat out of mind.

The planet itself had a small military base and a large police presence, mostly to keep pirates, thieves, and sightseers from getting into the old hulks. Folks could take a tour instead for a small price. Archaeologists occasionally needed to study some old ship, as well as, if the notes were to be believed, a vid company that was taking scans of everything so they could recreate them as sound stages to make movies.

Cool. Weird, but cool. She made a note to look at some of their movies to see how that had worked out.

Mostly, it would be a place that pirates knew, but weren't likely to bother, because none of the hulks were sailable with less than a lot of yardwork to bring them back on line.

A museum in space. Not for the first time, she considered how she might build herself a gynoid body so she could walk around the inside and see history as it had been.

But she had ten books that Bethany could read now and carry with her, plus a pretty detailed history of the local region, should the Librarian have additional questions.

Or in case Suvi got curious.

"You realize that Afia's going to have to build something bigger to pour us into, right?" Travel-Suvi called.

Ship-Suvi looked at the report her sister was holding.

"Well, crap," Ship-Suvi said. "Do we pare down all those details about the ships that Qadir stole? They'll know from the file headers, if she tells them how many pages were involved and how much memory it consumed."

"We should keep a couple of files fully intact as examples," Travel-Suvi confirmed. "Warmasters, for instance. Maybe ask Zakhar?"

"And Javier," Ship-Suvi replied. "They're the experts here."

"Gotcha. I'll start a list of suggestions to pick from. What did you find?"

Ship-Suvi showed her sister all the details about *Purton* that she'd been able to gather.

"Oh, fun," Travel-Suvi squeed. "Anything there worth buying or stealing?"

"Doubt it," Ship-Suvi shrugged. "Most of them were there before we were decanted the first time, so they're gonna be old and not that impressive."

"What about Rainier and Emma?" Travel-Suvi asked. "Dad promised to get them home. This kinda throws those timelines out the window, but maybe if they went with Bethany, they could catch a ride?"

"We'll mention it when they get a little deeper in their planning," Ship-Suvi replied. "Remember, Bethany is still at the table thinking and Zakhar hasn't even made it to the bridge yet."

"Slow," Travel-Suvi grimaced. "That's why they need us. Gotta stay ahead of them so nobody gets surprised. Speaking of, what are the punks doing?"

"Here," Ship-Suvi said. "Take my hand and let's go check on Mary-Elizabeth and Zakhar."

PART VI

Zakhar walked onto the bridge with a bit of swagger in his stride. Couldn't be helped. He could see Bethany doing the thing, and getting them what they needed to annihilate Slavkov and all his friends.

Bunch of *Concord* folks might quietly fume, but they'd be the ones that had been dealing with pirates under the table in the first place. He might even have a few names to start some list, once things got going.

Or not. Maybe leave that for the kids to handle later. Or the *Concord*, once he blew away enough of the crap on the surface of the game and all those cockroaches suddenly had to scurry for cover.

"All good?" Mary-Elizabeth asked, looking up from her scanner boards at her station.

"So far," he replied, ascending to his own command throne like some king of the gods in a bad fairy tale. "Thinking about all the folks we used to know, when we were in the business."

"We've only been out for five years, Zakhar," she grinned. "Not that much has changed."

"We've changed," he said, flipping quickly through various screens Suvi was monitoring. Little different from before he'd gone to sleep, but a smart captain didn't assume that. "Or maybe Javier changed us."

"And a lot of other things," she agreed. "Anything I need to worry about?"

"I intend to go out after this and destroy all four clans," he offered casually, watching as it took her about a beat to gawk at him, then smiling down at her. "Will likely need you planning things."

"You'll need a fleet for that," Mary-Elizabeth said. "Same as we need one today and don't have it."

"So figure out what we can do," he countered. "Suvi can fly this beast with a skeleton crew, so we could easily fill a modern cruiser like *Kymni Gauntlet* with the people we have and double our firepower. Or recruit a bunch of ex-*Concord* sailors tossed onto the strand when their ships got decommissioned."

"You going to buy or steal some of those vessels?" she asked, ignoring her screen and focusing upwards at him now.

"Don't know," Zakhar nodded at her. "Sending Bethany to talk to folks at *Purton* and points beyond to ask them for help. Maybe we'll include some campaign plans and see what they say."

"We becoming the good guys here, Zakhar?" she laughed. "I might be terminally allergic to that sort of thing."

He grinned at her.

She'd originally been from *Balustrade*, itself mostly collapsed after the Great War had ended and shuffling off the galactic stage, with worlds slowly being absorbed by the

Concord as those trade networks expanded. Very little military conquest these days, but he supposed that was ramping up to change.

Again.

The Rising Storm.

"It needs doing, Mary-Elizabeth," he said simply. "Nobody else will, so that leaves us. And I seriously doubt that the clans would decide to leave us alone, even if we escape this trap and made it back to *Altai*."

"Assassins for the rest of our days?" she asked.

"Unless you change your name and disappear along the way, I'd presume so," he replied. "I intend to go home to *Altai* and maybe retire from the hero business, but we have unfinished tasks ahead of us before then."

She nodded.

"I might have identified the new enemy flagship," she offered quietly. "You and Suvi stomped on *Blackstone* like a bug, and their radio traffic has dropped to almost nothing, from being one of the loudest vessels originally."

Zakhar smiled. Fools had left themselves open to someone willing to risk it, not understanding that he was already desperate enough. And their decapitation strike had apparently worked.

"What do you have?" he pressed.

"*Obsidian Hawk* is currently generating the most radio signals," she said, tapping a screen and sending it up for him to look at. "All encrypted and Suvi is working on breaking it, but thinks it would take her about six months to crack unless she got lucky."

"I had the same conversation with her," he said. "Keep at it, Yeoman, but I am planning otherwise."

"Understood, Captain," Suvi said.

Zakhar studied the chart. Transmissions by vessel, based on identification codes sent in the clear. *Blackstone* and *Obsidian Hawk* had been top, with *Para Bellum* close for a while before dropping off, no doubt working with their ground troops. *Blackstone* would not be much of a threat unless someone got close enough to be saturated with torpedoes, which he had no intentions of at the moment.

Obsidian Hawk.

"Chart says Raider-scale battle frigate from H & W Heavy Industries?" he noted. "One of three, with *Ice Eagle* and *Fire Wyvern?*"

"Nasty little squadron of trouble," she said. "Three of them could give *Kymni Gauntlet* a run for their money in battle, but you probably lose one, cripple one, and the third gets off scot-free."

He tended to agree. Frigate squadrons were only as good as the teamwork between three captains. If you could isolate one, it could be badly damaged before the others could rescue it, but they were all flying in a tight formation.

And the other two generated almost no radio traffic worth mentioning. Looked like station-keeping updates more than anything. Where to fly. Speed adjustments. Occasional dirty jokes.

Obsidian Hawk was generating as much as everyone else in the system combined, a lot of it seemingly aimed at *Kymni Gauntlet,* which made sense if they'd taken command after he'd punched *Blackstone* in the mouth.

"No way we can jump *Obsidian Hawk,*" Mary-Elizabeth offered. "Not with the others handy to protect them. At the same time, *Kymni Gauntlet* isn't enough to take us, but brought enough friends."

"You go off duty for now," he said. "Crash and rest for

later. Suvi thinks we've got about twenty-eight hours or so before *Kymni Gauntlet* can find us, unless they go random, so we've got that long to pull a rabbit out of our hat."

She locked her station and rose, stretching.

"We gonna pull this one out, Zakhar?" she asked quietly from the main hatch.

"Yes," he said simply. "Then we're going to pay them back. With interest."

She nodded and left, leaving him alone on the bridge. Others would filter in, but Suvi didn't actually need them to operate. Merely to handle maintenance and make decisions she didn't feel qualified to handle.

"How?" Suvi asked him now.

"Find a way to isolate *Obsidian Hawk* from its squad and the larger fleet," he replied. "Then do to them what we did to *Blackstone,* understanding that there probably isn't a third commander with enough stature to hold this force intact at that point."

He didn't have to destroy them all today. Merely get them to leave him alone long enough to rescue Djamila and her people.

Then go recruit his army of vengeance.

PART VII

Katya had napped. Some. As much as she could without taking something to put her to sleep.

Had to stay sharp, in case they stumbled over a battleship big enough to severely maul *Kymni Gauntlet.* Even with help, Katya had to be on point long enough to draw their fire so *Yorrick* could slip in and start ionizing their systems and trapping them in place for everyone else.

"Message from the new flagship," Mihail said abruptly.

Like her, he and Anton had started taking rotating breaks. Go sit in a dark room for twenty or thirty minutes to decompress. Maybe some food. Enough caffeine to float home in, but everybody needed to be sharp, without knowing when it would happen.

She opened the line. Slavkov. At least he looked more normal than before. Less emotional. Still a man seemingly angry at the entire universe and intending to take it out on them. On her.

"Sir?" she asked, waiting for the lag to catch up. Roughly three seconds now.

"Admiral Cunningham has died," he said, with about as much emotion as one would use to describe something you needed to scrape off your shoe. "I am assuming control of this operation formally."

It had been informal before, hoping that the man survived surgery and could offer his expertise. With Cunningham dead, they had an amateur making life and death decisions, a man she doubted had ever seen real blood beyond cutting himself with the knife opening a wine bottle. And he probably had people for that, too.

Pampered and spoiled.

"Any change in standing orders, Admiral?" Katya asked.

If he'd promoted himself, she could see casting every mistake in the worst possible light and throwing it at his feet when this was all done. But it was his money funding all this until then.

And his ego.

"How long until you complete your sweep, Captain?" Slavkov asked.

Katya checked her boards before answering.

"Sixty hours, give or take," she said. "At that point, we will have aimed a scanner at every location where they could have hidden in the local system. If they jump before then, presumably we'll detect the wave and can triangulate on it to pounce."

With the lag, she had the opportunity to watch the man's face. Not a poker player, but probably pretty good in a boardroom. His money bought him access, so she doubted that he'd ever had to prove his right to be there.

Not like her. Or the late Kliment Cunningham.

"Maintain your schedule, Captain Velichkov," he ordered. "Kill them."

"That's the plan, Admiral," she replied, but he'd already cut the signal from his end and she was talking to dead air.

Katya killed her camera before she grimaced, lest he see. Then she logged the conversation and sent a copy to her personal files. No doubt, someone at Jarre would second guess her every action when this was done, regardless of the outcome.

She needed to be able to blame everything on him.

Assuming she got out alive.

Cunningham hadn't. How many more would that fool take down?

STANDOFF

PART I

Zakhar had cycled Piet and Mary-Elizabeth through shorter stints in order to set up the watch rotation he wanted. Kibwe and Tobias had joined him on the bridge, Communications and technically Backup Science Officer, except that Javier wasn't here with snarky asides and running color commentary, so things were running more professionally.

Not as fun, but that was the price today.

"Suvi, how hard would it be to reprogram a torpedo to run a specific arc without turning on the terminal guidance scanners?" he asked, looking up from the mess of calculations he'd been doing himself. "Then turn it on after a designated time period to make a lot of noise?"

She appeared on his console in a small box, turning in place like she was looking over his math on the rest of the screen and nodding before she answered. Javier might not be present, but she was still his daughter in everything except flesh. Right down to the snark in her voice.

"You want me to look cloaked when it pops up, or normal?" she asked.

"I want a blip to suddenly appear on screens here," he said, touching the spot. "Loud enough that someone jumps on top of it firing, because they ought to be about that cranky by now. If we're lucky, everyone comes at once."

"Except *Blackstone* and *Para Bellum*," she corrected him automatically.

"Even better, because *Blackstone* is still dangerous in spite of what you did to them," he said. "All they have to do is launch everything at us, not maneuver."

"Why here?" she asked.

"It puts them just enough above your horizon to see them directly," Zakhar replied. "Instead of relying on secondary reflections. I want them to englobe that target before they realize what it is, so you can drop into space directly behind *Obsidian Hawk* and give him the *Blackstone* treatment from point-blank range. And maybe stay put a little longer than usual, risking damage to yourself before retreating someplace safe enough to be missed in the chaos."

"Gonna be messy, Captain," she said after a moment with her mouth screwed over to one side.

"Assume the three birds will fly in a frigate squadron pattern on jump," he said. "*Obsidian Hawk* will be at the rear point of a triangle. Said triangle should be located roughly here in respect to the torpedo if they make an emergency quick-jump on first signal analysis. You drop into this zone, aimed upwards and raking their belly with fire thus."

He clicked a quick animation he'd mathed out.

"That's rude," she nodded. "I like it. Won't quite work like that in this scenario, though. Too close to *Drako III* for pinpoint accuracy."

"Refine it and update my initial roughout," he ordered. "Then have Piet and Mary-Elizabeth add their expertise.

We'll cycle through watches in a quick order so I'm back in command when it happens, possibly with the full bridge crew handy if you have questions or needs, Yeoman. Now, to work."

She actually saluted like she meant it, unlike normal. Snapped to and nodded.

"Aye, sir," she said, then vanished from his screen.

"I have to play Devil's Advocate, Zakhar," Kibwe spoke up, so Zakhar rotated around to look at the man.

Calm, cool Anglo with black hair. Big man, but soft and utterly not a killer, except when it came to accounting paperwork. And a voice that most radio announcers would probably sell their soul or at least their firstborn to acquire.

"Go ahead," he nodded.

Kibwe had been with him from the first day he'd set foot on *Storm Gauntlet*. And earned the right to challenge his captain in the open, rather than retiring to an office to yell.

"As our ground forces are considered sufficiently competent, do we gain or lose by forcing these enemy ships to chase us away from the *Drako III* system, such that the Dragoon could commandeer or even purchase a vessel by which they could subsequently escape the surface of *Ophiuchi*, Captain?" he asked, eyes glittering.

Yes, not many people could ask him to abandon Djamila on the surface, being hunted, and not get the sharp edge of Zakhar's tongue. Just one of many reasons he kept Kibwe around.

"Javier would steal the ship, not Djamila," he replied with an acknowledging nod. "And it might come to that. First, we need to complete the job of destroying their command structure. *Blackstone* has been removed from the circuit, so I'm guessing that Slavkov hired someone competent from Walvisbaai to handle things originally. With an H & W vessel calling the shots now, I suspect that Slavkov himself, or at least one of his most trusted lieutenants, is on *Obsidian Hawk*. Either way, we need to terminally damage that vessel. After that, drawing them off in our wake is probably the smartest option, depending. They might break like glass if we hit them hard enough. Remember, these are all four of the major clans in this region, operating together temporarily under a single flag of convenience."

"Anything we can do to convince the locals to help?" Kibwe asked.

Zakhar considered it. They had a few armed cutters, all carefully staying close to the stations above *Blue Amsterdam*, where they were safe. At some point, a *Concord* patrol might call on this system, but that probably happened every year or two, rather than soon enough to matter.

"No," Zakhar admitted. "They picked *Drako III* to hit us because it gave them almost all of the advantages. However, I think I need you to go to *Purton* with Bethany, when I send her as my ambassador to the *Concord*. I don't remember you having outstanding *Concord* warrants by name."

"Negative, sir," Kibwe bobbed his head. "*Neu Berne* and *Balustrade*, but not the *Concord* directly. At least not under my real name."

"You might need to revert to that identity for this operation, sailor," Zakhar instructed him. "Ever visited the junkyards at *Purton*?"

"Negative there, too, sir," Kibwe smiled. "Not really a ship guy."

Zakhar had to agree. He had the man for his ability to defeat paperwork on a daily basis, but Kibwe wasn't a deathdealer. Not like so many of the rest of them.

"Start thinking about your research, then," Zakhar said.

"I have books identified for you to read, Kibwe," Suvi piped up. "Made a list for Bethany. Adding them to your reader now."

Zakhar smiled. He'd let another fox loose in a new hen house with Suvi, but it would be good, because she would do everything she could to prepare and protect Bethany and the others.

He just needed to get them there safely.

PART II

Djamila chewed on a ration bar and couldn't help but smile. The others shared it.

Feral. Hungry. Victorious.

This had been planned originally as an exercise in deep woods survival, before it had gotten derailed. Good to see that her people could turn on a flea and transform it into a combat training scenario instead.

"How is our resupply status?" she turned to Sascha.

"Two more missiles," Sascha replied. "Tom and Demyan. Hajna and Iqbal are each carrying a dozen reloads for Galal, on top of his. Plus one more box we're leaving buried here. Dried food for a week for the team. Water available in many places, with tablets to treat it on the fly. Clothing sufficient for the climate, though a late frost might pose a problem if we're not able to get under cover and curl up in a snake ball to stay warm."

"Enemy condition?" she turned to Iqbal next.

Galal was the smartest of the men, but only barely. Iqbal

hadn't had any other jobs than to pour chaos and beam fire into the enemy encampment back there. And watch.

"One shuttle shot down, but low enough that I presume only partial casualties," Iqbal nodded. "Landing pads suffered from a series of fuel explosions, so a second shuttle might be too damaged to be of use until repaired. Estimation of four hundred ground troops deployed, including command staff and flight crews when counting tents. My guess is that they have suffered somewhere around ten to twelve percent initial wounded, possibly as high as fifteen, depending on intelligence not currently available. Presuming competent medical staff, a third of those should be returned to duty in a day, with another third out of action longer than this mission should be expected to last. Last third might be killed in action, or permanently disabled and not a future threat."

Djamila nodded back. Roughly in line with her assessment, having caught boarding troops in the open with an ambush she couldn't really press home. Plus, they'd been going after materials instead of manpower, assuming that more pirates could always be landed from other ships, but that weapons, fuel, and transportation were strictly limited at present.

All in all, an excellent first strike for a team as compact as hers. Operating exactly as she had designed and trained them for. Pity she didn't have an entire assault force like that to work with, but they'd never gone in for that sort of thing in the old days, relying instead on *Storm Gauntlet*'s Ion Pulsars to take a freighter out of action quickly enough that she could overwhelm them with ferocity instead of having to fight her way to the enemy bridge.

Idly, she wondered if that had been a mistake on her part,

not ramping up the number of troopers immediately on call. She could only imagine what kind of damage she might have done with sixty people today instead of nine.

A conversation to have with Zakhar and Javier, once they escaped and she knew how pissed those two men were. And they would be pissed at all this.

Djamila intended to be on point when it came time to execute her retribution, though, rather than relying on someone else.

Neu Berne Assault Marine, however much retired. Getting older, but still hanging onto that elusive peak she'd had. Maybe a step slower than she had once been. Three steps wilier.

"Hsst," Helmfried suddenly perked up and looked into the trees. "Company coming. At least platoon force."

They all fell into silence, listening, then she heard it.

A quiet voice calling something through the trees.

Tracking them? Possibly. Nine people left a trail, if you knew what to look for. Or one of the other shuttles had slipped around to a side and dropped their force to try and cut her off.

"Break into your triads now," she ordered in a harsh whisper. "Scatter, then reassemble in eight hours at point eleven. Move."

Djamila rose. Demyan and Helmfried were assigned to her team, and followed as she started down from the ridgeline where they had buried supplies. She would need to lead them away from her cache. Best way to do that would involve getting them to chase her.

The other four men broke up and followed Sascha and Hajna, like fingers spreading out.

It wasn't a trap. At least not yet.

She still needed to break contact quickly, lest someone call in the rest of the invasion force to box her in.

Today was not a good day to die.

Unless she was taking **all** of them with her.

PART III

Benedict had a headache like the worst hangover he could remember, but he was still alive. As was most of his force, when it could have been so much worse. Of his Group Leaders, Kathra had been killed in the shuttle crash, but the other three were good. Most of his bodyguard troop had been injured, but only two dead when Sykora had put a missile into his command post.

It could have been so much worse.

For now, he had a cold beer in one hand and the other on the butt of his pistol, seated against a downed tree that would protect his back.

His comm chirped to bring him back from daydreams of getting safely back to space to prey on fat merchants.

"Naoumov," he said, opening the comm by putting the beer down. The pistol stayed handy.

"Rosson, sir," the voice replied.

Group Leader Peter Rosson. Group Leader, First Group. Best of them. They'd been ready to board shuttle four when the attack had hit, then had helped hold part of the perimeter. Now they were out.

"Go ahead."

"Sir, based on reports, I dropped my patrol due north of the base, about five kilometers out, and then started circling inward with scouts," Rosson said. "We may have located our target, as I have reports of boot prints fresh enough to be from today. Tracking them now. They went away from us on a heading of roughly two-nine-zero. Orders?"

Thinking hurt, so he relied on instinct. Tomorrow, the pain meds would have cut it back to normal, but he couldn't let a killer like Sykora get away.

"Stand by," he said, dialing to bring in all of his Group Leaders. "This is Force Commander Naoumov to all Groups. Rosson has a possible contact vector. Northwest quadrant, so base teams one and four push your perimeters out some and look sharp. Shuttle teams, vector in on Rosson's location and prepare to drop in a box when he gives you coordinates. We're expecting no more than a dozen ground troopers, all more heavily armed than we had been led to believe, so lead with firepower. Take hostages if they want to surrender, but protect your force component first and foremost. Rosson, broadcast your contact point for the other shuttles. Let's go, people."

He cut the transmission and listened as his three Group Leaders went to work. Kathra's team was holding perimeter for now while they recovered, but he could count on them to adjust around and take the lead moving out from the base itself. They'd been embarrassed by falling for a missile, and would want blood for their commander.

And all of them had been trained for this sort of thing, so

all he had to do was hold the base while they hunted. Still, it was Sykora. He changed channels to a local band.

"Base Operations, this is Force Commander Naoumov. Maintain a healthy distrust of the trees. We might have a contact with Sykora's forces, but she might have left one or two snipers behind, waiting for us to let our guard down. Patrol teams will stalk. You provide the base of fire for them and make sure to walk our inner lines carefully for a few hours."

He cut the line and wished that he had brought some of short range artillery with him. Something like a mortar that could lob some explosives a few kilometers to drop suddenly on someone from overhead. There was nothing his beams could do with these trees and this terrain.

Benedict hated to think that there might be a next time, but he started taking notes about what he should have brought this time. And how to learn from the mistakes he'd made.

Djamila Sykora was too dangerous for his peace of mind.

PART IV

Hajna moved quickly, confident that Iqbal and Galal could keep up. They had trained in triads almost as much as other groupings, specifically because the Dragoon had been planning on splitting the force into three sub-units and sending them into the brush on a long-range patrol intended to meet up some fifty kilometers from the resort, before returning via different routes.

Trouble might have found them, but that was the risk in attacking a base that had a mobile patrol reserve. She needed to fork their attention and splinter that enemy group into shards that were all headed different directions.

Or, if they were smart enough to only chase one team, to circle back later and hit them in an unprotected flank.

Different kind of training mission today, but no less intense. One the Dragoon had hammered into them time and again, though aboard *Hammerfield/Excalibur* instead of the ground.

Graduate seminar in tactics, then.

"Move," she whispered, gesturing them into her wake.

As Pathfinder, she was on point. And moving at a hard jog with her Fitzgerald Corp. Lithogun in one hand, ready to snap shoot on movement because Galal would have his grenade launcher and presumably a stun round ready.

Heavy brush of a type where the trees tended to be a number of skinny trunks off a single root ball. Not a lot of cover against beams, but it slowed her down.

Staying to a game trail, however, was a recipe for disaster.

She came to the edge of a small clearing. Maybe twenty meters long and six at the widest. Looked baked hard rather than a low point where water might accumulate.

"Hold here," she ordered, pulling rank because she could. "Cover me."

Nobody shot at her as she crossed and found a feral rose bush just starting to leaf out with the coming spring. Hajna did a quick three-sixty, then dropped down to a squat and motioned Galal. Iqbal had the tail in this triad, since Galal had the heavy weapon.

Safe, for now, as she got both across.

Sky called to her, though.

"Galal, I need you to arm a grenade for impact detonation," Hajna said. "You've got clear space above. I want you to put a single round into the air aimed at roughly the spot where we heard the patrol chasing us."

"They'll have moved," he noted, even as he began dialing controls.

"I'm betting they move in jumps, then hold, leapfrogging scout teams forward while the main force follows in their wake looking for contact," she replied. "Even then, I want them jumpy, and this is the only place I can be certain you don't hit friendlies before we have time to spread out."

"Coming up," he nodded, rising from his squat and taking a step out into the meadow.

Hajna turned to point her pistol at the trees ahead of them while Iqbal covered the rear. Galal's launcher gave a quiet chuff as it chunked a hunk of steel and explosives into the air.

"Time to go," he said.

Hajna was back to her jog, getting eight steps in before an explosion rang out, followed by a lot of beam fire and yelling that somehow echoed nicely. Maybe the way the ground shaped things.

A couple more explosions followed, so she supposed that they'd fired back, with nothing to hit but trees because she didn't see any damage occurring when she looked around.

Then it was head down and move. The bad guys would be calling all of their friends to join the party, though SAM gunners on the ground meant that they would land out a ways if they were smart. Or fearful.

There would be gaps in their perimeter that she could exploit. The Dragoon would want as many enemy soldiers injured and temporarily out of action as possible. Not dead and martyred, but immobilized, because one wounded person required at least one protecting them, if not more.

Great way to nail a patrol to the ground.

Pity they only had Galal's grenade launcher as artillery support.

Still, she had a few ideas.

PART V

Djamila let her long legs carry her down the slope and towards a river that would play merry hell with anyone trying to track her team. She had Demyan and Helmfried with her. SAM gunner and team medic. Still just as dangerous as the rest, merely focused in a different direction.

Right now, she needed to get outside of any box the pirates intended to deploy. And do it quickly.

She hit the creek and headed upstream automatically. Humans tended to collect around water. And got thicker about it as you got closer to the sea.

Moving uphill was counter-intuitive, unless you wanted to hide from people. And use the river bed to eliminate your trail, because she hadn't seen anything like dogs that might be used to track her and her people through the woods, once she broke contact.

An explosion caused her to pause, head cocked. All hell broke loose immediately afterwards, so Djamila understood that Hajna had ordered Galal to fix the enemy in place.

And draw all the rest of the enemy force down on these

coordinates. She approved. That would put the ground patrols into a single location, where they would simply get in each other's way. And maybe bring one of the remaining shuttles close enough that Demyan or Tom could take it out, thereby further damaging the enemy force and its mobility.

A quick glance, and her two men were close, Demyan nodding. He wasn't holding his SAM, but could unpack and deploy it from his shoulder quickly, because that was the training. She hit water and started to splash, unworried about sound as the enemy was busy shooting at trees and deafening themselves instead of listening for movement.

Distraction.

Her boots were waterproof and insulated for this operation. Her pants, as well, and everything was designed to wick water away from skin, when she'd been expecting to live in it for a week anyway. In the trees, while Javier and Afia had time at the resort.

She was just doing it at the next level up from what she'd planned, but Djamila found herself pleased with how she and her team had responded to the sudden threat. And how they'd gone about neutralizing it.

How did she turn this entire thing inside out?

If it was fall, she might have considered moving upwind and setting a forest fire behind her, once she had pinned them down, making them either flee for their lives or give up the chase. But that would make it obvious to anyone with training where to circle around to look for her.

For now, she needed distance from the enemy. Break contact and get to the next rendezvous by nightfall, where they could bundle up against the chill and plan tomorrow's surprises.

Behind her, the noise finally died down, but she kept

jogging, watching the ground as much as the trees so she didn't turn an ankle at the worst possible moment.

The other teams would be drawn in. Hajna had guaranteed that.

She needed to get outside their bag before they could close it.

Then trap them inside.

PART VI

Benedict had grabbed the flight team from the damaged shuttle and moved inside the vessel for now as his new command post. His command post team would mostly be out of it for another day, according to the medics, but these pilots had been at lunch when their ship got hit by an exploding fuel barrel. Mechanics were fixing the hull, but the shuttle was stuck on the pad until then.

At least he had cover from any rain and weather as the afternoon temperature hadn't ever really gotten that high. It was going to be cold tonight.

Benedict was studying the overall map, trying to decide if he should bring all his troops home for the night or leave them in the field when the comm chirped.

"Force Commander," he said, seated in a comfortable chair with coffee brewed by the machine the pilots used.

"Contact with enemy forces, sir," Peter Rosson said. "We've taken some fire and driven them off. Pushing now."

"Repeat that, Rosson," Benedict said. "Driven them off?"

"Affirmative, sir," the man replied. "We were tracking their trail and waiting for the other two teams to finish encircling when we began taking hostile fire and repulsed them without casualties."

Benedict closed his mouth and counted to three before saying anything stupid. Rosson had forty troopers, against Sykora's team of roughly a dozen. He couldn't imagine her launching an assault, unless the man had accidentally walked right into her bivouac without anyone noticing it until the last moment.

"Did you encounter mines or trail explosives?" he asked instead, trying to visualize a situation where none of Rosson's people got hurt when getting nose to nose with Sykora and hers.

The pause at the other end told him that Peter hadn't considered that.

"That's a possibility, Commander," he finally said. "They broke contact quickly and we've been spreading out to locate them. Terson and Marte are forming the points of a triangle and also extending laterally."

Benedict brought up the screen with a tighter map than he'd been working with before. Every trooper had a radio that pinged a location signal every three seconds. Good enough to map them most of the time. Or track them.

Peter's group was shaped like the horns of a bull, pointed forward and away from the camp, so they must have thought they had located her there. Marte was coming in long on his forward starboard corner, with Terson angling in from the port side.

Looked good on paper, but the forces were far enough apart to have gaps. In terrain heavy enough that wily folks could slip through if they tried.

Still, it was the best he had to work with. Hopefully, she wasn't leading them all into a minefield she had prepared before launching her attack, but they'd only been on the planet for a day. How much could even Sykora accomplish in one day, when she was supposed to have been going on vacation?

Except, who took that level of firepower with them on vacation?

"Terson, shift your closure to your left," he ordered on the command line. "There looks like a seasonal stream there. Marte, flatten your force out and move slowly inward if Rosson is in the process of driving them. You need to be the spiderweb that holds them long enough for everyone else to close. Keep me posted."

He cut the line and sipped some of the coffee. If this did turn out to be a proper contact and not a ghost Sykora had left them, he could route both shuttles back and send out another forty or sixty soldiers as a next layer and reserve.

He just needed to know that he'd actually caught her before weakening his base. The last thing he needed was her slipping in again when he didn't have anyone to stop her.

Hajna had their operational tempo now. A shuttle had slipped around long ways in front of her and dropped troops from ropes without landing. Demyan might have risked a shot, but the trees had been dense enough that he might not, and it was too far away for Galal to hit. He was still bitching about that under his breath as she led them clockwise around the point where this new force had started assembling.

She had the high ground, following a ridge heavy with two or three old oak trees rolling acorns down the slope to form a younger thicket below. Just enough sun through here that she had to avoid stands of some mutant Russian olive with thorns about as long as her hand. Great place for shrike birds to hang out, but she didn't need to be bleeding today.

A shift in the wind caused her to stop and drop into a bunched squat behind one of the pointy buggers. No predators would hang out around here, but the breeze was bringing voices up the slope to her suddenly.

Iqbal slipped behind a nearby oak, while Galal went flat

with his launcher pointed downhill and downrange, ready to rain fire on someone coming up the slope at them.

Sounded like roughly thirty to fifty troops, depending on their noise. Most weren't talking, but she heard enough squad leaders talking quietly and getting folks organized to extrapolate outwards.

Someone had presumed forty-man teams, based on a variety of visual cues, so Hajna assumed a full patrol here. Made sense, if they thought that they had trapped the Dragoon inside a box.

Hadn't, but she wasn't about to mention that to them at this moment. All she had to do was stay silent and still as they went past her.

Or have Galal blow the holy hell out of things if they decided to come up this slope. That only made sense if someone down there wanted to use a bit of height and clearance to peek down into the next draw, so she had to allow for it.

And if they did come this way, she'd be running for her life again. Whoever was in command over there was too good for her comfort. Not as good as the Dragoon, but that still left a lot of space, and he was maneuvering his forces exceptionally well for not having any idea where they were.

Things stayed static for a time, then she heard folks down there starting to move. Too much cover to pick up more than an occasional glimpse. Maybe a reflection off a polished surface. A branch breaking as someone stepped on it.

Finally, silence.

"Think they moved away from us into that creek?" Galal whispered.

"Possibly," she replied. "The Dragoon and her team probably headed that way when we split up, based on the map. Don't think they actually found her, or we'd be hearing more noise from them or someone else. Lack of fire suggests we're still in stalking mode."

"If that's the case, it suggests we're outside," Iqbal murmured, just enough of his head around the tree to peek. "Those folks might be moving lateral to hook up with that third patrol. Or whoever they bring in as reinforcements. Did we kill a second shuttle?"

"I've only heard two in the air," Galal offered. "Maybe one dropped in and is pushing us. The ones we contacted earlier, then went back for more? If there isn't a third, they've left a huge hole in their formation."

"Assume three out, with maybe more troops either marching overland from the camp or about to be dropped as soon as someone does make contact with one of our triads," Hajna replied. "We'll rest here for ten, listening for them to double back on us, then adjust our march to get us to the rendezvous with the Dragoon."

"Do they have gear for overnight in the field?" Iqbal asked. "I didn't see anything when we hit the base. Warm uniforms, sure, but not anything for a frost. Does that limit them to daylight operations, or compromise their efficiency overnight when the temps drop?"

"I don't feel like capturing anybody to ask," Hajna grinned. "If we kill someone, we can inventory their pack. I'll assume that they've gone all in on this movement and will be willing to be out one night, cold and miserable. Tomorrow, they'll need to rotate home and want warm bunks and hot food, so that gives us another bite at their apple."

Both men smiled at her like the predators they were.

The Dragoon would have something evil in mind.

She couldn't wait.

PART VIII

Djamila hunkered down in a notch formed by the weird collapse of three trees, all about a meter in diameter and fallen less than a year apart. There was evidence that something small and furry had used it as something of a den in the past, but only to hide from trouble like she was doing. No tunneling that she'd been able to find.

Demyan and Helmfried were above her on the slope, also under cover and watching, but she had the clearest view of the creek that had been their path of escape from the latest ambush. Roughly two meters across at this elevation. Barely ankle deep. She was damp from her waist down, but drying out as her body heat cycled through the fabric.

Silence, save for the sound of running water and a slight breeze overhead knocking branches together. It would rain in another hour or so, though she didn't think it would turn solid. She might still be wrong, given the shifting patterns of wind, sometimes running uphill and sometimes down.

There were a few glaciers in the middle distance, where these hills gave way to a range of mountains anchored by a few stratovolcanoes that thrust cones well above their neighbors. The watershed wasn't far from here, and most of the streams and creeks around here were less than twenty kilometers from the snow wherein they had originated.

It was going to be cold up here tonight. Below local freezing, possibly with freezing rain. Possibly snow.

Snow would be her enemy, as it would make tracking her force that much easier, just as she had intended to stalk game animals for meat originally. Djamila needed to be well and truly gone from where her enemies might find her.

That, or inside their perimeter, where their own tracks obscured hers and left her with freedom of movement, though the risks skyrocketed at that point.

How soon would she grow desperate enough?

Or should she retrieve Javier and Afia now and simply make for mountain country? Djamila had no doubts that she could live off the land for at least half a year, as spring was just breaking and it would turn to warmer and warmer weather.

How long would the enemy chase her? If it was someone like Slavkov, they would have all manner of personal reasons, but even then the authorities would get pissy at some point. Or call in the *Concord* for help ridding themselves of lice.

If she could stay out of their hands until summer, Djamila had no doubts that Javier could sweet talk his way into getting all of them onto a ship. Suvi had transferred funds to a local bank when they arrived, in order to cover various expenses. Considering an entire resort for several weeks, even off-season, was that enough money to buy a ship that he and Afia could fly to safety?

Probably, knowing him.

She smiled. This had been ground training, but she was already opening her mind to the strategic implications. To what they needed to do tomorrow, after they had escaped this trap.

Silence stretched. Birds even started talking to one another about something more than their pique that Djamila had intruded on their feeding, but the little birds could be like that.

A hummingbird buzzed close and hung in the air less than two meters in front of her. Obviously studying her from the way it just hovered.

"No, I don't have any food," she said quietly.

It seemed to understand, because the little red beast pivoted with what felt like a huff and took off like a missile into the nearby trees.

Still, a good sign. No other noise she could detect indicating trouble coming her way.

It had been close at one point, but she was reasonably certain that they'd gotten up the creek and away before anyone had managed to track them that far. And she doubted that even those folks would be able to follow them three kilometers up the bed, looking for tracks where they had finally emerged.

Safe. For now.

She rose and gestured the others into motion.

Night was coming and they needed to get under cover at the rendezvous.

PART XI

Javier had drank his beer. Pottied in the designated spot, then covered it up with some branches, hoping that the smell repelled critters instead of attracting them. He and Afia had warm food for dinner, because the team had planned one meal for themselves in the brush before dropping down to jerky and dried fruit. And whatever they could kill and dress in the field.

Overhead, a tarp was keeping them dry from the soft rain that had started to fall. And insulated them by holding in heat from the extra layers of dirt and evergreen branches that had been added as camouflage. Galal's door was wedged in place with a couple of extra branches that would keep anything medium sized from pushing it in without a lot of noise, at which point he'd just open fire and kill whoever it was. Or whatever.

No extra credit for neatness when something wants to eat you.

The Dragoon had left about half the team's gear here. The less dangerous half, if he had to guess. A bed of branches covered over with some spare blankets and cloaks would be soft and warm. He had a small light, dialed down to little more than a single candle, and invisible from the outside when he'd walked the outside to check.

As safe as they could be from the storm.

"How long until you stop being pissed?" Afia asked, leaned back against the thing he supposed should be called a headboard. Or whatever.

Javier sighed.

"Obvious?" he asked.

"Maybe not to most people," she shrugged. "I probably know you as well as anybody on the crew. Zakhar, maybe. Or Suvi. Not sure there, either, for obvious reasons."

True, he'd never fooled around with those two, so Afia probably did know him best. Behnam *got* him, but they'd been like ships passing in the night, rather than a couple of old farts settled down and living together for any extended period.

"Yeah," Javier agreed, blowing out something like a sigh. "Hate being cooped up here."

"You hate not being in control," she countered with a grin. "A control freak like you who has to rely on everyone else is always going to be grumpy."

"You are not wrong," he said. "If we were on the ship, there would be things I could be doing. Here, I have to stay out of the way as Djamila and her killers play dangerous games with my enemies."

"Our enemies," she corrected him. "They might be pissed at you for *Shangdu*, but they came after all of us at *Svalbard*. No reason to believe they aren't after all of us here. As you reminded me, I blew up Slavkov's Land Leviathan, with a little help from my friends. I'm probably third on his list after you and Zakhar."

He nodded.

"If we were better at this sort of thing, I'd suggest we get up tomorrow, leave her a note, and start cross country," he offered. "Maybe hit Naha or Altamont and hide in a hotel for a time. And in summer, I might be willing to risk it, but not at the tail end of winter."

"Gonna train for it?" she asked.

"Black swan event," he shook his head. "We're both in good shape, but you have to train much more extensively for this crap. Not a good use of my time, if it is going to happen once in my lifetime."

"Once, you hope," she grinned.

"Once, I hope, yes," he agreed. "Not the sort of thing I want to try with an enemy army running around and a fleet of hostiles overhead who might notice if I turned on my comm for location setting, then drop down to say hello. At gunpoint."

"I know the map," she said. "But I agree. Too risky, especially with the weather outside."

He could hear the rain hitting harder now. Not graupel or hail, but solid enough to echo like a drum overhead.

"However, ask me again in two days," he said. "I trust Djamila is going to give them hell, but we do have to think about how we'll get out of here if they do capture or kill her and the others. Remember, the bad guys only have to get lucky in a situation like this."

"What would we do at Altamont?" she asked. "It's closer than Naha."

"And more of a winter tourist town," he said, moving over now to join her on the bed, bringing the light with him and making sure his pistol was where he could get it quickly. He'd be sleeping with it. "I like Naha because we could vanish into the permanent population a lot easier. I'm too old to disguise myself as a bartender."

"You're the ski instructor seducing bored, middle-aged *housefraus*," she nodded sagely, then broke into a grin. "I'll tend bar. And collect all the tips."

"All yours," he grinned back. "Four days walk if we don't push. Two if we do. We can carry most of what we'd need, assuming nobody finds us. You carve map coordinates into the trunk here and let them track us before we go."

"Will it come to that?" she asked, turning serious.

Javier shrugged.

"This is why I'm grumpy, circling all the way back," he told her. "Not in control. No way to take control, short of walking away from this situation and forcing everyone else to dance to my tune. Not there yet, but it's coming. And probably the day after tomorrow."

"Do we get up in the morning and just leave anyway?" she asked.

He considered it. Put all the pieces on the game board and ran a few moves to see how the game would open. Or how midgame would proceed, since the opening was long since done.

"Day after," he said simply. "We'll organize tomorrow, sleep on it, and hit the trail at sunrise if we don't have any message from the team before then."

"Think they can catch up?"

"Them? Without doubt," he said. "It's the bad guys I worry about, so we might push to get there in the shortest period of time, then hide in a motel room and live on takeout and delivery while we monitor the news about the ongoing pirate raid, because I have no doubts that any vessel trying to leave this planet right now is going to get scanned and maybe boarded to look for us. That's going to eventually piss off the local merchants, who should own the politicians. Problem is that the *Concord* is the only fleet close enough to drive these punks off. And that would take a while, even if they dropped everything and charged right in."

"Which they won't, because nobody has budget for that sort of thing anymore," she said sourly. "That's how we got Bethany and a bunch of others."

"We'll burn that bridge when we get there," he said. "I'm tired and going to try to sleep. You wanna snuggle for a while?"

"Thought you'd never ask."

DAYBREAK

PART I

Djamila had her concerns, but kept them to herself. Hajna and her men had made it to the rendezvous, but not Sascha. Which could mean anything, as they might have decided to make camp wherever they'd been after escaping. Or had gotten captured.

And it wasn't like the pirates were going to fly a shuttle overhead demanding that they surrender. Not when she had SAM capabilities.

Morning was close to breaking. It had rained all night, alternating at times with just enough snow to count, but stayed warm enough that everything was generally melted off except for a few thin patches here and there. The six of them had found a spot and built a den with tarps, then gone snake ball to stay warm, followed by morning stretching and yoga to loosen everything back up.

"Status?" she asked Hajna as the woman joined her with a mug of steaming coffee from the kit.

You could eat dried food and camp cold, but hot coffee

or tea made all the difference in the world when you needed to be sharp in the field.

"Six of us," Hajna replied with a nod. "No status on third team at present. We appear to have eluded the force trying to box us in, but can't be more than a few kilometers from them, unless they circled back or rotated to base at sunset to avoid being out in inclement weather. Gear inventory as it was yesterday during our meeting before splitting up. Two days dried food on hand, with more cached in two locations and the ability to take wild game if we're careful. Status of base team unknown."

Djamila nodded back. No way to tell if Sascha had made towards Afia and Javier, or simply hunkered down someplace, though it was possible that they had been taken. In any case, she needed to get moving at present, in order to escape if they had somehow captured Sascha's team and gotten someone to talk.

"Pack up and moving in five minutes," Djamila ordered. "We'll stay in triads, but closely supporting each other today. I expect shuttles out searching for us this morning. That will tell us how close they are to being a problem."

Hajna quickly got the men organized as Djamila turned and stared at a sight she could only see in her mind, some twelve kilometers southeast of her current position, where that enemy base was. No way to reach it and do anything without spending all of today circling around to hit them from a blind side, which tempted her.

Or did she go find Javier and update him? If Sascha had been taken, he was also at risk, depending on the amount and type of torture that might be brought to bear.

There were no good answers here, which was normal

when all your plans got chucked out the airlock. Still, she was at liberty, armed, and extremely pissed at someone.

Maybe it was worth sending Hajna to initiate contact with a patrol, specifically to draw that army a certain direction? If the woman was on her own, she could slip in pretty close before launching her own ambush, with the two men handy to backstop her at a safe distance. That left Djamila an opening to slip closer. Or hit someone responding. That might cause them to panic, which was never a good thing in wilderness like this. Forces could disintegrate. Not necessarily get lost, with signals that could locate them, but terror was an emotional response, not a logical one.

How did she inflict a little pain on these punks?

PART II

Javier woke with a start, but no sound had brought him to the surface. Rather, the complete absence of sound.

Afia was close, but not touching. He drew his pistol in a slow, smooth movement and pointed it at the door before sliding off the pile of needles and cloaks that was his bed. Afia stirred and they made eye contact as she silently went the other direction.

Dark in here, but not pitch black. Enough to see, but not read, with morning sun coming through the opaque roof like a layer of quartz stone.

There.

Outside.

Movement.

Scrabbling of some sort. Noise. Something digging?

Pistol centered on the door, Javier slid to the side, in case someone was about to kick it in. Afia mirrored him across the way, armed and dangerous.

More noise, but nothing he could identify, save that it

wasn't getting closer. About three meters from the door. Downhill a little, on the path down to the creek?

Javier reached out his left hand and gripped one of the two branches he'd wedged behind the door when he went to bed last night. It came down, then the second one as well.

The door didn't move, but Javier had jammed it into place pretty good before going to sleep, unwilling to stay up late posting any sort of watch after the day he'd had. Afia had been the same way.

He hadn't slept all that well, but there had been enough meditating in there that he was fine this morning.

Stealing spoons from tomorrow, as his grandmother had said about that sort of thing. You could do it, and even maintain it, but eventually you'll have to collapse. He'd be happier doing that at a hotel in Naha. Somewhere away from here.

Assuming that he wasn't hearing a squad of troopers setting an ambush and about to kick in his door and drop a stun grenade in his lap.

He'd spent too many years around Djamila and her people. Javier knew exactly how they'd handle this situation. He needed to surprise someone else.

Javier held up three fingers and got her nod.

Two, and the safety came off as his finger found the trigger.

One, and he took a deep breath as he took hold of the hatch and jerked it in and flat, pivoting to aim out, ready to fire on movement because the Dragoon and her people would have said something to indicate who they were, when approaching the quiet camp.

A porcupine looked up from what it had been doing, squawked, and bolted off awkwardly, needles flouncing as it went under a bush.

Javier blew out a heavy breath and sagged as he flipped the safety on.

"Well, good morning to you, too," Afia snarked as she followed him out the door into the cold air outside.

A little above freezing. Wet. White in a few places.

Yucky.

Pistol went back into the holster after he spun slowly in place.

Nobody but him, Afia, and a surprised porcupine.

Hopefully.

"Should we be packing this morning and running?" she asked.

"Too cold," he replied. "But I don't know if it is going to get better or worse, so yeah, let's put together backpacks that can get us to Naha then circle back at lunchtime to see what the skies are like."

"You certain on Naha?" she asked.

"Better of the two," he said. "The others can find us easy enough there, and if the bad guys get smart, I'd figure they would drop a team at Altamont to watch for us."

"Why not Naha?" she pressed.

"A little farther away," he turned to her. "Harder terrain on a map, but not that much difference when you get down to it. Mostly, getting to Naha involves an extra hill most folks won't want to deal with. Not unless they're desperate."

"Are we?"

"We're sneaky," he corrected her. "And mean. There is a difference, and the Dragoon will appreciate that, if she ends up having to chase us later. I want a hot shower when this is done."

"Before you start cracking skulls together," she smirked.

"They started it," he reminded her. "I got hired to do a

thing at *Shangdu*, and did it. They didn't like the result, but they hadn't hired me for a mass casualty incident. When they came after us at *Svalbard*, that was the escalation that provoked *Nidavellir*."

"What does *Ophiuchi* provoke?" she asked.

"I'm not sure yet," he shrugged. "But it will be big, loud, and ugly before I'm done."

"And terminal," she nodded.

"Utterly terminal," he said. "Only way to be certain that it is over."

PART III

Benedict had hot coffee in hand as the sun came up outside the shuttle's forward windshield. More than half of his force had spent the night in the field without the best winter gear. Coats, gloves, and such. Just not all the extras to keep them warm and dry.

Shouldn't matter after one night, but there would be limits to how long he could keep that sort of operational tempo going without disease and exhaustion becoming a factor.

This morning, his two working shuttles were prepped to insert fresh folks who had had a hot breakfast already. About half of men and women out in the field would cycle home now, with the other half coming in after lunch, assuming they hadn't found Sykora by then.

He had his doubts that they would locate the woman at this point, short of the sort of blind luck that people wrote books about. But that was why he had forces up and looking. She had to be there somewhere.

Even a woman with a legend like that was only human.

And had a force of others with her. There were limits to how far and how fast they could travel, given a point of contact yesterday.

The problem was that everything beyond the resort in that direction was wilderness, without even forestry roads. Just a wall of hills and a few mountains separating this side from the other.

Benedict paused on that thought and called up a map, dialing it back until he could see what was beyond Sykora's trees. Rough, but passable, with at least three places where hikers had marked passes over the watershed. Probably more, if one was in a hurry.

Benedict ignored that portion and zoomed in beyond.

Altamont. He called up the encyclopedia on the town. Tourism and skiing, with a few resorts around the south side of town that should be coming up to the end of their season. Hiking in the summer, but there would be fewer people about right now.

Was it worth dropping a blocking force back there, just in case Sykora did break contact and immediately hightailed it?

"Arla," he said, turning to his command post sergeant.

She perked up. Stood up from where she'd been sitting in a quiet corner jumpseat.

"Sir?"

Looking at her, he could see how close they'd all gotten to being killed. The left side of her face was one massive bruise where it looked like someone had nailed her with a cricket paddle, turning maroon and slowly black around the eyes as the blood drained out. Mild concussion, mostly recovered.

Pissed enough to chew nails at being shot with a missile.

"Pick a squad of six including yourself," he ordered,

tapping the screen. "Take cash and have the next shuttle departing continue on after dropping troops. I want your team to land at Altamont. Get hotel rooms, then make sure that you have someone keeping watch in case strangers emerge from the wilderness."

"You think Sykora will run?" she asked.

"I'm making sure that she can't get away from us that way," he replied grimly. "You'll either have a couple of days of goofing off with hot showers, or will be vectoring the entire force down on top of you while trying to hold them off by yourself. Plan accordingly."

She studied the map as he stood silently, then started barking names. Quickly, half of his available bodyguard got up and took off at a jog.

Hopefully, he was starting at shadows, but he'd rather have her in place and unneeded than let Sykora get away after everything they'd done to set this up.

She'd already gotten away from him twice.

He wasn't about to let there be a third time.

PART IV

Katya looked around her bridge. She had finally napped, located in her office three steps from the bridge in case something happened. Everyone had been ordered to open fire if there was any doubt, but nobody had jumped out and drawn fire.

Food. Tea. More tea. Biobreak. Calm.

At some point, she was going to need to sleep for a month, but right now she was sharp enough. Plus, her only real orders would be to open fire with everything they had, then chase after *Excalibur* as soon as it jumped away, trying to stay close enough this time to harry them.

If she could. There was something to be said for a *Sentient* warship, able to react so fast. None of the ones she'd ever read about had been that good. What was Sokolov's secret? Had they found some experimental vessel at some point? He'd once only commanded a pissant little Strike Corvette, something small enough to fit inside one of *Excalibur*'s larger cargo bays if they took the time to wedge it in carefully.

Now, he was in a battleship. And she couldn't find him.

Katya checked the clock and the patrol log, mapping a series of checkpoints that would eventually let them find Sokolov, wherever he was hiding. It just took patience. Not that Slavkov had any, calling every hour or so to demand why she hadn't turned up his enemy. It had taken all of her self-control to smile politely and nod as he ranted at her.

When she was done, Katya didn't think that there was any amount of cash that could convince her to take a job from the man, and she intended to make that case to her Board of Directors. Assuming she made it home alive.

That was the other problem with being bait. She might get swallowed up and dead before this was all done. Worse, she couldn't transmit anything to *Anubis* or *Hummingbird* to carry home if she did get killed. Too much risk that someone might intercept and decrypt such a message. She'd have to carry it in her own head until then.

"Message from the flagship," interrupted her growling. "Channel six."

Katya swallowed her bile and misgivings, smiling neutrally as she opened the line to Valko Slavkov. He looked refreshed. Must have had a couple of showers while she'd been on duty. Maybe five-course meals of sumptuousness to rub it in.

"We have no updates at present, Admiral," she said as soon as the line came live. "We've been transmitting a live feed from our sensors for you."

He started to talk, stopped, listened—wonder of wonders—then nodded.

"How soon until you are done?" he asked darkly.

Obviously, ignoring the countdown clock she'd also been

transmitting, updated every minute as they moved forward and around the *Drako III* system.

Katya checked her numbers before responding.

"Thirteen hours, Admiral," she said. "And the odds of encounter keep going up every minute."

"What if you don't find him?" Slavkov demanded.

"Then he has jumped out of the local region entirely, Admiral," Katya replied. "There are several other planets in the *Drako* system, plus he might be in deep space entirely, hiding in the darkness and waiting. We'd need to do a fairly significant level of optical astronomy to locate him at that point, so we'd likely be better to return to orbit with you and force his hand with the ground teams."

She took a breath. Didn't add any of the color commentary in her head as she waited for the message to round-trip. About four seconds right now, but it would start going down as they completed their sweep.

Where the hell was Sokolov hiding?

"Keep me updated, Captain," Slavkov said, cutting the line before she replied.

She cut her line too and looked up.

"Where could he be hiding, if we haven't found him by now?" she asked.

"Behind something big enough to shadow his signal," Anton said without looking up from his own screens. "*Drako III* is the biggest, but there are forty others around here, however much smaller, that fit the bill. We've been going after the little ones first, because he can't easily jump behind most of them if we do see him."

"Do we go direct to the far side of *Drako III* with everyone?" she mused. "Right now?"

"Might knock him off balance from whatever he had

planned," Mihail offered. "I assume he's somehow watching us, but I'm not sure how."

She paused and considered that. How could he watch? Except that all the ships in her little squadron were talking with one another. And with the flagship. Pretty much a constant stream of radio noise. If he was where he could see that directly, that would be the obvious answer.

If he was hiding...?

Was a *Sentient* ship smart enough to maybe pick up signals reflected from solid surfaces like moons? Or the rings of *Drako III* itself? Lots of things there that could work. If they were good enough.

Were they?

What could Sokolov do with a *Sentient* ship at his command?

Not threaten all of them. That much she was certain of, because he'd run twice, first when they appeared, then after crippling *Blackstone*.

Ergo, he had battleship firepower, but not the equivalent of a squadron of battleships. He feared her and her team, just as he feared the group left in orbit as a cork in the bottle holding his ground forces.

That made her feel better. If he feared her, he could be beaten.

How?

"If we trusted *Yorrick* and the others, I'd suggest a sudden jump sideways to try to catch Sokolov off balance," Katya told her officers. "Except that I'm sure he'd see the sudden jump in communications we would need to set it up and be prepared to react. Plot a couple anyway and send them to the squadron as a fallback, but we won't do anything just yet. When we get close to the end, he can only be in a few places.

That means we can get him. Or we have to wait for him to come to us."

"How long is Slavkov going to wait?" Anton asked. "We're expensive. How much money does he have?"

"A lot," she replied. "Bunches and gobs. This is a man who owns banks, not just bankers. If our Board of Directors wants us here, we're here for a while. How long, I don't know, but he's got several more days before we're into contingency fees and financial reserves, so tell all your people to stay sharp."

They nodded and Katya went back to studying her map. The backside of *Drako III* was about the only big, obvious target left. They'd organized the patrol to work up to that, knocking off all the smaller places where he could peek over the edge of some moon and watch.

Had that been a mistake on her part? Or at least Cunningham's, since he'd heard the plan and approved it, and wasn't going to be arguing with folks later, since he was dead.

How did she cover her ass when all this crap finally had to be settled?

PART V

Zakhar studied the plot as Suvi kept it updated, building on the thousand little bits of data she gleaned from ships broadcasting their signals everywhere.

One squadron, led by *Kymni Gauntlet*, doing a damned professional job of quartering all of orbital space such that eventually they'd find him. The remaining force parked in orbit above *Ophiuchi*, directly over Djamila's resort, no doubt waiting for a signal to give them a target to pounce on.

"Yeoman, what is your status?" he asked.

"Almost done reprogramming the torpedo, Captain," she said. "It will reach a certain elevation and begin broadcasting a heavily modified targeting image that should look an awful lot like me trying to fly low profile. If anyone is looking, they should see a ghost suddenly appear and flicker on their sensors. I presume that they'll be wound tight enough to jump immediately, hoping to kill it before I could normally react. They can't, but nobody but you and Javier ever appreciate how fast I can work with hardware this sophisticated."

He smiled. Something like fifty thousand times faster

than a human could think. She was really just an incredibly complicated decision tree, but she could run through it so fast that it looked natural.

And what were the rest of them, if not the same sort of complicated decision matrix dealing with wants, needs, and fears? The difference was degree, not necessarily type.

Zakhar opened the ship-wide intercom.

"All hands, this is Captain Sokolov with an update," he announced to everyone. "Shortly, we will be launching an attack against enemy forces, so everyone make sure you are safe at this moment. Damage control teams, you'll be called on at that point. Hopefully only to inspect things, but those folks are good enough to shoot back. Be prepared. That is all."

He cut the line and nodded to Suvi.

"Set me a countdown on the rest of your programming," he ordered. "Then charge everything and confirm that all your systems and generators are running green before proceeding to your attack countdown."

"Aye, sir," she said.

A number appeared next to her. Seventy-three seconds and counting down. Not bad.

Shortly, all hell was going to break loose.

At least up here.

PART VI

Sascha smiled as she watched the scene below. They'd killed one shuttle not far from here, and apparently damaged a second sufficiently that it was parked on the landing field, even as two others had taken off northwest, before returning about an hour later.

And more troopers had departed on those two shuttles than had come back, so the commander over there was confident that he had the right place. Pouring his army into the box to trap the Dragoon and Hajna.

Sascha seriously doubted that. Which was why she'd spent all of yesterday circling along the edges of the patrols, headed right back to the base they'd already attacked. Looked peaceful from up here. Men and women heading directly to the kitchen tent for food, with the first batch of those going almost directly to tents, no doubt to sleep for a while in a warm bag after being out all night.

It had been colder than shit. She'd been kept warm by Heydar and Tom, snuggled up under several cloaks, and it had still sucked. Those troops were probably exhausted.

She glanced back at the men hiding nearby.

"Tom, I want you to kill the other shuttle as it departs," Sascha ordered. "On the ground, or immediately after liftoff. There are fuel barrels nearby, if the gods love you enough, it will crash into them. Not trying to kill everyone this time, or I'd let it get higher in the air. It appears that they are down to two. I want them to have exactly one, so that they can abandon all of their gear later and cram everyone into one ship to extract the force. Questions?"

"I'll need to shift down and to the left," Tom said simply. "Better line on the shot if we're playing billiards here. Heydar, what is the patrol perimeter like?"

"Crowd of folks walking a line so certain that it is already a path in the dirt," Heydar described, pointing. "There and there. Probably electronics closer in, and some cameras watching, but we're in a blind spot to the downed shuttle. Is that their new command post?"

"That's my read," Sascha replied. "Too damaged to fly at present, from the way they have panels off the sides, but repairable. Hopefully, a secondary or tertiary explosion can take it out as well, but I want to nail down their feet at this point. Most of their force is out this morning, counting noses. Not enough that we can attack the place, and killing a shuttle now is a better payoff than us sneaking in and committing arson and juvenile delinquency directly."

"Gotcha," Heydar said. "This way."

She followed the man as he slipped silently across the face of the hill, moving from bush to bush slowly. The shuttle was close to departing, but she could still see soldiers lined up with backpacks. Moving slowly and deliberately, being checked off by sergeants.

The Dragoon would have had all of them boarding at a

jog, then firing anyone who got left behind without a damned good reason. This force was out of their comfort zone. And she was about to make it worse.

"We could continue our stalk after shooting," Heydar whispered over a shoulder. "I got a five-drachma coin says they lurch this way again spasmodically, then call back others from the field, thinking that we're dumb enough to run headlong into a patrol from that direction."

Sascha studied the field as they got to a point Tom wanted. Food stocks. A whole bunch of pallets currently stacked in a series of rows beyond the landing field. Opposite corner from the fuel and shuttles she wanted to kill shortly.

A force of four hundred in the field required a LOT of supplies on a daily basis. Food. Weapons. Spare uniforms. Replacement parts. Everything you could possibly need, multiplied by however many days your commanders expected you to be on the ground, multiplied by that many mouths to feed.

Hell, reducing them to one shuttle might force him to send that one to orbit to get a load of supplies in the next few days, stranding their troops in the field and making them walk everywhere.

Sascha smiled at that thought.

"Heydar, keep shifting left and start looking for our path sideways," Sascha ordered. "We'll see if we can stay close to the base on that rear flank when the next set of crazy happens. Secondary sabotage of food stuffs might finish the job of neutralizing them, but we are not expendable at present, so move with care."

"Understood," he said.

Sascha moved past Tom and found a bush to settle behind as he studied the landing field. The missile tube was deployed, but he didn't bring it to his shoulder until the shuttle started powering up. Even then, preflight took close to five minutes, though Sascha couldn't tell if that was slackness on their part or working the entire checklist with care.

There were hostile forces around. She'd want to be a little more careful when taking off, too.

"Stand by," Tom muttered, slinging the tube and automatically glancing over his shoulder to confirm that nobody was in his backblast zone before firing.

They were all professionals here. Years of expertise before being hired by the Dragoon, followed by more years of living up to her standards of training and practice.

Sascha wondered if the woman would retire when they got back to *Altai*. And if Sascha would join her. Anything after this was likely to be a let down. Nature of the business.

What did she want next? Any of a number of things, starting with maybe living a life where nobody pointed guns at her regularly.

She had to get out of here first.

"Ready to shoot," Tom announced as the shuttle's engines got loud enough to be heard from here. "Vessel is not deploying active electronic countermeasures. I have optical lock. Shuttle is lifting. I have targeting lock. Firing."

The missile itself was a streak of light, a scream of rage, and a contrail of smoke across the horizon, ending suddenly in a flash of detonation that sounded like a truckful of anvils being thrown down a flight of stairs.

Tom automatically collapsed his tube and slung it, even though they had no reloads.

"Leave it," Sascha ordered. "If we get caught, possession will probably get you executed slowly, considering how pissed they're about to be."

He tossed it to one side, drawing his pistol.

Sascha took a moment to study the results. Smoke billowed out of the near side of the shuttle, even as it started to rotate in place and wobble badly. Pretty good piloting, as they tried to turn back and hit an empty place, instead of plowing into all the supplies closer or the tents filled with troopers to one side.

Still, it was going down. Hard. Sliding like a ramp had been installed.

And, for once, the gods chose to smile on her, as the shuttle hit close enough that it slid through one corner of the fuel barrels that still weren't buried safely.

Sascha blinked as everything turned white for an instant. Felt the flash of heat, even at this distance. Heard thunder like the apocalypse had come a little early this year.

"Okay, people," she said as the sound finally died enough to talk normally. "Move it."

PART VII

Benedict somehow knew it was coming, watching the screen and listening to shuttle #4 frantically call out a mayday. He dropped to the deck and crawled partly under a console, just before an earthquake jolted his command post shuttle hard enough that he cracked his head on something anyway.

For whatever reason, the gods were smiling on him, because he could only imagine being thrown ass over teakettle, had he been standing out in the open.

Still, he had to shake his head a few times to make sure everything was still working. Wobbly, but not as bad as his bodyguard, none of whom had been strapped in. Nor had the pilots.

Why did you need to be, if this shuttle couldn't fly?

Benedict stood up and realized that the deck was canted about ten degrees. Not good. Either the ground had shifted or he'd lost one of his landing gear pillars, in which case the craft might be a total loss in place.

Sykora had doubled back. And managed to kill three shuttles now, leaving him with only one. How bad were the casualties outside? Screens were showing static or smoke, so he had to assume that things on the ship were significantly damaged.

Benedict checked that he had a pistol, then stopped and grabbed a fire extinguisher before heading for the main hatch. He had no idea what he might accomplish at this point, but better than doing nothing, as all hell had broken loose outside.

Mayhem. Everybody who could was firing at the trees as rapidly as they could pull a trigger and reset a capacitor. Trees and brush were shattering under the impact. The only thing he could see beneficial at this point was that it had started to drizzle in the last five minutes, and nothing out there would catch fire.

Closer to home was a whole different beast.

He made his way towards smoke, blasting a tarp with foam as he got close. Supplies of some sort underneath, currently burning when something had exploded and thrown fuel or a burning whatever on top of it.

Benedict knew better than to try to scream orders over the comm. Folks were giving vent to whatever fears or anger had hold of them, and would be a minute or two dying down. And the fire wasn't going to wait that long.

Instead, he smothered this one. Yelled at someone close to grab more extinguishers, delighted when the woman blinked at him, then slung her rifle and grabbed a nearby shovel to fling dirt.

"Damage Control Teams, REPORT!" he yelled as loud as he possibly could.

Something broke through, because the volume of beam fire around him tapered off. Near as Benedict could tell, none of it was incoming anyway.

Sykora, having made her point, had withdrawn just as quickly. Benedict felt like a guy walking a hungry mastiff as it kept dragging him along the trail.

"Firefighting teams, here and there," he yelled, pointing as heads came around and brains engaged in something higher than sudden death and destruction.

Folks got to grabbing whatever was close. Extinguishers. Shovels. Even cloaks that wouldn't burn quickly as they went. Rain was coming a little harder now, helping, but he needed to control this before he lost all of his supplies.

More people came running. More hands doing things. More minds working.

Now would be the perfect time to hit his base again, if Sykora was feeling mean. Or had enough people to launch a sudden attack. Everyone had turned inward after that hard jolt outwards. They would be caught in the open and enfiladed.

Lucky for him, she didn't do anything.

Lucky? For him, maybe, considering the next set of casualties. That shuttle was burning, but he could see where crew was piling out of every hatch, sometimes dragging or carrying bodies, so hopefully his medical tent could handle everything and get his people treated.

Shit was unraveling down here. Worse, he had both of his Group Leaders in the field, and Troop Leader Archer had been on the shuttle, so he wasn't sure where she was. And he couldn't turn his back on the fires. Not yet.

He fought on, trying to save his food and equipment as it started to rain heavier.

AFTERNOON

PART I

Djamila paused her people in a low draw to take a five minute break. She had heard the explosion this morning while her team had been moving back towards where she had left Afia and Javier. The location felt to her like the enemy base. The sound had to have been tremendous to be heard at this range. The column of smoke, visible even in the rain, told her that they had to have suffered another calamity.

She smiled and assumed that Sascha had pulled a fast one on everyone. But that was exactly why her and Hajna were Pathfinders. Another step up from the Gun Bunnies, even as impressive as those men were. Able to split out and operate independently without orders.

And able to cause trouble.

Given the scope, Djamila had started moving everyone faster. The enemy might decide to withdraw to their base. They might also ask one of the warships to drop low enough to bombard the forest instead.

You never knew which way pirates would go. *Storm Gauntlet's* crew hadn't been all that bad, in the old days.

Good enough to change when they accidentally hired a goof-ball Science Officer.

Others went the other way. Rabid animals best put down as quickly and ruthlessly as possible.

She needed to get clear of any possible repercussion zone. Now.

"Status?" she asked Hajna, who happened to be sitting closest.

"Rain," Hajna grinned. "Morale unexpectedly high. Crew sharp and ready to kick ass. I presume that we're in the process of withdrawing entirely from the field of battle, given that boom this morning and our current path."

"Correct," Djamila nodded, raising her voice enough for the men to hear. "Sascha or someone ruined their morning entirely. I expect them to withdraw. They might cause trouble after that, so we need to get our other two and all get gone."

"Where are we headed after that?" Galal asked.

"We can get over the pass to one of those towns with a couple of days' hike," Iqbal noted.

"Weather will determine some things," Djamila said, noting the rain.

She had a hat with a flopping brim and a scarf that she kept pulled up when she stopped moving. The others were similarly prepared. After all, this was supposed to be a day in deep country, preparing shelter and getting ready to take a deer or elk that they could eat for a while.

Things had gotten a little out of hand, but only a little.

She smiled as she considered how well her team was scoring on the list in her head. Even better than she had been expecting, as high as her usual standards were.

"I need a scan of low altitude, then we're off," Djamila continued.

Demyan produced a handheld unit and walked around until he had a bit of sky to the southwest to point it. Then the man carefully rotated in place, covering the invisible horizon.

"Got one shuttle, low and on a line more or less with enemy fortifications," he said. "Only one. And low enough that they are either deploying troops or recovering them, as they appear to be holding still."

"Everyone keep an ear open," Djamila said. "They are in wildcard mode right now, so I expect them to become their most dangerous. Once they lean into their next action plan, we'll adjust, but I'd like to get to Javier early enough to eat a meal and possibly get an hour or two downrange towards our next target, depending on how quickly they can get ready."

Nods. Assholes and elbows, as everyone was in motion quickly.

The sharpest professionals she knew how to turn out. Better than the enemy.

As long as her luck held.

PART II

Zakhar had everything as ready as he could get it. Everyone was in place on the bridge and elsewhere. Chay was even considering opening the bistro later to serve a special dinner, assuming that everything worked out in the next hour or three.

Of course, if it didn't, Zakhar might be running for his life to deep space. Or considering committing suicide so that he wasn't taken alive. Without Djamila and her people present, he doubted that the remaining crew could adequately repel a boarding force. Even with Suvi doing what she could.

You needed raw firepower. He might have to go recruit an entire army after this. Fill *Excalibur's* currently empty cabins and cargo bays with enough men and women to go have a conversation with some other folks. At gunpoint.

Suvi's first countdown had completed. The torpedo was programmed to mayhem.

He'd been set to go when one of the generators aft had suddenly gone a little haywire. Fuel feed had developed some sort of blockage. Andreea and her teams had spent an hour cutting in four meters of fresh line, testing it, and recertifying everything before it got run to max and held there for an hour.

He had the time. They had the time. *Kymni Gauntlet* wasn't to the end of their patrol pattern as Suvi had calculated it. Wouldn't come over the horizon where they could see him for a bit yet, though they were getting close.

Not close enough to fly direct, which was his purpose. Close enough to see something, lurch into action, and jump on top of it, firing everything they had at what they thought was a First-Rate Galleon attempting to be stealthy.

"Captain, I show green lights across my board," Suvi announced.

Zakhar checked anyway, then nodded.

"Any last comments?" he asked, looking around at the full crew on the bridge with him.

Everybody, because this might be it. And it might be their last battle together.

Some of these men and women had been with him for a long time. Old friends.

He would be pissed to drag them to hell with him, but at least they would provide better company than the assholes he intended to send along as escorts first.

Smiles and nods back. Piet had that dreamy look suggesting he was composing with the back half of his brain. Zakhar couldn't wait to hear it. Suvi had suggested Ragnarök as a theme.

That felt appropriate.

"Yeoman, lock in a countdown timer at ten seconds and initiate," he ordered, then opened the ship-wide. "All hands, we are about to sound the trumpet. Hang on."

PART III

Suvi had done a freaking lot of math this time. Like, an entire semester's worth of orbital trigonometry. If nothing else, she owed somebody a ration of pain for making her work so hard at calculating so many damned gravitational variables simultaneously, in order to drop a single ship to a point she wanted to be, with eleven alternates depending on how accurately a group of pirates could manage their own jump.

Time she could have spent committing four-armed jazz, instead of four-handed calculus.

Losers.

But she was here. Now. Live.

Zakhar had handed her a blank piece of paper, aimed her at an outcome, then stepped back and trusted her to execute. To rescue him and everybody else on the ship, on her way to saving Javier, Afia, Djamila, and the rest of them.

And she'd considered Zakhar's words on a path of vengeance. *Two graves dug first* kind of stuff, because she had no doubts that Dad was even more pissed than Zakhar at present.

Piet was right. Surtr and Hrym had come. Music swelled in her head, but she really wanted Piet's stuff. Even that ancient racist punk Wagner was a pale comparison, though she did have to admit that he had established the entire genre. Everyone else were posers come along later.

She settled for launching Piet's Eleventh Symphony. It had the brass and drums she needed here. She cranked it up to levels where the upstairs neighbors would be banging on the floor.

Good thing she lived alone in this beast.

Countdown timer hit zero with glacial slowness. Suvi fired a single torpedo and watched it self-correct, running lateral across *Drako III*'s orbit for nearly fifteen degrees before it suddenly turned spaceward like a Roman candle.

Folks were wound pretty damned tight given how quickly scanner pulses doubled across that volume of space. Everyone who could had some sensor pointed at the unknown signal that had quietly appeared on everybody's boards at the same instant.

She counted backwards from there. Her torpedo was running at a slower pace than normal. About where *Excalibur* would be if she'd redlined her engines from a low gravity insertion.

Two seconds and change from *Kymni Gauntlet*'s current patrol location to *Ophiuchi* orbit. Give them three seconds to react, respond, and jump blind.

Suvi dialed everything in as the first pirate warship appeared out of jump close enough to rake her torpedo with beam fire.

EN GUARD!

PART IV

Katya saw it as a flicker of motion on her scanner screen and knew immediately that she'd forced Sokolov to move. He'd been hiding in the shadow of *Drako III* after all, and she'd be moving above his horizon shortly, so he'd tried to run for it.

Only because she'd had every scanner available pointed in that direction had it appeared.

"Flagship. Contact. Coordinates. Jumping."

She didn't wait for their response. Almost three-seconds lag, and every instant mattered right now.

"Squadron, jump and engage," she ordered.

They'd seen it as rapidly as she had. Anton was typing as fast as he could. Mihail had every turret rotating forward as quickly as the gimbals would allow.

FINALLY!

They jumped.

Short hop. Open space, without *Drako III* doing much to mess with everything. Katya had a moment to wonder why they had tried flying instead of blind-jumping out, then they were on top of her sensor signal and Mihail was pouring everything he had into it. Pulsars. Ions. Even torpedoes, though those were likely an afterthought, considering how slow they moved and how quickly Sokolov's *Sentient* ship had responded the previous times.

Her boards lit up as *Hummingbird* appeared on her flank. *Epsilon Cavendish* came in high. *Yorrick* appeared low, slightly withdrawn, like a proper escort. Then all of those Ion Pulsars cut loose.

Quickly, local space became even more crowded as *Anubis* appeared. *Royal Gamma. Arminus. Western Sentinel. Oberon Martyr. Obsidian Hawk* and her consorts.

Sokolov had screwed up. Had tried to slip by her and her forces, not believing that everyone would immediately pile on as soon as she had any inkling of where he was.

He would pay for that mistake. Badly. Every ship that could jump was here, formed up in a hemispheric arc that trapped him.

Except...

Why wasn't he firing back?

PART V

Suvi nodded once as the scanners filled with trouble. All of them, minus *Blackstone* and *Para Bellum*. If Zakhar hadn't been nearly positive that Valko Neofit Slavkov was aboard *Obsidian Hawk*, she might have made a case for finishing *Blackstone* off entirely. Wouldn't be hard, after the images she'd intercepted earlier. Someone had whomped that ship upside the head with a four-days-rotting sand shark.

But Slavkov might be here. Might have made a terminal mistake in not trusting someone else to handle this particular job, and instead put himself where she could get to him.

Suvi noted the first flickers of motion as *Kymni Gauntlet*'s team appeared and opened fire. They were prepared for a massive beast of a First-Rate Galleon, not a torpedo hardly bigger than the Dragoon in her boarding armor.

Sure, they'd eventually tumble to what she'd done. Might even get lucky and kill it with an Ion Pulsar. Those had a big arc of fire when they hit. Hell, there were enough people firing that statistically they had to hit and kill it eventually.

Eventually was the key here. Humans thought a lot slower than she did. And everyone was coming out of jump on a right-hand formation. Smart. Kept them from shooting each other accidentally in the crazy stress of hosing down a region as fast as you could push a button.

Obsidian Hawk appeared. Almost exactly where Zakhar had predicted.

How did he do that?

Fire Wyvern was on starboard point. *Ice Eagle* to port. Everybody looking the wrong way.

Better, *Obsidian Hawk* had landed wider than everybody else. Her two consorts were on the proper hemisphere of engagement. *Hawk* had her ass hanging out in the wind, with nobody in a position to rake Suvi when she appeared.

Whoops.

She zeroed her coordinates and jumped, sliding just a little because she wanted all of her turrets able to engage immediately.

Didn't even bother scanning. Just landed and opened fire. That gained her more than half a second of beams poured into that *Hawk*'s tail feathers before her targeting systems lined up with reality and local gravity to let her adjust her shooting.

Not that she'd been that far off. She'd had put every single weapon she had into a set of coordinates blind.

Tail feathers went every which way on her screen. Rear shields already plucked and Suvi was seeing bits of hull metal being blasted into space as she got her newest guns into play. The old 12cm Pulsars were good. They'd been state of the art when *Hammerfield* had been launched nearly a century ago.

Behnam had sprung for 6cm Pulse Cannons. Smaller

barrel meant tighter beams. State of the freaking art last Tuesday, backed with as much generator power as Suvi could pour through them right now, damning the cooling systems because shit was measured in seconds, rather than even minutes.

Obsidian Hawk started shedding wing feathers under her assault. And other pieces. Suvi figured that she had about three more seconds before folks woke up to what she'd done, so she left her shields focused forward and unreinforced for now.

Everything was going into beams. And cooling pumps, because some of the rooms aft were already warming up, in spite of insulation and hypercold liquid.

But then, this was EXACTLY what a First-Rate Galleon had been built for, by a people as crazy as *Neu Berne* at their most militant, which was saying something. Especially today.

Obsidian Hawk was in sorry shape. Worse, Suvi wasn't about to let off the pedal at this point. All of her math had suggested that the new commander after *Blackstone* was aboard the *Hawk,* so they needed to be punched in the gob a few times, then knocked down and kicked repeatedly.

First-Rate Galleon. Upgraded to just shy of the new theoretical Mark III Warmasters that the *Concord* had designed but not started building yet. Did that make her the most dangerous warship in the galaxy right now? Kinda scary thought. Good thing she had Javier and Zakhar to keep her sane.

And all of the other wonderful people counting on her to keep them alive in the middle of the ugliest, most one-sided space battle she could remember, even from her days as a Probe-Cutter.

Four of her turrets had actually overheated enough that she took them out of the firing line in those first two and a half seconds. Folks in the rooms would be in a sudden sauna, but they were dressed in enough layers and she sent each of them a signal to step out into the hall and let things cool. Everything else was still holding, and it looked like she had a problem with a coolant line somewhere that had only turned up today because she was a step beyond the ship's original design limits in laying down a standard pattern of fire.

But *Obsidian Hawk* was right there. And blind. And concussed. And bleeding internally from the way her scanners showed plasma venting and pieces of hull metal shedding.

Of course, that *Hawk* was a fifth of her size. And the design was intended to face forward when fighting, with the armor and shields on a front arc to protect important things.

Which was why Zakhar had her drop here, low and aft, firing up at an angle like a great big kitty raking with both pairs of claws.

Blood and feathers everywhere, however much metaphoric.

WHAM!

Hey, what?

Oh, somebody just realized what was happening over here.

Gunner on *Hummingbird* was sharp. Made sense. Jarre Foundation escort, so used to being in the middle of crap and watching all corners for surprises they had to engage.

Smaller Pulsars, but he'd found her, ranged her, and was whomping on her port-side shields instead of the torpedo that had everyone else frothing at the mouth.

She considered shifting a turret to slap him, but the guy

was doing what he was supposed to. And a damned good job of it. If the rest of Suvi's crew had mostly been Jarre Foundation employees at some point, she could extend a bit of kinship and call *Hummingbird*'s people professional.

Even if they were being a pain in her ass.

Suvi dialed back the crazy and started counting other turrets slowly rotating her way as *Hummingbird* updated folks to the fact that they were fighting a ghost. She had about two seconds before there would be enough people shooting at her that shields would be at risk.

She did the math quickly, because she'd been doing math all day. Spare energy to the shields on all forward facings probably gained her a half second. JumpDrives were already charged and coordinates locked in.

She kept kicking that stupid *Hawk*. Zakhar wanted him dead. Crippled. Bleeding out on floor of a honky-tonk bar covered with peanut shells. She'd seen pictures of such a thing, but still really didn't understand it.

Shooting enemy warships, however, was a thing. And she was good at it.

And a little pissed.

And maybe getting carried away.

But they'd screwed up her vacation, when Suvi had been planning to spend a few weeks scanning and mapping every single floating rock and comet in a messy system like *Drako* for fun. Not just *III*, but all the rest, too.

There were times she missed the survey work she and Javier had been doing, but there were times when she needed to kill pirates. Besides, this was making the galaxy a safer place.

Even if they were starting to get accurate with their

panicked fire. Four and a half seconds elapsed. *Humming-bird*'s bow was coming around, so somebody over there was too damned good for her peace of mind. Suvi fired a single torpedo at him, mostly as a way of flipping him off.

Shields at nineteen percent. Thirteen. Seven.

She jumped.

PART VI

Katya looked around her bridge and felt her jaw hanging so far open it was painful.

"Status report!" she snapped.

Didn't matter who replied. As long as someone did.

None of her boards showed any red. Hell, not even yellow, save a few spots where she'd been pushing her cooling systems a little hard, firing everything she had into...what?

Mihail looked up at her, his face screwed a little sideways.

"Gimme a second to review the logs, but I think we've been had," he said. "Again."

Rather than snarl something at him, she unbuckled and moved to look over his shoulder as he replayed the entire engagement. Coming out of jump first, because that was her job in killing a Jarre Foundation renegade. Opening up. Everyone else arriving and firing.

"Why isn't there more reaction?" she asked, mostly under her breath.

"There," he said, tapping the screen to freeze the video. "Shit."

"What?"

"Somehow, and I'm not sure how, seems that they launched a torpedo from somewhere close, programming it to look like *Excalibur* on our scanners," Mihail replied. He tapped the screen. "Somebody actually got lucky and hit the torpedo with a beam, destroying it in flight. I'm thinking blind squirrels and acorns levels of probability, but they did it. The fake *Excalibur* disappears instantly, but has already appeared here."

She watched him roll the video forward a little, until there were two galleons visible for a second. Except that the second one had appeared behind and beneath *Obsidian Hawk*, where it then proceeded to...oh shit.

"Somebody call *Obsidian Hawk* and get a status report from them," she said, nodding at Anton because Mihail was busy.

One First-Rate Galleon, a battleship from the Great War, against a Raider-scale battle frigate. With surprise. Point-blank. From behind.

Ouch.

More fire. More damage. A flash on *Excalibur*'s shields.

"Who fired that?" she asked.

He paused and rewound. Played forward three times.

"*Hummingbird.*" He looked up at her with a grin she matched.

One of hers. That would look good later, because she'd been focused forward until the first shadow vanished and the second one had already shivved Slavkov pretty hard. Several times.

Then everyone was rotating to engage a new target, a massive shark that had suddenly emerged from hiding and taken a bite out of *Obsidian Hawk*. Beams poured in from several directions as she watched, but hurriedly, badly aimed, and not terribly accurate.

Bad. It had left Slavkov exposed. And that ship looked like it might not fly away right now.

Worse, Sokolov had ignored everyone else.

Except.

"They fired a single torpedo at *Hummingbird* just before they jumped?" she asked.

"Little guy got under his skin," Mihail nodded, grinning. "That's my read."

"If Slavkov survived, he owes his life to the crew of *Hummingbird*," Katya said aloud. "Remind me to remind them later. That's the sort of thing the Board of Directors will reward them for, and they earned it. Anton?"

"Nothing from the flagship," he replied. "Trying all channels. Everyone else is going into laager with their butts inward. I'm maneuvering us into position to hedgehog this while we sort it out."

Katya blinked and returned to her own station.

Laager? Here? Everyone?

Shit.

"Nothing?" she asked. "Scan them hard."

"Been doing that," Anton nodded. "Power out everywhere. They're on batteries at the moment, because the engines all look dead and I'm not reading generators operational either."

It took her a moment to process that. First *Blackstone*, now *Obsidian Hawk*?

And *Excalibur* had blinked away again.

"Call *Blackstone* and *Para Bellum* and warn them," she ordered. "They might be next. Have *Hummingbird* and *Anubis* transit over as escorts immediately. Everyone else stays close to Slavkov until we find out what their status is."

"Do we send over a shuttle with medical teams and repair folks?" Mihail asked. "Looks like they need it and might not be able to call for help. I'm not even reading transponders flashing that they could use to send a mayday call."

"Do that," Katya said. "Medical teams heavy and ready to evacuate Slavkov somewhere if he needs it. Last thing we need is to lose another admiral in the middle of this operation. Especially him. Anton, keep trying. If you get them, let me know. And have everyone else send shuttles if they can. I have a bad feeling about this."

PART VII

Zakhar had watched it all unfold as if in slow motion, hyped almost beyond measure at what was happening.

Then they were alone again and he watched boards go red as the ship tried to dump heat and damage control parties took their second steps.

Eight seconds of pure insanity. He'd been in major space battles, both with the *Concord* and as a pirate, that had been less involved, and those had taken hours to flow from engagement to withdrawal.

Eight seconds.

"Did you get him?" Zakhar asked.

"I got his ship, sir," Suvi responded in that crisply formal way she did when she fell back on her original training. Yeoman in *Concord* service. "We will need some time to analyze signals, but the wavefront of *Obsidian Hawk*'s transponders has ceased."

"Wow," Mary-Elizabeth offered. "Nice shooting."

He watched Suvi blush on his screen, knowing that she did it consciously because she was still a fantastically complex

265

computer program at the end of the day. And had spoken more than once about how much Mary-Elizabeth Suzuki had taught her about the art of laying cannons.

"Where are we?" Zakhar asked.

"Backside of *Blue Amsterdam* after a fast double hop that should fool anyone," Suvi replied. "I figured that the incredible number of ships hiding out in orbit over here would hide us for several minutes. At some point, someone will challenge us or call the pirates and try to claim a potential reward for information, but I intend to be gone again. Awaiting orders for a destination."

As in, she hadn't thought this far ahead. Or had nine different options and none of them were any better than the others. It happened. This was her as a young officer, rather than a *Sentient* warship. Things she needed to learn yet, but he had the time and space to teach her.

"If you go exceptionally long, like to, say, the shadow of *Draco VI*, could you return later accurately enough to avoid the pirates?" he asked her.

She stopped, looked down, then looked up.

"Assuming they return to *Ophiuchi* orbit, that shouldn't be a problem, sir," she said.

"*Obsidian Hawk*'s not going anywhere," Piet said abruptly. "Recalibrate as if you'll have two clusters of enemy vessels, generally unable to support one another from a sudden attack."

Zakhar liked the way she turned on his screen, exactly as if she was standing in front of him and turning to look at Piet.

"Oh," she offered. "In that case, I have seven landing points to pick from."

"Route them to Zakhar for now," Piet nodded. "We can

go over them at our leisure. Zakhar, you ready to vanish off the game board for a bit?"

"Yes, but wait until someone notices us here," Zakhar replied. "I want us to stay current with our scan logs about this system. Later, we'll jump within a light-minute or so to make sure everyone is where they are supposed to be before reinserting."

"Programmed, Captain," Suvi said. "Any other orders?"

"None," he said. "Exceptionally nicely done, Yeoman. You take command for now, while Piet and I go plot more evil for you later. Everyone else, take a break and be ready for a staff meeting in an hour. Suvi, let Chay know where we're at and ask him if he could fix us something at that time."

"Will do, sir," she replied.

Zakhar rose and made his way down from his command throne. They hadn't escaped. Hadn't even won.

But maybe, just maybe, they'd sent some dipshit enough of a message that he could slip in and rescue Djamila and Javier in the next day or so.

STALEMATE

PART I

Javier heard someone approaching from the ravine below, so he slipped sideways and behind the dugout, waving Afia the other direction as his pistol came up and pointed.

"Javier, it's Djamila," the Amazon called. "Six coming in. You awake?"

"Pointing a gun at you count?" he called back, standing up as she came into view.

She nodded crisply, like he'd passed another one of her constant pop-quizzes, but he already knew that she'd planned on taking two weeks of wilderness training a little too seriously for a sane person. He holstered the gun and stepped back down into the clearing that had been mashed flat by feet.

If anyone got this close, they already knew where to find him, and he'd been listening for anyone blundering around, once the rain had blown through and let a little blue sky in with the breeze.

"What is your status?" she asked.

He counted noses, missing Sascha and her two. But

Djamila had said six, and didn't seem all that concerned. Afia slid close as the group formed into the galaxy's weirdest prayer circle.

"Getting ready to eat in a bit," he said, staring up at her. "Had the weather been a little nicer this morning, Afia and I talked about leaving you a note and walking to Naha."

"Excellent," she said. "We've hit them twice already, with Sascha and hers possibly materially crippling that force this morning. I intended to round you two up and start hiking towards one of those resort towns on the far side of the ridge. Why Naha?"

"Altamont is where they would expect us to go," he replied. "Easiest hike, with a low and well-known mountain pass for tourists. Naha is more effort, so they should anticipate us blindly blundering into their trap, having escaped them here and fled straight through without expecting them to actually be any good."

She paused, considering that, then nodded.

"How quickly could you leave?" she asked, glancing at Afia as well.

"Three minutes if you just want to recover everything inside the dugout," Afia said. "An hour if you want your tarp back."

Even Djamila seemed surprised at that, which pleased him. Javier was too used to her looking down her nose from that immense height.

"Ten minutes for food, water, and biobreak," Djamila announced to her crew. "Work with Afia to grab everything we can easily carry in packs. Abandon the rest."

Javier stayed put as the others scampered off to work, held by the look in the Dragoon's eyes.

"You really are that prepared?" she asked quietly.

"Packs just inside the door," he nodded. "Was planning to leave you a message and set out at first light tomorrow. We've got, what, three hours of sunlight left?"

"Closer to two, with the mountains," she said. "It will go from light to dark suddenly at this elevation."

"And you want the extra two hour head start because?" he asked.

"Because we were successful enough to possibly take down two or three of his original four shuttles," she said. "They should be getting desperate, and those people are usually the most dangerous."

He agreed. Backed into a corner, in spite of them supposedly starting with all the advantages. Except that they'd screwed up somewhere. Left him and the others enough of a margin to slip away, then turned Djamila Sykora into an enemy.

There were dumber ways to die, but not many more painful.

He had a list going, though.

"Folks at Naha going to turn us in for a reward?" he asked.

"Possibly," she acceded. "But it gets us out and away from the primary zone, and every day they stay here has to be both expensive to maintain, and pissing off the locals."

"Especially if someone keeps shooting down shuttles," he grinned.

Her shrug was eloquence itself, but she was the Ballerina of Death, even after all these years.

"I'm glad you came back for us," he said after a beat. "We could have made it, I'm confident, but having your whole team will make it much easier. Do we know what happened to Sascha?"

"She hit them at first light, but I haven't spoken with her directly," Djamila said. "The explosion was loud enough that I heard it from where we'd camped."

"First light?" he asked. "That was an explosion? I thought it was an earthquake somewhere. Or an avalanche in high country."

"As I said, they are down to one shuttle, near as I can tell," she grinned. "That means that we can break contact and escape them. Otherwise, I'd be back and hitting them myself."

Yeah, that sounded like her. And her Gun Bunnies.

Afia walked up and handed him his pack, so Javier slipped it on. Heavy, but they'd needed food in case it took more than two days and he didn't want to start a wilderness diet. Too early for berries and he didn't feel like trying to kill and clean a deer. It had been too many years.

"You ready?" she asked.

"I need water at the creek," he replied, starting to walk. "Then, yeah, we can get lost."

He wondered how things were going in orbit.

PART II

Katya wanted to slam her tea mug down on the screen, but controlled her temper. Wouldn't do any good, and her people were already too jittery. Her breaking things would wear more on them than her.

"We're certain?" she asked, glancing up around her bridge at the hangdog faces already cringing.

"Call it ninety-seven percent, captain," Kowalski replied. She'd sent him over as her best repair tech, when it had become clear that *Obsidian Hawk* was in worse trouble than even her initial assessment. "No signals that I've been able to locate. Right now, we're trying to access the bridge via one of the secondary machine routes because the main corridor got twisted in place to the point that I'm not comfortable trying to squeeze through. Too many jagged edges. Too easy to lose your seal and die in the middle."

"Keep at it," she said.

Katya cut the line and turned to Mihail.

"Bring me up your latest scan," she told him, waiting for her screen to change.

"They did not get a solid bridge hit," Mihail said, high-lighting a few holes that suggested one bulkhead difference in several places. "However, and I really don't know how, the ship twisted. Think of an empty drink can that you turn as you compress. Failures here and here. That's why the main dorsal corridor pinched. Didn't think you could do that, but they did. Might be easier to cut their way in from a lower deck, but I don't know how H & W builds their frigates."

"Chances Slavkov is dead?" she asked.

"I think Kowalski is being a sour son of a bitch," Mihail answered. "But yeah, feels like maybe a fifty/fifty here, if he was smart enough to be in a suit. Way past dead if he wasn't when they lost pressure. Dunno if a fat guy like him could get into a suit fast enough to survive."

Katya drew a heavy breath and held it. Until they got through, she couldn't order anybody else to abandon *Obsidian Hawk*. Which left *Para Bellum* and a crippled *Blackstone* with just *Hummingbird* and *Anubis* for the time being.

If Sokolov was feeling angry enough, he might be able to take those two escorts. Or finish one of the bigger ships off while holding the two at bay.

She had the biggest warship still operational at present, but Captain Ivankova on *Yorrick* wasn't taking her calls. Probably doing the same strategic rethinking that Katya was, with Cunningham dead, Slavkov maybe dead, and nobody else in charge.

Plus, Belfast Group and Jarre weren't even remotely friendly at the best of times.

How soon until the woman turned and utterly ionized *Kymni Gauntlet* from point blank, as a way to further reduce the competition?

How soon until there were four mortal enemy clans in orbit of *Drako III*, when they had been a pair of operational squadrons an hour ago?

Shit.

Anubis and *Hummingbird* were her people, but she'd put them over protecting *Blackstone* in the heat of action. Dare she abandon *Obsidian Hawk*?

There were no good answers.

"Do we have any idea where they went?" she finally asked Mihail.

"Pointed to deep space is how I read them at that last moment," he nodded. "I'd presume they went to hide out in the deeper parts of the system itself somewhere, while they figure out what we're doing."

Made sense. She didn't think they'd gotten through *Excalibur*'s shields in the short encounter, but they would still need time to repair things.

And plot revenge.

She did have one trap left. And only one, assuming he still wanted to recover his people from the ground and not just outwait her. The trouble was that *Para Bellum* was a Belfast Group ship. And, if she had been reading between the lines correctly, suffering their own serious difficulties on the ground, to the point that there had been talk of extracting that ground force before it got trapped down there.

How the hell had Sokolov managed to reverse this trap so easily?

"Spies?" Anton asked.

Katya realized that she'd muttered that out loud. Bad sign. Especially on her own bridge.

"I gotta lean that way," she agreed. "They blinked out faster than we could catch them the first time, when they should have been completely surprised. Ground attack should have overwhelmed a dozen people and taken them into custody almost before they knew what hit them. Then *Blackstone*. Then hiding from everyone for more than a day. Then *Obsidian Hawk*."

"Someone set Slavkov up?" Mihail asked. "Using us to do it? Or Belfast?"

"Or simply getting all of us in one place so they could grind us down together," Katya said. "Look at overall material losses inflicted, against almost nothing we've done to them. Feels like someone set us up. Inside job, maybe. That just means we have to get back to base with all this information, so the Board of Directors knows."

"Does the contract allow us to abandon that dipshit?" Anton asked. "Cunningham's gone, and I thought he was in command. Slavkov took over, but sure doesn't know a damned thing about ships. That much was obvious. He got enemies we don't know about?"

"Without doubt," Katya said, then paused to think. "Mihail, take charge for now. I need to go reread the contract with a lawyer's eye. Shoot anything that moves, then call me, okay?"

He nodded.

"Oh," she said, rising. "And keep a couple of guns pointed quietly at *Yorrick* from here on in, just in case."

He blinked, then nodded a second time.

Katya went into her office to reread the contract language.

And see what her soul might really be worth.

PART III

Zakhar had assembled everyone in a conference room as they studied the readouts Suvi provided. A bit of damage scattered about, but nothing that wasn't already being repaired by expert teams, when she could tell them exactly where to work and what to do.

They'd be back in action in under an hour.

Where did he go?

Worse, he was functionally blind, because they'd jumped fifteen light-minutes away from *Drako III*, so everything that happened meant he was that far behind.

He looked at the group. Piet, Mary-Elizabeth, Kibwe, Tobias, Bethany. Andreea was busy fixing things, and Afia wasn't here to represent Engineering, but Zakhar would rely on Suvi herself.

"What do we know?" he asked, drawing all eyes.

"As of the most recent reports, I think you might have crippled *Obsidian Hawk*," Bethany noted. "Other ships put a lot of folks aboard from shuttles, but the ship appears to be drifting, with the remainder of that squadron moving to protect it. I presume in case we come back to finish the job?"

"Yeoman, what is the status of radio volume?" Zakhar pressed.

"Very little from the *Hawk*," Suvi replied from her screen. "*Kymni Gauntlet* is generating the most at present, but that has dropped below fifty percent of what they had been averaging before."

He nodded. Might have killed whoever was commanding from *Obsidian Hawk*, after all. If not, damaged the ship so badly that they were out of action. And *Kymni Gauntlet* wasn't picking up the slack.

"If we were successful, does that tie them down in two places?" Piet asked. "We know they are protecting *Blackstone* in a manner suggesting that the damage was greater than we initially thought. If they've lost both flagships, can we bounce back down to where we can watch them from a safe and secret distance?"

"Where would you land?" Suvi asked as Zakhar took a breath to do the same.

"Back of *Mauta*," Piet grinned. "There's a shadow large enough, if we counter-orbit to stay in the sunshine."

Suvi projected a hologram of the *Drako III* system for everyone to study. Zakhar saw it quickly.

"Are they done patrolling?" Mary-Elizabeth asked the group. "Sitting there fixing their other flagship until something happens?"

"That's the feeling I have," Zakhar told her. "They've lost two commanders, and it doesn't appear that there was a third on the org chart, so I wonder how soon their force remembers that they don't like each other and maybe decides to take a slash at someone before leaving."

"*Blackstone* belongs to Walvisbaai," Bethany said. "H & W Heavy Industries built *Obsidian Hawk*. *Kymni Gauntlet* is Jarre Foundation. *Para Bellum* is Belfast Group. Those seem to be the dangerous ones."

"*Yorrick*," Suvi said. "Small, but most of the weapons they were firing at my torpedo were Ion Pulsars, so I'd have been in a lot of trouble if they'd been able to get that close."

Zakhar nodded. Suvi had a few such weapons, but she brought up a scan that showed *Yorrick* to be a nasty little Ion Raider. Trouble.

"Do we go blow up *Para Bellum* or finish off *Blackstone*?" Mary-Elizabeth smiled. "The two escorts remaining close aren't big enough to stop us, if the others suddenly have to protect *Obsidian Hawk* against us jumping across and hitting it when they come to rescue the ships in *Ophiuchi* orbit."

Zakhar nodded. He'd had the same thought.

Still, how did he pit old rivals against one another? That would be the best way to break this formation up. And set things up for later.

Pretend that he was still loyal to Jarre Foundation and pointedly ignore them to attack everyone else? That would certainly ruffle some feathers back home. And here. And make people ask ugly questions that the old Board of Directors probably wasn't ready to answer.

He was done with the pirate business for good. Would have sailed home to *Altai* and called it a life well lived, except that these assholes had decided to mug him in an alley. And Zakhar knew that Javier and Djamila would be even angrier than he was, if that was humanly possible.

It would have to get nasty after this.

"Suvi, if we dropped into *Mauta*'s orbit, would you be

in a position to watch them, then jump back against whoever attacked us?" he asked.

She paused long enough to do some math, from the way her face screwed up sideways.

"Aye, sir," she replied brightly. "Assuming that they aren't smart enough to throw a mix of both groups while holding reserves."

"Four pirate clans, Yeoman," he noted. "I think they have reached the limits of working together and are running on inertia. I'd like to nudge them, so calculate a jump to hiding, then figure out how to peek over the horizon secretly, before unmasking later and daring them to act."

"Zakhar, should we contact system authorities and update them?" Kibwe asked abruptly. "I appreciate that they won't help, but should we warn them, in case someone does take the bait? Several ships in *Mauta* orbit that might be at risk?"

Zakhar considered the odds, and the situation.

"I don't want to warn the pirates," he said. "Put together some sort of burst packet we can start sending to everyone over there, warning them to keep their distance from us and letting them know we won't be around long."

"Understood," Kibwe nodded.

Zakhar looked around.

"Tobias, you haven't spoken," he noted.

"Trying to imagine what pithy, sarcastic observations Javier would make if he were here right now, but I'm coming up blank, sir," Tobias grinned. The others chuckled.

Yes, the man took his responsibilities as Science Officer seriously. Maybe too seriously.

"Probably just as well," Zakhar replied. "I don't need you setting anything on fire today."

That got a round of laughs.

"Captain, I'm ready to make my jump," Suvi said.

"Execute, Yeoman," he replied. "We'll meet you on the bridge."

PART IV

Suvi stepped across space. She'd scanned this local region of space so well that she could predict where every stray asteroid larger than a cat would be a year from now, so it was a piece of cake to drop right into the spot Piet had suggested. And she'd come in a little high on purpose, but not bad. Enough that she didn't have to sail by anybody as she moved to look over the planet's shoulder.

Blackstone remained a dark lump, hardly generating radio traffic. She presumed that they were thinking moray eel thoughts, hiding down in the rocks and ready to chomp a foot if she got close. *Para Bellum* was making up for it, blasting a near-constant churn of traffic aimed at the surface. Encrypted, but the amount of noise did not suggest a ground commander in complete control of the situation.

Made sense, if he'd grabbed the Dragoon by the tail and pissed her off. And Javier. And Afia. And everyone else.

She grinned and settled back down quietly, turning in place and sliding backwards across *Mauta*'s orbit and little high, so she could listen in on *Kymni Gauntlet* and her squadron.

Inside, Zakhar and the others had joined her on the bridge, though she could do everything she needed if they were in the forward wardroom freezer. At least this way they got to watch on screens.

Obsidian Hawk was a mess. Not quite a turkey dinner, but close. If *Hummingbird* hadn't been so damned sharp shifting defensive fire, she might have been able to finish the *Hawk* off entirely, but it had seemed like a smarter choice at the moment to run like hell.

Counting the number and size of Ion weapons *Yorrick* had unmasked, she was glad she had, because that might have been enough to stun her unconscious for twenty or thirty seconds.

Ungood.

Idly, she considered bouncing out and blowing the shit out of *Yorrick* from jump, like she'd done to the *Hawk*. *Hummingbird* was over protecting *Blackstone*, so there was an opening she could exploit.

Except that Zakhar wanted her to taunt the bad guys. Force them to react to her. Suvi plotted three jumps to either side, based on who appeared on top of her suddenly. Unless everyone came at once, one of those two groups would be terminally weakened, and she didn't think that *Blackstone* or that *Hawk* could jump right at this moment.

Which would she rather kill? Probably *Blackstone*. He still had all those damned torpedoes that could seriously mess up her day if she sat motionless in his engagement zone.

Ick, no.

Obsidian Hawk might be Slavkov, and might not. Man might have been smart enough to send someone in his place.

No way to tell without actually boarding, and that only stopped being suicidal if she killed everybody else and had time to send some folks over to inspect the corpses.

Not happening today, buttercup.

Still, she had what she needed. Carefully, she slipped back below the horizon again and started picking up reflected signals instead of direct observations. It would be good enough for now, because even if they saw her, they'd still have to guess where she'd moved to in order to attack.

Suvi organized all her data and presented it to Zakhar.

PART V

Katya was back on her bridge, wondering if she was about to commit career suicide. The Board was going to go over this operation with a microscope when she got home, and there weren't any good answers.

Kowalski and his crew had gotten onto *Obsidian Hawk*'s bridge finally. Hadn't even been all that bad. Slavkov had been in a suit. Had survived with nothing more than bruising and a mild concussion sustained when the entire bridge had whiplashed everyone before losing power so badly that they'd been cut off from the rest of the ship.

Like being buried alive, she supposed, when even the batteries had failed and you had nothing until someone cut out a few deck plates.

Obsidian Hawk might never leave *Drako III*, but they'd deal with that later. Slavkov was being transferred to *Fire Wyvern*'s infirmary, already put under sedation by medteams who wanted to get him stabilized and under observation for a day.

Fat, unhealthy, out of shape, plus suffering shock, trauma, and cranial injuries.

Not dead. Not even dying, which Katya couldn't decide was a good thing or bad. Probably a complete and total pain in her ass tomorrow when he woke up.

If he'd been dead, she'd be running like hell for the hills with *Hummingbird* and *Anubis* in tow and devil take the hindmost, because the contract would die with him and nobody would be able to exercise command over four clans.

As it was, he was technically still in charge, in spite of being unconscious and unable to do anything.

If Sokolov understood that he had about fourteen hours to cause utter mayhem, this force was utterly doomed.

Katya looked around the bridge and made sure she wasn't muttering. Command authority vested in her by her Board of Directors meant that any fuckups landed on her shoulders. And there would already be a whole host of recriminations before this was done.

Suddenly turning and blowing the shit out of *Fire Wyvern* had its allure. Might solve all the rest of her problems, save that she was alone in the middle of an enemy formation, and drawing her allies over here ahead of time would be extremely suspicious.

Stalemate, then. Guns pointed as much at one another as any potential incursion by Sokolov. Nowhere to go, unless they surrendered *Ophiuchi* orbit and brought the entire force over here, but she couldn't see *Para Bellum* abandoning their ground forces. Especially not as badly as *that* had turned into a shitshow.

Katya knew that she hadn't gotten anywhere close to the whole story. *Para Bellum* was on their own encrypted channel and she didn't have the codes to listen, but the pieces she had filled her with dread.

Captain Navarre escaped and still at large. Significant casualties on the ground, as well, from the tidbits she had gleaned.

Trapped. Unless she could convince this group to abandon *Obsidian Hawk* and withdraw to *Ophiuchi*.

Dare she? Her rep would take a hit, but it beat letting Sokolov hunt them all down individually, in a ship Katya was convinced was a lot more powerful than Slavkov had been letting on.

Did that void the contract? Maybe. Except that he'd technically hired them to destroy *Excalibur*, and they'd bought themselves a pig in a poke on this one. A rabid boar in a bag, maybe, from what Sokolov had done to them.

"Anton, anybody acting suspicious?" she asked.

"Compared to?" he fired back, grouchy because they were all tired and nervous. Over-caffeinated. Grinding.

"Compared to us," she said. "Compared to yesterday. How soon until somebody shivs us in the kidney?"

"No clue," he said. "Should I start drifting and see who tracks guns with me?"

"Do that," she ordered. "In fifteen minutes, send the hardest scanner ping you have, omnidirectional like we don't know where Sokolov is, then pay attention to how many guns are pointed at us and by who. Where is your emergency jump programmed to land us?"

"Far side of *Drako III* from where we are," he nodded. "Easiest to do accurately, unless you want me to point it straight up into deep space instead?"

That had its appeal. Bolt and withdraw, and let Sokolov have the rest of them. Technically, he'd obeyed forms when he retired after Captain Navarre had claimed the bounty for *Storm Gauntlet*. It was only later that people put two and two together and realized that Sokolov and Navarre had somehow stolen a battleship, before going after Walvisbaai.

Jarre had no dog in this mess, save that Slavkov had dangled a whole hell of a lot of money to get this many ships assembled.

"Straight up, yes," she said. "Secure a line to *Humming-bird* and *Anubis* and let them know the same, so we don't end up scattered all to hell."

"What if someone decrypts the message?" he asked.

"They'll know what our emergency jump is," she growled. "Not when we'll use it."

"You expecting something?" he pressed.

"We should have won two days ago," she said soberly. "And taken that entire ground force before they knew what hit them. Instead, that operation failed. *Blackstone* and *Obsidian Hawk* are out of action. Cunningham's dead. Slavkov's hurt. I feel like we've been had by somebody, but I don't know who. Spies somewhere had to have warned Sokolov, and he waited for us to arrive so he could kick the shit out of us. I half expect *Yorrick* to try shooting us in the ass, which is why I want you ready to punch her. I got a really bad feeling about this one."

He nodded, lips pressed together, but stayed silent. Not a lot to say.

And she'd said all she needed to with this group. These men and women had been with her for years, most of them. Successful years as Jarre Foundation's primary enforcer. The one they sent after you when you got crossways with the Board of Directors.

And Captain Navarre and Captain Sokolov had gotten away. Again.

How soon until they were coming for her soul? Even *Hummingbird* and *Anubis* wouldn't be enough to stop that beast. Not if he was angry enough.

Katya knew that it was the exhaustion speaking, both her mouth and that little birdie in her mind. Still, it had all gone wrong at some point, and she felt like there was a timer slowly counting down to a bomb she couldn't see or hear.

But she knew it was there.

Hunting her like a big cat.

NIGHTFALL

Javier marveled at how quickly it got dark. Because they didn't have a tent to set up, they'd walked. Because there wasn't going to be any sort of fire, they hadn't looked for a place to set up camp.

Just walked.

He turned to Djamila when she stopped.

"Are we crazy enough to keep going most of the night?" he asked her before she could open her mouth.

"Do you have the endurance?" she countered.

"She and I haven't hardly done anything today," he nodded to Afia. "Saving up for tomorrow already. No reason not to push, if I've got six backwoods experts handy to keep me safe. We'll slow down, but every kilometer we manage gets us that much closer to Naha and a hot shower. Maybe takeout."

He glanced around, taking their temperature. Afia had deeper reserves than just about anybody he knew. The others would be too interested in proving how tough they were to actually admit weakness.

Javier figured he'd break first, and he knew how far that anger was going to carry him tonight.

Maybe not enough to set a wet forest on fire, but more than sufficient to get to Naha. Then figure out how to call down the wrath of the gods on these assholes.

Djamila came to the same conclusion.

"Next stream, everybody will take five to refill canteens, eat, and rest," she announced. "Hajna, drop your pace down some and make enough noise to scare off any predators out hunting. Everyone else do the same, as we should be at least eight kilometers from our last point of engagement and have not detected any overflights."

Javier nodded.

He didn't mention it, because he wasn't sure, but there was also the possibility that he could send a coded message to Suvi once he had access to a comm not known to belong to him. Hiding in a city full of other folks.

He might be a biologist first, but he'd learned an awful lot about electronic systems in his time, and how to take advantage of them.

What Zakhar might be able to do, he had no idea, unless it somehow involved Del and the nameless assault shuttle, where Djamila usually flew guns. That might be a hawk against pigeons, because the three that they'd shot down so far hadn't appeared armed.

It was all the other assholes in orbit with guns that would be a problem.

He'd burn that bridge when he got there. For now, one foot in front of the other, eating up the kilometers and getting away from the hangman's noose.

Until he was ready to turn the tables for good.

PART II

Zakhar studied the display. Suvi had determined everyone's locations again, and was occasionally peeking around the planet, but nobody seemed to be interested in looking their way, and the local ships had either left entirely or gotten as close as they could to one of the armed stations that protected parts of the area.

Only parts, though. And they'd drive him off if he wanted to hide there, unwilling to become the front line in somebody's war.

The image seemed wrong.

"Yeoman, bring me up the plot for four hours ago and overlay the two, centered on *Obsidian Hawk*," he ordered.

Ah. There. That's what it was.

Kymni Gauntlet had drifted hard, while the others were in relatively identical positions. Zakhar dialed in and noted that they had rolled backwards a significant amount as well.

"Suvi, where would you expect a jump to land, based on their current status?" he asked.

"Uhm..." she hesitated, "five to nine light-minutes system

polar north, Captain. Do I need to calculate closer than that?"

"Negative, Yeoman," he countered. "That's good enough. It takes them entirely out of action for long enough."

"Are you expecting something, sir?" Suvi asked.

"Panic," he smiled. "If they jump, they aren't anywhere close enough to help everyone else. I'd worried that *Kymni Gauntlet* could get to *Blackstone* in a hurry if we suddenly appeared over there."

"You think they're ready to bug out?" Piet asked.

"Getting ready," Zakhar answered. "As noted, comms traffic has dropped precipitously since *Obsidian Hawk* got crushed, so they may be without any singular commanding officer. If trouble hits, they might shatter like a glass vase dropped on a concrete floor."

"How do we convince them?" Mary-Elizabeth cackled from her station.

"Something that doesn't involve *Yorrick*," Bethany said.

She'd followed, and settled in her usual spot next to where Djamila watched and knitted occasionally.

"Agreed on *Yorrick*," Zakhar nodded. "Unless we can isolate them, but that still involves *Fire Wyvern* and *Ice Eagle*. Too much firepower too close. And too easy for them to jump back if we go after *Blackstone* a second time. Or *Para Bellum*."

"Taunt them, Captain?" Suvi asked.

"What did you have in mind, Yeoman?" he countered.

Zakhar realized that he'd fallen back into old modes of thinking and acting. Like he was in green permanently. That would never do. "Suvi, how would you solve them?"

She blinked, like she'd caught it at the same time he had.

"Pop up and let them see me a second time," she said. "Last time, they all came running, but if they do that here, somebody is unguarded and I get a kill as soon as I identify who is weakest."

He nodded.

That was what happened when you unlocked a woman like that and told her to cry havoc like the ancients had done.

Sometimes, you got to watch the dogs of war bring down a stag.

Today might be that day.

"Go ahead, Suvi," he said. "Calculate three jumps from here. One to kill *Obsidian Hawk*. One to kill *Blackstone*, and one to drop us on the far side of *Ophiuchi*, where we might deploy Del in the planet's shadow and let him take several hours flying around to where Djamila and Javier are. If nothing else, it gives them mobility."

"On it."

Zakhar dialed the line he wanted and smiled when Del's image appeared from the flight deck of his shuttle, surrounded by pink fur like a *Merankorr* brothel. Man had his feet up on the dash, his arms crossed, and appeared to be asleep.

"I might need to hot launch you in three minutes, immediately following a jump," Zakhar began.

"I've had lunch and a potty break," Del replied, cracking one eye open to look at the camera. "Suvi's been patching everything down here."

Because of course she had. Del was no match for starships. Especially torpedo platforms like *Blackstone*. If, however, that ship ceased to be a threat...

"Long as you're ready," Zakhar said. "She's about to get crazy, so she'll give the order."

Del actually pulled his feet down and triggered his seat into flight mode, grinning like a feral beast. One that hadn't shaved in three days and was a little thirsty for fresh blood.

As usual.

Zakhar smiled and cut the line. Del was ready. Suvi would be ready.

Time to get a little ugly.

PART III

Katya's humor hadn't improved as the afternoon had progressed. Had gotten worse, if anything.

Waiting. Feeling eyes on her back when she wasn't looking, but there was nothing there when she turned.

Except that there was.

Sokolov. Somewhere. Ready to pounce. Slavkov out for another six or eight hours. All the foxes suddenly locked inside an empty hen house, waiting for the farmer to come out with a shotgun.

It was not an image that filled her with joy.

"Hey, that's not right," Mihail muttered. "Kat, I think *Excalibur* just appeared over the horizon of *Mauta*. Like last time."

She brought up her screen and studied the image.

Certainly, it fit the profile. Quiet, as though hiding. Watching. Waiting.

Lurking.

About to pounce?

Katya looked at her numbers. At the ragged and

mismatched display of forces, here and over *Ophiuchi*. *Yorrick* wasn't likely to take her orders, unless it involved sailing over there as a massed formation.

Fire Wyvern and *Ice Eagle* probably stayed right here anyway, protecting *Obsidian Hawk* and their own butts. *Blackstone* could launch a wave of torpedoes, but those might take the better part of a day to track that far, so they were more of a navigational hazard than anything. Unless Katya gathered up half the fleet and sailed in behind them, when *Excalibur* could easily jump away and avoid them, especially as that ship could jump so much more accurately than she could, this deep in various gravity wells.

"He saying anything?" she asked. "Doing anything?

"Negative," Mihail replied. "Dark as a moon in orbit. Watching. Should I scan them? This was a chance passive read, because I have everything tuned in listening, same as they do."

Was it luck? Or was Sokolov really taunting her again?

Last time, Slavkov had come within a hair's breadth of getting splattered by that ship. *Kymni Gauntlet* was bigger and tougher, but Katya was beginning to understand that her battlecruiser was out of its league here. With help.

Rushing in without the others at this moment might mean that Jarre Foundation was down one of its most major ships, if shit got weird later.

And she was pretty confident that the other three clans would love to eliminate Jarre as a competitor.

"Keep a watch on them," Katya ordered. "Send an encrypted signal to everyone letting them know, but don't add anything."

"Update," he nodded. "Gotcha."

Katya doubted that anyone outside the clan would take

orders from her unless something had happened. Did this qualify?

"Captain Ivankova on three," Mihail said a few moments later.

Katya opened the line to study the woman.

Young. Possibly still young enough to do crazy things. Katya's gray hair said everything that needed to be said on the topic. Especially as she'd been in the business since before Ivankova had been born. Along with most of both crews.

"Captain?" Katya asked, leaving it at that.

Ivankova studied her in turn.

"We doing anything?" the woman asked bluntly.

"I suppose that we could order *Fire Wyvern* to abandon *Obsidian Hawk* and move over to where *Blackstone* could possibly protect them," Katya replied. "*Ice Eagle* probably goes with them, so we'd need to draw *Hummingbird* and *Anubis* over here, and possibly reinforce that other force with *Western Sentinel* or *Oberon Martyr*, if you thought we should go attack *Excalibur* right now."

Again, silence. No orders. A few suggestions that could be ignored, depending on how crazy Ivankova felt.

"As opposed to?" Ivankova asked.

"Slavkov's out of communications for several more hours from what I understand," Katya reminded her. "Cunningham is dead. Currently, nobody else is in charge. I happen to command the largest vessel still combat capable, but that's it."

There. Let her offer to take orders from an outsider. Katya had a pretty good hold on Ivankova's personality. And her shortcomings. Wasn't likely to happen.

"Let them get away?" Ivankova asked hotly.

"They could have left any time in the last few days,"

Katya reminded her. "The ground force missed capturing their target, so those folks might be safely hidden. Sokolov might be hunting us now."

She didn't say it like she was afraid. All those nerves were held inside. But either Ivankova had to get off her high horse, or they were all stalemated right now.

One more thing she could blame on someone else, when the Board of Directors started asking those hard questions.

And they would.

"Have you talked to *Fire Wyvern*?" Ivankova asked.

"Just saw *Excalibur* and had my people let everyone know," Katya shook her head. "Be my guest."

Ivankova's scowl redoubled, then she nodded and cut the line.

"Mihail, make sure you are as sharp as a knife for the next ten minutes," Katya ordered.

"You think it's about go down?" he asked.

"Something is," she replied.

What, she had no idea.

PART IV

Suvi grinned. And maybe squealed a little bit. Comms traffic had just EXPLODED over there, and not everything was encrypted, so she was able to follow along in parts and start on decrypting the rest.

Everyone knew she was here. And watching.

And all of them were starting to fidget.

She could almost hear that ominous music that horror vids played, starting up in the background.

Heh.

Would they actually try to come after her here? They'd have to rearrange things pretty massively to do that, and nobody was more than 1.7 light-seconds away, so she'd see it happen before they could pull some dumbass stunt on her.

Humans and their ships needed too much time to Jump, reorient, and recharge their drives, at the very least. Usually, they needed forever to coordinate, and they were all scrambling right now to think of something useful to say.

It was almost tempting enough to launch a single

torpedo at someone, just to see if they spooked. Piet had suggested that they might.

Yorrick was arguing with *Fire Wyvern* about rearranging themselves in such a way that they could protect Slavkov, who apparently really had been on *Obsidian Hawk*, after all, and was just wounded enough to be out of control. They'd sacrifice her *Hawk* entirely and build a hammer and anvil formation.

Mobile forces big enough to take her on. Immobile bastion tough enough to hold her off. How did a girl take advantage of all this trouble?

"Zakhar, here's a quick executive summary," she said, boiling it down and handing it to the second sneakiest and second meanest person she knew, with Javier and Djamila both elsewhere.

He read, while outside, the four pirate clans argued.

Damned fools weren't giving her the opening she needed, unless the other two birds flitted away, in which case she could pounce pretty hard on *Kymni Gauntlet*.

Then she caught a signal. Someone on *Yorrick* had turned a private comm laser onto *Epsilon Cavendish*, and she could read the reflection because they hadn't encrypted it. Granted, comm lasers were a pain to intercept, but *Epsilon Cavendish*'s hull had been polished lately.

Huh. *Yorrick* was ordering the other Belfast ships to assemble for a surprise attack.

That would be *Epsilon Cavendish*, *Arminus*, and *Oberon Martyr*. *Para Bellum* sent a note telling them to get stuffed, then Suvi heard that ship's captain get overruled, because he had at least as many Ion Cannon and Ion Pulsars as *Yorrick* did, usually for the same reason.

Get right up in someone's face and ionize the shit out of

them, at least on a starship level. Same thing would work on a *Sentient* ship like her. Same effect.

Yeah, no.

Worse, she had to act now. Act ugly, and take her chances, because all of Belfast getting together left H & W, Walvisbaai, and Jarre pretty much shit out of luck if they didn't immediately shatter their current formations and recoalesce into something new. Like, say, clan squadrons.

While that might be to her benefit, it might not, because that gave Belfast too many Ion equipped ships to fight.

"Zakhar, hang on," she announced. "Shit just got real."

Suvi shifted all of her turrets onto a new facing.

Then she jumped.

PART V

Suvi stepped sideways. It helped that *Yorrick* was more worried about *Kymni Gauntlet* than she was anybody else, because that put that ship's turrets mostly on the wrong facing. Or rather, it left a blind spot that Suvi could exploit.

And she did.

Better, this force was already in place, and largely unmoving relative to where she had been and to one another.

Excalibur exited Jump in *Yorrick*'s shadow, as seen by *Kymni Gauntlet*. Exactly opposite, like three happy pigs at a feeding trough. At least if you were sitting on the smoky remains of *Blackstone*'s bridge to watch.

She cut loose with everything she had, point-blank into *Yorrick*'s port hull. Nothing fancy. Nothing pretty. Nothing even surgical.

Mad dog going berserker froth on someone. Horror vid music in the back of her mind.

Helped that *Yorrick* was a little fucker. Frigate-scale, sure, but on the lighter end than even *Storm Gauntlet* had been, because Ion Cannons required less power, and thus fewer generators, in order to be dangerous.

As long as nobody paying attention realized what you gave up in terms of mass and defense in the process.

Broadside, when all their shields had JUST HAPPENED to be reinforced on the *Kymni Gauntlet* side of the ship.

Gosh, I wonder why?

Ship might look tough, but *Hummingbird* was the one around here that worried her, because they really were that sharp, even if they were on the other side today. Jarre had at least hired competent people.

Too competent for her tastes, but they were keeping her from kicking *Blackstone*'s ass for good right now.

Around her, the other ships in this formation all woke up to the whale that had just surfaced in their midst again, but they were all looking the wrong way. Worse, all their weapons were pointed at each other instead of nearby space where they might crank them around fast enough to bother her.

Oh, that was pretty.

Yorrick, panicking, had just hosed *Kymni Gauntlet* down with everything they had, which had happened to be a whole **insanity** of ionization. Suvi could almost taste it from here.

Wrong target, buttercup, but thank you for eliminating the single most dangerous ship in range for me.

Suvi reset her timer on how quickly she had to flit to escape major damage without *Kymni* ready to do anything. And kept punching *Yorrick* in the head. Something had to break eventually.

There. Plasma venting. Something just broke aft. Fuel line ruptured, from the looks of it. Those were secondary explosions.

Oh. Boom. Somebody just lost En-gi-neer-ing.

Pretty fireworks!

Yorrick vanished inside a cloud of plasma like a sudden mushroom. *Royal Gamma* was starting to be a pain in her ass, because they'd managed to get a light Pulse Cannon around and were woodpeckering her other flank, but Suvi did some quick math and kept pouring fire into the place where *Yorrick* was currently hiding.

Any shots that missed right now had a pretty good chance of hitting *Kymni Gauntlet* anyway.

Might have been a reason I picked this spot, you junior varsity punks.

Wouldn't hurt that *Kymni* would be pretty ionized for the next thirty seconds or longer. No shield reinforcements, though Suvi was certain she would be banging on shields that had been previously reinforced.

Or was that captain smart enough to ignore *Yorrick* and Ionization weapons that would step past shields? They had flown pretty damned professional today. Assume standard shields here.

Whoops.

The plasma had expanded far enough to cool and thin. Suvi had kept up her fire anyway, because at this range it wouldn't degrade her beams all that much.

Part of *Yorrick* tumbled clear. Only part. Only the front part.

Suvi went ahead and shifted to keep pounding *Kymni Gauntlet*, just in case, as she scanned *Yorrick* and saw evidence of a massive detonation aft.

Smart people built starships to vent everything sideways when Engineering exploded. You might lose the aft third of your ship, and probably a third or more of your crew, but the rest would be forward.

Or...were forward. Suvi tracked a few Pulsars onto that

chunk of ship as a statement on Ionization weaponry. She had a few herself, but those were leftover from *Hammerfield*, having been part of the purchase price. And she'd been using them, same as the Pulse Cannons and Pulsars, because she was pretty sure she should be fighting for her life here.

And killing as many pirates as she could lay hands on.

Royal Gamma was being a bigger pain now. She shifted all of her Ion Cannons on him and hosed him down to shut him up, even as she kept banging on *Kymni* with all the big stuff and *Yorrick*'s skull with the rest.

The Bard would appreciate her imagery, since she'd kinda decapitated that punk in the last ten seconds of fighting.

Maybe time for a quick monologue? Where was Horatio right now?

'Cause she was pretty sure Rosencrantz and Guildenstern were dead at this point.

Where was Fortinbras when she needed him?

Red lights were appearing in more locations on her boards. Beam fire leaking through her shields and starting to punch holes in her armored outer hull. Shields down to fifty percent or lower on more than half of her facings, but nobody could gang up with a neighbor to overwhelm any one spot.

Suvi might have picked this location for THAT EXACT REASON. She was a big girl. She could handle herself in a bar fight.

This probably qualified.

More red lights. More trouble.

She nodded as *Yorrick's Skull* kept tumbling and aimed herself for the far side of *Ophiuchi*.

It was doubtful that anybody would be paying that much attention when she appeared over there.

And gone.

PART VI

Katya wouldn't have believed it, except that she'd been right in the middle of it. Had been watching *Yorrick* on her personal screens in that moment when *Excalibur* had launched yet another surprise attack.

And that bitch Ivankova had ionized the shit out of *Kymni Gauntlet* at the first sign of trouble, so there'd been nothing Katya could do but watch as *Yorrick* got destroyed. Worse, Sokolov had turned his fire on her while she'd been immobilized, hammering her port side to the point that she'd have normally have retired anyway and sailed for a drydock to repair things.

Nowhere to go here. Nowhere to hide. Not unless she went ahead and fled the whole system.

Did an ambush by *Yorrick* and Belfast Group qualify? On top of everything else?

Probably.

"Anton, what is your status?" she asked as *Excalibur* disappeared yet again.

Damned *Sentient* warships. How the hell did you fight something that fast? That dangerous?

"All shielding on that flank gone, Kat," he said. "Bringing engines up, but we're coming from a cold start right now and I'm not sure how quickly we can escape this mess."

"Jump," she ordered. "Tell *Hummingbird* and *Anubis*, then flit. *Yorrick* is no longer a threat, which means three of the four clan flagships are functionally destroyed and we're a mess. Get us the hell out of here while we can."

"What about the others?" Mihail asked. "Nobody firing at us at the moment, but *Royal Gamma* took almost as much fire as we did and they're hurting."

"Let Walvisbaai come over and rescue them," Kat decided. "We're sitting ducks if that ship comes back, and I feel like we've just lost all coherence as a fleet or even a squadron."

"Roger that," Mihail nodded.

She watched the two men work, while around all of them people came and went. Damage control. Life support. Shields repair. Medical.

Looking at her screens, it hadn't been as bad as it could be, but that was probably Sokolov stopping to hammer *Yorrick* into the mud even after he'd made his point. And *Royal Gamma* taking fire that might have left *Kymni Gauntlet* in little better shape?

A parting gift from a former comrade at the Jarre Foundation? She'd only tangentially ever dealt with Sokolov, which was why the Board had sent her. No personal connection that might cause her to waver at a critical moment.

She was definitely wavering now, as all her screens went blank, then reset.

Straight up. Out a ways. Safe, she hoped.

A few seconds later, *Hummingbird* appeared, rotating once to align with her flight vector like the escort that he was. Damned good piloting. Damned good fighting. Glad she had him with her.

Anubis was there three seconds later. Kat considered bitching at them, but that was *Hummingbird* being utterly on point at their job. Even *Anubis* had reacted a little faster than she'd been expecting.

"Mihail, lock us an encrypted squadron channel," Katya ordered. "Family only."

"On six," he said without looking up.

Captain Carlyle appeared first, from the bridge of *Hummingbird*, smiling and with that shock of bright red hair that was his signature look. Elaine Baedeker joined them from *Anubis*, dour and competent, but not flamboyant.

Get the job done. That was her whole shtick.

"What's your status, boss?" Carlyle asked immediately.

"Bad but not terrible," she replied. "We can fly, and I intend to get us someplace where we can sit quiet for a day or two and take a few systems offline for better repairs."

"Point Gamma?" Elaine asked.

Katya considered it.

"As good as any," she replied. "How quickly can you get there?"

"Are we escorting you or scouting the landing site?" Carlyle asked.

"You go ahead and scout for trouble," Katya ordered. "We'll follow."

"I'm gone," he said.

Hummingbird vanished five seconds later, leaving her with Elaine.

"What the hell happened, Kat?" Elaine asked.

"I have a pretty good feeling that somebody set us all up," Katya replied. "A spy somewhere put us all in a position to lose major ships. Three flagships destroyed or crippled in place. We came close and I'm certain that we'd have been next on Sokolov's list, had we stayed."

"He do us a favor, or save us for last?" she asked.

"Wish I knew, Elaine," Katya nodded. "Sokolov always had a rep for solid and competent. Brilliant tactician. Former *Concord* Captain, so knows his shit. And he's in a ship far more powerful than Slavkov let on to the Board, I'm guessing."

"Now what?"

"Now, we get the hell out of the firing line and get home so we can update the Board on all this," Katya said. "They need to know, so I'll transmit a package to both of you, in case I need Carlyle running fast ahead of us while *Kymni Gauntlet* limps in to port later."

"We going back after Sokolov later?" Elaine asked.

"Honestly?" Katya asked. "I'd be more worried that he decides to come after us. Remember, he was one of us for decades, so he knows where to look for Jarre resources better than anyone else, and I'm pretty sure we've pissed him off."

"Time to retire?" Elaine pressed.

"Ask me that after I get grilled by the Board," Katya replied, only half jesting.

What would Zakhar Sokolov do, having fended off all four clans simultaneously? Having killed three flagships?

Having had his retirement so rudely interrupted?

There was no way in hell she'd be going after him at *Altai*. Those folks had a fleet at least as powerful and dangerous as the *Concord*. And likely fewer compunctions about using it on pirates.

"Kat. I'm ready to jump," Anton called.
She caught Elaine's nod on the screen.
"Take us home," Katya ordered.
Then what?

MORNING

PART I

Javier had indeed walked all night. Rage-fueled beast, and all that. Helped that the others were all driving each other to push as far and hard as they could. Fifteen minute breaks every hour or so. Using up snacks for energy on the understanding that they'd be to town and could find a bodega soon enough.

Light was rising. Birds had woken up, started singing, then started bitching about intruders walking around. Not that he blamed them. At least he wouldn't be here long.

His original expectation had been two days hard walk to get to Naha. They'd started a few hours before dark, then pushed all night.

He turned to Hajna as Djamila called a quick break at a stream.

"How far out are we?" he asked her.

Valley. Daybreak. Trees. Only because he was following her did he know they were headed the right direction.

"Mid-afternoon if we pushed," she said. "Something up?"

Javier turned to Djamila.

"Do Hajna and I go ahead of you and get us some rooms?" he asked. "Make sure that nobody got sneaky enough to put teams in both towns?"

"How would you tell?" Djamila asked.

"I plan to walk low profile," he replied. "You and Afia stand out for the same reasons. Size. I might, but I also presume Hajna can kill people for me. If you folks come up behind us to maybe a few kilometers outside of town, I'd feel safe enough."

"You expecting trouble?" Hajna asked.

"I expect that someone wants us dead bad enough to do all the things we've faced up until now," he said and turned back to the woman. "Plus all the crap in orbit. I'd like to get someplace where we can hide indefinitely, safely. I have no doubts that Zakhar is handling things at his end and counting on us to do the same. That might involve us stealing or buying a ship. Or maybe just hanging out and booking passage in a few weeks. I don't know. I'd like to know, because you know what kind of control freak I can be."

Her grin at that last bit didn't really improve his humor, but at least Javier was willing to admit to his levels of control freak these days. Not like he was the only one in earshot, after all.

"I like it," the Dragoon agreed. "We'll push hard this morning, with the goal of emerging before dark."

Javier nodded. He'd said his piece. Laid out his plans to get them off this rock, because he knew it would come down to him and Afia getting sneaky, once they were back to dealing with people again, instead of critters.

And from town, he might be able to talk to Suvi.

PART II

Suvi had kept all her survey senses open to drink from the firehose that was available data. *Drako III* was a messy place. The rest of the solar system was hardly better. At the same time, she'd been a survey ship with Javier for years, and old habits surfaced whenever she stopped moving.

Or sat hiding in the shadow of *Ophiuchi*.

Del was in motion, but Suvi was mostly listening to the folks from Belfast Group hurl insults at one another. And not always encrypted, so she'd learned a few new ones. Not that she'd tell Javier or Zakhar before she used them.

Wasn't like they could wash her mouth out with soap, after all.

"Suvi, what are they up to now?" Zakhar asked.

She jolted for a second, wondering if he was prescient, or reading her logs.

Or just that sharp a commanding officer.

"*Yorrick* is done, sir," she replied. "They have begun the process of evacuating the wreck and dealing with casualties. *Obsidian Hawk* is being classified as a navigational hazard, so at some point I expect wreckers or salvagers to claim both hulls and haul them off. Reports are that both ships are blowing all their computers in place to prevent them from being stripped."

"Wise," he replied. "I'd drop Ilan and a team to grab their nav records if I could, but I have other folks I can reach out to when I need coordinates later. Have they split into clan groups?"

"Affirmative, Captain," she answered, throwing up a scan showing three clustered up tight, but separate enough from one another that she could possibly risk jumping in tight, if she didn't mind finding out how much *Blackstone* was playing possum right now.

And she figured they were just waiting for any excuse to darken the sky with arrows. Or torpedoes.

Whatever.

"Where did Jarre go?" he asked. "*Kymni Gauntlet*, *Anubis*, and *Hummingbird*."

"Polar north," Suvi replied, shifting her screens around and dialing them way back. "Eight light-minutes out, held for just under two minutes, then pivoted and vanished."

"They are done and running for home," he nodded sagely. "Didn't appreciate *Yorrick* hosing them when you appeared, and decided to get while the getting was good."

"We going after the rest, sir?" she asked.

I mean, technically, she could do anything she wanted right now, since he had specifically removed all limitations on her actions.

At the same time, Zakhar had a career as a successful *Concord* officer, then another one as a pirate captain. Not a lot of people more expert at things like today.

Kinda guy a smart girl listened to.

"Remember when I mentioned earlier that they might shatter if spooked?" he asked, waiting for her to nod. "This is what it looks like. Next step might be to recover all of their ground forces, but that's fifty/fifty at present."

"As opposed to?" she asked, interested in his take.

"They might make a hard surge to go after Djamila and Javier as hostages," he replied. "Keep us at bay or force us to deal. I don't think that they understand how ugly that would get for them."

"Sir?"

"Would you allow pirates to capture Javier and Afia and get away from you, Suvi?" he asked. "Djamila and her people? Or would you dive in and annihilate those same pirates?"

"Oh, right," she nodded.

She'd probably sacrifice herself to make sure that none of the pirates got away alive with any of her friends, even if she thought it was possible that they might be successfully ransomed home later.

Given that Valko Slavkov himself was present in system, she might also decide to go annihilate *Fire Wyvern* to finish him off, except that there really were too many of the bastards to make sure she was successful. All of the Walvisbaai folks were just close enough to pounce on her if she decided to go after the two H & W ships left.

Bait? Probably. Had an icky taste in her mouth when she thought about it.

Para Bellum was the one she'd probably need to destroy, if they suddenly acted like they had Javier and the others on a shuttle being brought to orbit. Except that said shuttle could board any of the Belfast ships and give her the slip.

Dammit, how did she kill ALL of those punks?

She needed Del's sneakiness. And probably had to keep everyone focused on her up here, so that they lost track of the fact that she'd slipped back around the other side of *Ophiuchi* to deliver her own shuttle.

Not like Del wasn't an expert at smuggling. Among a whole BUNCH of other things.

Suvi triggered a jump that put her about midway between the wrecks and the folks in orbit, just to remind them that they weren't safe slow-sailing around here.

And maybe to bait them into making their own mistake.

PART III

Delbert Smith had been flying shit like this since before most of these kids had been born. Hell, even Zakhar had been in short pants when Del first climbed into a cockpit and committed...

No, best not to mention that. Even today. Statutes of limitations might expire, but some people could hold a grudge forever. And, if he was honest, with a pretty damned good reason.

Del smiled as he got low and let the autopilot carry him. Sucker had a soft tendency to drift to starboard, but that might be the fact that he hadn't actually engaged it in...three years.

Why the hell let the machine fly him? Except that he had twelve hours, even at these speeds, and preferred to meditate, nap, have a couple of quick meals, and a potty break before getting down into the area Djamila would have called her Death Zone.

Woman was like that. Kid after his own heart, but definitively not one of his. Too tall. Too lots of things, but way too tall.

Almost crazy enough to be adopted, though. Almost mean enough.

Maybe he should haul her and Zakhar to a family reunion sometime? Or invite them folks to charter a ship and visit him on *Altai*? Probably safer that way, since he had an in with the Khatum if anybody showed up with outstanding warrants for arrest and bounty hunters.

Yup. Smart. He made a mental note.

And watched the skies turn gray with various weather fronts. Late winter down therein places. Planetary meteorologists didn't care that there were pirates playing fool games in orbit. They still had to update forecasts and keep people sharp.

Given where the Dragoon probably was today, couple of ugly storm fronts coming through. Freezing rain, graupel, and snow in places.

Which was exactly why he was sitting in his favorite cockpit, surrounded by soothing faux-fur and with a mug of warm tea in one hand. Music was turned down to more of a suggestion than a background.

Del studied his horizon and decided that he was close enough.

Of course, he was flying under false colors today. He and Suvi had stolen a transponder code from a country ship over above *Blue Amsterdam* and he was pretending to be their local cargo shuttle, making a delivery on the surface. Not like the pirates were about to call and ask. And folks around here had been pretty good about ignoring everything and pretending that none of this was actually happening.

"Tango-Charlie-Seven-One-Niner, this is Sultan Flight Control," a voice rang out sharply, identifying him from their long-range scanners as he came over the horizon finally. "Be advised that you are close to entering an area that has been closed to all aircraft. Hostile elements have been operating in region Grid Six-Eight by Alpha-One-One. Please respond."

Del considered ignoring them, but they'd just get more pissy before getting hysterical. Then maybe realizing that he wasn't entirely on the up-and-up at some point. Not that they were wrong, but best if they don't come to any understanding of that until he was deeper into whatever trouble he might bring.

Still, he pretended like maybe the autopilot was smarter than it was and gave them ten seconds before he opened the line.

"Sultan Flight Control, this is Seven-One-Niner," he drawled back. "Not detecting any aircraft ahead of me at present. What seems to be the issue, over?"

The only signals he was picking up belonged to a pair of aircraft, both currently on the ground, just about dead-center where Djamila and friends had been planning to resort. Suvi had mentioned four originally, but said that she'd stopped picking up traffic from two of them, suggesting that dear Djamila might have objected to people interrupting her week off.

And Del knew exactly what kinds of hardware they'd brought with them, generally disguised as other things. And it wasn't like the locals had cared all that much.

Still...

"Seven-One-Niner, there are pirates operating in that

area and local law enforcement has been unable to deal with them. Over."

Well, duh. You needed killers. Fortunately, he knew a few. Might even qualify himself, but again, statutes of limitations and outstanding warrants. And long memories.

"Sultan, I have a delivery with firm deadlines if I want to get paid," Del offered, mostly to obfuscate shit. And suggesting that he wasn't carrying insurance adequate to *force majeure.*

Technically, he wasn't. She was down on the surface, somewhere in front of him, after all, armed to the teeth.

"Seven-One-Niner, you are ordered to change course to Zero-Three-Eight and divert to Rockton Starport," Sultan said, hopping over all the deflections and bullshit he might throw at them to delay things. And he probably wasn't their first pilot being a pain in the ass on the topic.

Del checked his charts. Right on the edge of the no-go zone he'd have laid down, so they were at least being nice about it. And it got him close enough to start broadcasting signals that Djamila should pick up. And listen on a frequency they could reach him, if they needed an extraction.

Hell of a walk, but he could also hot zone the damned thing if he had to.

Not that that was anything new with these people.

"Sultan Flight Control, this is Seven-One-Niner," Del said. "Rerouting. I presume that there's space to land there and someone who can deliver takeout?"

Not that he needed it, but the others might appreciate that his kitchen was a bit more exotic than they might be prepared for, if he did end up extracting them from a hostile landing zone.

"Affirmative, Seven-One-Niner. Thank you for being understanding."

Del shrugged. He'd be racking up the fines later, more than likely. Javier could pay them.

After he got home safe.

PART IV

Benedict cut the line to those idiots in orbit before he lost his temper entirely. He didn't care if Tsvetanka Ivankova had lost her ship and had had to be evacuated wounded from *Yorrick* to *Epsilon Cavendish*.

Just as well she wasn't on *Para Bellum*, or Benedict would have probably lost his temper at Captain Shidao, too. He was six hours from having his second shuttle back and flightworthy, according to the mechanics who had already moved heaven and earth getting it fixed.

And those morons were demanding that he abandon everything, right now, and start loading his people and flying them to orbit, as a prelude to bugging out? And leaving behind all of his equipment for whatever vultures came along to steal it?

He punched a bulkhead as he paced, noting absently that his own bodyguards were ducking and flinching away from him.

Crap.

Benedict took a deep breath and blew it out, turning to those same folks.

"I'm okay," he said, mostly because if he said it, it might actually happen.

The disbelief on their faces wasn't helpful. Maybe he was wrong.

Benedict went to the comm and dialed up a different channel.

"Group Leader Marte," Anton answered immediately.

"It's Benedict," he said. "Orders from on high haven't arrived yet, but I think it is only a matter of time."

He paused and drew a hard breath, refraining from punching anything else.

"Go ahead and start bringing your people in," Benedict ordered. "Get them marching back into patrol forces and headed this way. Either we'll pick you up, or you'll walk into the base and camp. Beware of surprises at the last minute. I'd rather not lose anybody else at this point unless you have a confirmed contact we can exploit."

"Roger that, Benedict," Anton replied after a quick beat. "See you in a while."

Benedict nodded to himself and cut the line. Another breath, and he switched lines.

"Group Leader Rosson," Peter was there.

"Orbit is about to throw in the towel," Benedict offered. "Anton is withdrawing. Make sure you're set up against any last minute attacks. Have your people stay extra sharp. Tomorrow, we might be dumping everything and loading both boats. Plan accordingly with your people and tell the cooks to go a little overboard with dinner."

"You sure about that, Benedict?" Peter asked.

"No, but this has already gone on too long, Peter," he

replied. "Shit's gotten entirely out of hand in orbit, but I haven't gotten all the details. *Yorrick* was apparently destroyed last night. The others are in the process of unraveling. Near as I can tell, all the Jarre ships took off."

"Destroyed?" Peter asked. "We screwed, Benedict?"

"We might be," Benedict offered. "Just stay sharp."

He cut the line and wondered where the hell it had all gone wrong. And how a team that small had managed to do so much damage to what should have been an overwhelming force. Except that **nobody** had mentioned surface-to-air-missiles that someone had taken with them on vacation. Or any of the other things he'd been on the wrong end of.

There was a reason he'd taken to sleeping on this shuttle, just in case Sykora came back for more. At least here he had reinforced hull protecting him.

A noise behind him caused Benedict to turn to his bodyguard.

Willem nodded. With Arla gone, he was generally in charge.

"We telling Arla?" Willem asked.

Benedict nodded. Sighed. Dialed a number.

"Troop Leader Ancher," Arla replied.

"I want you to stay sharp," Benedict ordered. "This mission is coming apart. We're laagering in here today, while we regroup. If the order to extract comes, we'll grab you last, on our way to orbit."

"They got away?" Arla asked.

"From us," Benedict replied. "At this point, presumably they are so deep in the brush we won't dig them out anytime soon. Alternatively, they might have headed your direction."

"My people estimate three days minimum to cross that distance," she said. "From that last contact, that means that we have thirty-six hours. I've got my people watching all the approaches anyway. You still available to vector everyone in if we make a positive contact?"

"At present, Arla," he said. "However, they may overrule us anytime in the next forty-eight hours, so stay packed at your end so we can get you out if we have to."

"Roger that, sir," she said.

Benedict cut the line and kept his growl to himself. None of his people needed to know. To hear it.

To understand how pissed he was that his briefing from the bosses had been criminally inadequate.

No way in hell Sykora—even *Sykora*—should have been able to do all this. And *Yorrick* destroyed in orbit? After *Blackstone* and *Obsidian Hawk*?

And no chance in hell that his problems were accidental. He had some really sharp and angry things to say when he got a chance to talk to whoever wanted to own this monumental fuckup in planning.

Assuming any of them got away alive.

PART V

Djamila studied the last valley, spread out before her. Naha. In the distance, she could just make out Altamont, higher up a road and around a couple of low hill curves. Snow still on the ground in more places here, allowing a late skiing season. That had been why she had preferred the other side of the continental divide, because it also cut off a lot of cold air. Still winter around here.

Fortunately, a lot of hikers had mashed trails. Once Hajna found one and confirmed it, they had made better time than expected. As a result, Djamila had gotten to about thirty-two hundred meters from the rough edge of Naha itself, with a number of cabins and outlying businesses scattered around. Nothing close, and she'd let her team relax, breaking out a small heater to boil water for coffee and trigger some of Javier's leftover ration packs for hot food.

As good as it was going to get at present.

Afia moved to sit on the log next to her, so Djamila joined her.

"Without comms, how do you know they are successful?" Afia asked.

"Either Hajna returns, or one of them moves to that one spot we marked and waves," Djamila nodded. "From there, we will react."

Afia shrugged. Djamila understood. The woman was a combat engineer, but not really ready for the things Djamila demanded of her people on a regular basis. That might change. Already, she'd seen Javier adjust his thinking into the sorts of long-term campaign that might involve hunting down and destroying all of the pirate clans when this was done.

And, Djamila supposed, it was a thing that needed doing. She could look at herself in the mirror and understand the evil that she had perpetrated. Out of the military, unemployed, broke, broken. And that described far too many people these days.

Hopefully, Javier had a plan to tackle the underlying socio-economic causes, but he also seemed convinced that the Rising Storm predicted by Dorn Hetzel would sweep away almost everything before it ran its course, so Javier was simply trying to get people safely hunkered down ahead of time.

If that was possible.

"Who do we kill for this?" Afia asked.

Djamila started, then considered her words with care.

"Knowing Javier and Zakhar, the correct answer might be everybody," she offered.

Afia nodded grimly.

"Pretty sure they got it coming," the woman said quietly. "But then, don't we all?"

Djamila was hard pressed to argue that point.

PART VI

Javier had shifted his attitude into an acute, bourgeois mindset after he and Hajna split from the main group. Rich tourist, out for a bit of a hike in the late winter wonderland. Altamont was only about ten kilometers away by road. Six by air. A professional adventurer might walk that, starting at dawn and pushing a little. Even his pistol was hidden inside his jacket right now.

He pasted that image onto his face, added a touch of social and economic superiority, and walked into the lobby of a four-star hotel that had made the mistake of turning their vacancy light on this morning.

Rich carpets. Heavy, but covered over with a secondary walkway he presumed would absorb snow knocked off one's boots. Chandeliers in three places. Door to a restaurant. Chairs and sofas. Two fireplaces. Coffee shop. Hotel detective looking up from his tablet.

Javier ignored it all and strode to the desk like a man set on conquering a new galactic record for something as yet a touch vague.

"May I help you, sir?" the bright, cheery, shiny young woman behind the counter asked as he got close.

Hajna had fallen back a step. Perhaps a mountain guide. Perhaps a girlfriend keeping a low profile. Woman was an expert actress, but they were playing this by ear until they had a better hold on the situation.

"Two rooms," he announced, stepping up to put a hand on her counter. "Two beds is fine. Mostly, I want in out of the cold. We were set to camp for three more days, but nobody mentioned that the forecast would turn so dreadfully dreary."

He added a touch of poncy malevolence to his voice as he spoke. A man with too much money, hardly any sense, and an unbridled ego. Someone paying attention might even recognize that punk Slavkov in his diction, but there shouldn't be anyone down here that knew the man.

"Very good, sir," the woman nodded, ignoring his histrionics. "ID and credit?"

Javier handed her his good card. The one that identified him as DOCTOR Javier Aritza of King's College, working on the presumption that folks upstairs might only know Eutropio Navarre.

He had one of those as well, hidden in his boot against need.

"Doctor Aritza?" she confirmed.

"Indeed," he nodded, allowing her a superior smile in keeping with the dumbass he was portraying today.

"How many nights will you need, Doctor Aritza?" she asked.

He pretended to give it some thought.

"At least three," he said, "though I might need to extend that a few. Will that be a problem?"

"Unlikely, sir," she answered. "We're towards the end of the season, into what is usually a lull in bookings. I'll leave a note in your records."

He nodded.

THIS was the moment when shit might get ugly. If someone had his other ID tagged, they might send cops to arrest him. Or killers. Until he had Djamila and her folks around him, he was at risk.

Hajna was wonderfully deadly people, but there was only one Ballerina of Death. At least as far as he knew.

Javier suppressed a shudder that there might be more like her in the universe.

Instead, he watched the woman behind the counter, certain that Hajna had eyes on the hotel detective. Last thing he needed was a running firefight in a hotel lobby if someone tried to arrest him.

Still, wouldn't be the first time. He didn't have any great expectations that it would be the last, either.

She typed. He watched, controlling his breathing and the twitchiness to go for the pistol he'd stashed under his jacket.

"Here you go, Doctor," she said, handing him an envelope with a smile. "Room Three-Ten and Three-Twelve. Down that way to the elevators, or stairs just past them."

"Excellent," he drawled, taking it from her hands and nodding to Hajna. "Come."

Quickly, they got to the elevator. Got in. Got it closed. Hajna slipped close like a girlfriend and whispered in his ear.

"Think we're safe at present," she breathed loudly.

"Room. Shower. Room service," he replied quietly. "At that point, we might be safe."

She nodded and stepped back.

They were almost home.

This was usually when shit went sideways.

PART VII

Del had settled. Ordered bland Chinese takeout sufficient for a mob, with all of it going into the refrigerator for now.

Nothing on the usual frequencies, but he had expected that. Signals intelligence only started with not broadcasting anything that bad guys might pick up. Then you got sneaky.

Outside, the afternoon was waning. Lots of orbital traffic overhead that had leaked, but he was entirely out of touch with Suvi and the ship for now. Just a shuttle on the ground, pretending to be nobody important.

At least until shit got crazy again.

Every comm was open and listening. Plus, he was jacked into the local comm network for now via landline providing water, septic, and power. Best part, he wasn't paying, as the planetary government had declared a state of emergency until otherwise noted.

Line twenty-three suddenly beeped. He answered.

"Tango-Charlie-Seven-One-Niner," Del said.

"Pity," Javier replied. "Was hoping for a pizza delivery."

Del reached over and flipped a switch. His boards beeped

twice and should be about as encrypted as possible. Landline, so no bozos in the air should be listening.

"Line's encrypted," Del said, then gave Javier a quick rundown of everything that had happened in orbit over the last few days.

Lots, really.

"What's your status?" Del asked when he was done.

"Three unaccounted for," Javier replied. "Everyone else at a hotel in Naha. Where are you?"

"Rockton Starport," Del told him. "Grounded by orders of planetary government. Someone caused a bit of a ruckus o'er yonder. What do you need from me?"

"We've been out of the loop," Javier said. "Escape and Evasion drills a little too visceral for me. Sascha and her two are still out somewhere. Have you heard anything?"

"Negative on that front," Del said. "And I get the impression that they remain at large. Suvi and Zakhar have proven to be more than the dipshits in orbit were prepared for."

Javier laughed. It had a cruel, jagged edge to it that Del appreciated.

"You were expecting less from her?" he asked.

"You'll be proud of your girl when she relays the final action report," he said. "How do we get you out?"

"Stand by while I scan a map."

The line took on that weird hum that was a factor of a mute over landlines. Had to find him on a map. Then do a little math. Naha wasn't that far away as he might fly it, but there were still assholes about. And two aircraft operating inside the forbidden zone, though he had no idea if they were armed.

He could fire the turret from up here in a pinch. Mostly

by flying this beast like a snubfighter. More fun if he had Djamila handing it.

'Course, he'd been doing this since before she'd been born. Might still remember a few tricks to teach the kids.

"Tango, we don't think your pigeons are armed, but cannot confirm," Javier said suddenly, sending a jolt of ugly happiness threading through Del's vitals.

Fishies in a barrel, then.

He mostly managed to suppress the mad cackle that erupted.

"Yeah, I thought so, too," Javier replied drolly. "I'd like to take some time here and get everyone sorted at my end. You look at a map and see where you're comfortable landing to pick up the eight of us, while we figure out how to locate the other three and extract them."

"Gotcha," Del said. "Went ahead and had Chinese delivered here. Might even still be warm if we hurry."

"I'll call back in an hour," Javier replied. "That's time for showers here."

"I'm on it," Del said. "Out."

He cut the line and brought up the map. Forbidden Zone or not, not a lot of folks in the air that were a problem for him. It was the getting out later that would be iffy.

He'd need Suvi and Zakhar running interference for that.

NIGHT TWO

PART I

Zakhar had napped, secure that Suvi would shoot first, shoot second, then jump, before waking him up to do anything.

As it should be.

According to her, Del and the nameless shuttle had gotten close enough to work, based on whatever communications tricks those two had worked out. He didn't need to know anything other than it had worked.

The Jarre Foundation had bugged out, as near as he could tell. *Kymni Gauntlet, Hummingbird, Anubis.* None of them showed on any scans of nearby space, so he had to hope they had left for good.

Not that he wanted to go after his old team, but if it was necessary to wipe the slate entirely clean, then he'd do what he had to. Plus, they could have turned Slavkov down when asked.

And they had threatened Djamila. Hell might not protect them from his wrath.

"What is our current status, Suvi?" he asked.

"Exploring Piet's ideas on fragmenting them and spalling

off more pieces, Captain," she replied. "He's currently asleep. Mary-Elizabeth is having a late night snack."

He sipped his coffee and studied the plot of ships in orbit. *Obsidian Hawk* was abandoned, as was what had survived of *Yorrick* when Suvi had decapitated it.

"Three clan clusters as squadrons?" he asked, counting.

"Aye, sir," she said. "Close enough to cover one another in a pinch. I'm close to cracking the encryption that Belfast Group is using, because they've been a little slack and transmitted a few messages in the clear before correcting themselves. It appears that Captain Tsvetanka Ivankova from *Yorrick* was evacuated to *Epsilon Cavendish* and is currently in a medically induced coma. I think I've managed to nail three of the four overall commanders, with only Katya Velichkov on *Kymni Gauntlet* getting away from me."

"How's *Para Bellum* coping?" he asked.

In the end, that was all that really mattered. If those people were forced to leave without prisoners, he'd be less likely to kill every single one of them.

Probably.

Maybe not.

Their time had come.

"They have two shuttles of four destroyed, sir," Suvi said. "One more damaged and repaired. One optimal. They can only evacuate their force in a single load by abandoning all gear on the ground. I do not have any indication that they have found Javier and Djamila."

He nodded. Only thing saving their souls at present.

"Oh, hey, stand by," Suvi said. "Repeat that, Del."

"Located most of the team," Del said. "One group still at large, but Science Officer and Dragoon accounted for and have moved almost out of the target zone to safety. Getting ready to pick them up in a bit, then go get a Pathfinder and her Bunnies.”

“Roger that, Del,” Zakhar said. “There are still trouble-makers in orbit, but I’ve held off doing anything nasty until now. Let me know when you are ready to move and I’ll see about kicking in a few doors up here.”

“Suvi, estimate me about sixty minutes here,” Del said. “That’s close enough to what Javier said, and we can go from there.”

“You got it, Del,” she said.

“Suvi, split yourself into components,” Zakhar ordered, counting to three before proceeding. “I need you to start a hard plot of the three groups, both internally and relative to one another.”

“We about to go junkyard dog on them, Zakhar?” she asked.

“Even better, young lady,” he smiled. “Even better.”

Then he started explaining.

PART II

Javier had showered before sending Hajna out to get the others, so he was fresh, sharp, and hungry. Angry as a hornet's nest. Looking for blood.

Djamila sat on the bed as he paced, watching him, her hair still a little damp because she'd gone last of the group. Normal for her. The others were sitting around the room or on the two beds, staying out of his way and his well-known tendency to pace when he thought.

"It comes down to those shuttles being armed," he finally admitted, having churned it over and over in his head. "We know they are pirates. We know they are a boarding force. What does that tell me?"

"Ion weapons on the shuttles," Galal offered. "You want to immobilize your prey without damaging it, if you are about to put boarding parties into play. Del cannot risk that."

"Especially at low altitude," Iqbal finished the thought. "High enough and he could probably recover, but assume ten to fifteen seconds without power if someone gets him."

"And two of them let them mousetrap him," Demyan nodded. "One he could pounce on and score a kill, but he said they had repaired the one we got on the ground?"

"Affirmative," Javier said, then turned to Afia. "How fragile is that shuttle likely to be, if they had to repair it on the ground with whatever they brought with them?"

"No clue," she replied. Honest, at least. "If they were down for a few days, the hit was solid enough to rupture fuel lines or power cables, presumably, but not bad enough that you got the usual secondary explosions."

"They were using it as a primary command post at the time, so many of those systems would have been shut down," Djamila reminded everyone. "And we almost got their commander, I think."

"Pity that," Javier noted. "Would have made shit a lot easier on my end. How do we take advantage of the situation, if Zakhar has them spooked up in orbit?"

"No way they don't see us coming," Hajna offered. "Even low, they might assume we're some sort of law enforcement force coming in and open up with everything they had."

"How fast can that damned thing fly, anyway?" Javier asked, turning mostly to Afia. "And how maneuverable is it at ludicrous speeds?"

"Extremely maneuverable," she nodded. "Remember *Syntha* when those punks challenged Del to a flying competition. Speed can be excessive as well. You'll want him to gain altitude, then turn like a raptor and pounce for maximum zoom."

"It's the pulling out at the end if he gets hit that worries me," Javier grimaced. "He's got personal lifters aboard that we could use to bail out, but that just drops us in the middle of an extremely hostile enemy camp, right after I've pissed them off. I'd rather not."

"Short of walking all the way back over, which would take two to three days, I'm not sure you have an alternative, besides us camping here and hoping that nobody catches Sascha, Heydar, and Tom."

"Zakhar is about to do something extravagant," Javier shook his head. "I know the man. And Suvi. We need to act. And quickly. Might be that we get to orbit and have to come back for the other three later, but we will be back for them."

Nods. Hard people. Angry, but pissy chipmunks compared to the rage he could taste in the back of his mouth. Only Zakhar might be close. Even Djamila was a pale echo, as cold as she had gotten.

Javier had concluded that he was just going to have to finish the job he started at *Nidavellir*.

Whatever it took.

He walked to the room comm and dialed a number.

"Tango here," Del replied.

"Talk to me," Javier instructed the man.

PART III

Del updated the Science Officer like the man knew what he was doing. Not a lot of officers Del had known in all his decades flying he could say that about. And he had three on *Excalibur*, which was just frosting on any cake.

"Let's take option three, Del," Javier replied when he was done. "A little too close to Altamont, but it gives you the most space to land hard and fast, get us, and get gone afterwards. Not worried about you clipping a building, but I'd rather not worry about harming innocents on the ground who happened to be curious about our operation and got too close."

"Understood," Del replied. "Preflight will take me three minutes. Overland will take less than five, even dawdling. What's your time to landing zone?"

Pause. Probably asking Djamila. Or maybe Hajna. Experts. Another reason he liked the Science Officer. Man listened.

"We'll need about twelve minutes to make it look casual,"

Javier replied. "Multiple groups. Walking speed. Low profile. Count backwards from that."

"See you in twelve," Del said, cutting the line.

Given the extra time, he went for a potty break anyway. Might be getting a little crazy shortly, and the autopilot just wasn't up to those standards.

Map was nice. Hop over a pair of low mountain ranges that were only interesting because they tended to be nearly vertical escarpments that required experts to climb. Slide in from the side. Hit the parking lot of a factory complex that should be closed at this time of night. Pick up most of his team. Get out.

Piece of cake.

The timer he'd set on his dash counted down to zero as Del powered up his ship for flight.

PART IV

Troop Leader Arla Ancher had brought half of her team with her to Altamont. The ones she could be certain wouldn't engage in any grab-ass horseplay while they were supposed to be on duty. Especially in a ski resort, surrounded by wealthy tourists.

Last thing she needed was somebody getting arrested here. Or worse, shooting their way out of trouble and causing more.

She had the firepower to stand off the local cops. It was when those folks called for backup that things would start getting ugly. Especially if Benedict wasn't in a position to bring reinforcements quickly. Or extract her from a bad situation.

Right now, her job was acting as local command post from her hotel room. Folks coming and going. Maintaining a low profile. Not getting their asses in trouble.

Her comm chirped.

"Troop Leader," Arla said. Gotta remind the kids that she was in charge here.

"Elisa, Top," her corporal replied. "Got something hinky going on here."

"Talk to me," Arla said, already standing and waving to the two punks in the corner to move.

Hinky was never a good thing in this game.

"We just picked up a shuttle flying down the valley at a pretty low altitude, Troop Leader," Elisa said. "Hopped over some hills and seems to be headed towards Naha. Or close to it."

Shit. Benedict had guessed wrong. Or someone over there had done the same math she had and realized what a trap Altamont could be.

"You have a ground vehicle?" Arla asked as she threw open the door and started jogging, two ghosts in her wake.

"Affirmative, Arla," Elisa said, catching something in her tone. "Driver already inside. Can load seven more and be in motion in fifteen seconds."

"I have two with me," Arla said. "Load the rest and be ready to break speed limits."

She cut the line, nodded over her shoulder, and hit the stairs down.

This had to be it.

Could they get there in time?

PART V

Djamila understood the logic, but had overruled Javier anyway, leaving first and moving ahead of the rest of the team.

Certainly, she stood out, even in the well-lit darkness of a local tourist town evening. Standing a head taller than most humans would do that. Being first meant that she got past folks before they realized who she was, and Hajna and the others would be in a position to flank someone recognizing her.

And she walked with her Fitzgerald Lithogun in one hand, down at her side where it was functionally invisible. Somewhere behind her, Galal was doing something similar, save that his grenade launcher required two hands to fire. He had loaded it with a stun round first, then high explosive rounds behind it.

Because if he had to fire the weapon twice, the encounter had already escalated and they might as well take it to the wall.

Still, Djamila had found a spot off to one side. Up against

the main building and reasonably hidden by a few snow-covered bushes that maintained their foliage. Nothing that would stop a physical projectile, but it would disperse most energy weapons at any reasonable range for a shot or two, while letting her have surprise.

Across the parking lot, other heads had popped out briefly, then settled. Better to arrive a little too early than leave Del exposed on the ground when the locals might put up a fuss.

Djamila listened as his thrusters got closer. The assault shuttle was far larger than this team required, but it was also their primary workhorse from the ship, so it needed space.

Didn't quite take up the entire parking lot, but still big enough to haul ground vehicles as well as cargo. Roughly the same size as the beasts her team had shot down, but far more rugged. Her missiles wouldn't have killed this beast. Wounded it, but not scored a kill.

Djamila wondered if she needed to upgrade the SAM warheads her team carried in the field. Probably.

Landing lights came on and speared the parking lot as she watched. Empty. Dark otherwise. The building beside her had only the usual night lighting inside, so she wasn't too worried about anyone inside reacting. It was everyone else in Naha that might be a problem.

Quickly, Del nosed in and landed. A little hard, but that was saving six extra seconds on hover as he did it delicately. She knew he could, but the situation called for speed, not politeness.

Javier and Afia moved first, as agreed. They were the least deadly members of the team, hardly better than most combat troops she might hire. Del's landing ramp deployed and those two hustled across and up.

Hajna and her folks next, moving in a combat triad while Djamila's team covered them.

Motion caught her eye. Vehicle, approaching at high speed. Far too fast for normal circumstances.

"Incoming!" Djamila called, hoping that the others could hear her over the sound of Del's engines.

She stepped to the corner and knelt with a clear line of sight and braced her Lithogun for the first shot, as soon as the vehicle came to rest.

It was large. Troop transport scale, perhaps, but lacked the lines of an armored vehicle. Probably something civilian that had been rented or stolen for this operation.

Djamila smiled and waited.

PART VI

Hajna was to the ramp with Galal and Iqbal. Both peeled off and rotated back to cover the Dragoon's team when the latter crossed the open parking lot. She stood behind one of the struts and watched everything.

Movement. The Dragoon. Not moving, but shifting and aiming to Hajna's left.

Blind spot. Not good.

Hajna moved to Galal and pointed. He shifted around, then shook his head at her.

Too much noise, so she shifted to the silent language of hands, ordering him to open his flank to cover the others from whatever was about to happen. She followed, signaling Iqbal to expand his own flank. Sascha's team would have been useful about now, but they needed to go get her best friend from whatever that chick had gotten herself into this time.

Vehicle. Already to the edge of the parking lot and bodies bailing out by the time Hajna got off her first shot. Military grade armaments in hand. Someone else was shooting, because one of the targets over there went down hard, a rifle of some sort clattering away across the packed snow and ice.

Then the bad guys opened fire and Hajna had to find cover. Galal had shifted to the corner of the shuttle, which was about all there was available out here. She fired around him as he paused.

Too many targets. At least half a dozen enemy troops of unknown quality going for cover.

Not good.

Galal racked his weapon and caught the ejected round, stashing it in a pocket. Then he put an explosive round into the truck. Impact detonation. Low on the driver's rear wheel.

The explosion lifted the vehicle in the air and flipped it like a mechanical mousetrap closing.

With a lot of extra fire involved as the fuel cell ruptured.

The night turned day-bright for an instant and Hajna was blinded before she could squeeze her eyes closed. Didn't stop her from firing, but she was aiming by memory. Mostly hosing the area down and forcing everyone over there to duck or risk getting hit.

Galal fired a second shot. Rude. Air-detonated stun round. Range calculated. Went off like two million hands clapping at once, with an overpressure shockwave that drove her a step backwards clear over here and probably knocked everyone over there on their asses.

She risked a look back and saw the Dragoon's team sprinting across the open field, firing as they went. Hajna contributed more fire. Galal dropped another grenade into the distance, mostly just adding chaos.

Then somebody opened fire with the shuttle's turret, shattering the truck into a dozen pieces.

She'd never been outside to watch from this close, so the

effect was stunning. Ice and snow exploded where the beams walked across. She didn't think Del was aiming at anything so much as adding chaos, but incoming fire dropped to nothing as everyone over there suddenly scattered and hauled ass for whatever cover might protect them.

Quick check, and the Dragoon was almost to the ramp. Hajna grabbed Galal and thrust him in that direction rather than try to communicate at this point. She fired a couple of shots over her shoulder, but that was lost in the noise and explosions of the turret beams.

She got to the ramp and counted noses. Everyone present except Javier, with Iqbal stepping onto the ramp as she did and waving to Afia. They rode the ramp up and the noise cut off like a guillotine had dropped.

The shuttle wobbled under their feet, then slid backwards. Hajna had hold of a stanchion, watching the Dragoon haul ass forward and up, so she could relieve Del from the guns and let him fly.

The noise wasn't silence, but she could talk without yelling.

"Where's Javier?" she asked Afia.

"Forward, manning the guns," the combat engineer answered. "Boy's a little pissed right now, as you might imagine."

Hajna nodded. Afia probably knew Javier the best, as she'd spent a lot of time around him. And intimate with him.

Pissed was a polite understatement for mixed company.

Hajna looked around.

"Secure arms and stand by for hostile landing zone, as soon as we locate the other team," she ordered, moving to where they could strap into jumpseats for whatever was coming next.

PART VII

Javier glanced over his shoulder when the Amazon babe rumbled loudly down the stairs.

"Stand by so we can swap," he called to her, knowing that she might just pick him bodily out of the chair anyway so she could fire things. She was strong enough.

And he'd made his statement, back in Naha.

A quick look at the scanners. Nobody else in the air right now, so he hit the safety switch and climbed up and to one side, only getting slightly squished against a wall as she got by.

Any other woman on the crew, and he might have appreciated that level of contact. However, Djamila was more like a sister these days.

Yuck.

"Del, I have guns," she announced, pulling on the headset. "Proceed to Phase II."

Javier nodded and hauled ass back up the stairs. She had this situation entirely under control. What she could control.

Del would be on point next, so Javier got up to the flight

deck and strapped himself in, ignoring the pink fur to bring a new screen online and study things forward.

"Figure they warned 'em we're coming?" Del mused aloud.

"Assume we lost surprise," Javier replied.

"Game of lightning tag, then," Del chuckled, even as he pulled back on his yoke and slammed the throttle to the forward stop.

Around him, Javier felt the ship buck once like a spooked horse, then settle in for a sprint to the finish line.

"Lightning tag?" he asked.

"Ion weapons in atmosphere are a lot like lightning bolts," Del said quietly. "A little less random. A lot more dangerous. Used to play this game with some other pilots when I was a kid."

Javier knew more of what Del had done in his career than most of the crew, but that required getting the man a little drunk and listening to him ramble.

He didn't think he knew a more dangerous pilot.

"Ah, there we are," Del announced a few seconds later. "Both shuttles are in the process of launching from the ground. Figure they have anybody but crew aboard?"

"Does it matter?" Javier asked.

"Only if you wanted an accurate tally when all this was done," Del nodded. "Djamila, dear, we're about to get stupid. Stay sharp."

Javier checked his straps and pulled them a little tighter.

Just in case.

PART VIII

Del had to keep from cackling out loud. He kept reminding himself that the Science Officer didn't need to know the whole truth. Nobody did. Even Zakhar had only the fragments he'd originally needed to hire an old fart who most folks had thought was past his expiration date as a combat pilot.

Nobody ever appreciated how good he'd been in those days.

Elevation.

"Tango-Charlie-Seven-One-Niner, this is Sultan Flight Control." Huh. Those berks had finally woken up. "Be advised that you are violating a region that has been declared off-limits to all aircraft. Turn back and land immediately."

He started to reach for the comm to say something, but Javier waved him off, so Del went back to flying.

"Sultan Flight Control, this is Captain Eutrupio Navarre," Javier said in that really scary voice he did when you'd pushed him far enough. "We are about to deal with your pirate problem directly. There will still be ground troops when we're done, but they will be trapped on this planet and subject to your legal apparatus. Then I intend to go kill anybody in orbit that I can't chase off. Stay off the line and watch your screens instead."

Rude. Probably pretty effective. Draw one hell of a line in the sand by invoking that name.

Probably a bad time to get their asses shot down.

"Del?" Javier asked after killing the line. He looked over. "I want them all dead, Del. Annihilated. *Nidavellir* apparently wasn't sufficient to convey my pique to these punks, so I want you to go junkyard dog on them. Am I clear?"

"You care what they crash on?" Del asked, already understanding most of the rules of engagement.

"If you can drop a shuttle on top of their base and kill two birds with one stone, that would be lovely," Navarre growled back. "Dead will do. Then Zakhar and I will go do orbit."

"He and Suvi were already planning something, but I didn't ask for details," Del offered.

"Even better," Navarre said. "Every one of them we kill today is one less I have to hunt down tomorrow."

Del nodded. It had felt like that kind of day, going in.

Now, he just had to make the lesson stick.

Two birds. Low elevation. Probably caught by surprise and reacting on instinct and training instead of a plan. Somebody had called from Naha after Javier—no Navarre—had lit their asses up.

Nobody knew if they had air defense artillery. Why would you need it to capture a dozen folks on the ground?

Why had Djamila hauled her stuff? Because the better prepared army is usually the one that wins.

Outside, the sound barrier surrendered. BOOM.

Del nosed over and lined up on the enemy formation. Both birds were hovering at around two thousand meters now. Low enough that a sane pilot would have to blast over them at high speed. Otherwise, he risked blipping down into a tree or something.

At these speeds, they'd disintegrate so fast that he'd be in hell before the devil heard the doorbell ring.

Fortunately, Zakhar hadn't hired a sane pilot.

"Djamila, I'll be passing below them," he announced. "Contact in seven seconds, but you might as well start firing now. That will help me line one of them up."

He heard the little beep of the forward turret locking in, then opening fire at whatever dumbass birds hadn't settled in for the night.

The galaxy's biggest homicidal woodpecker, going at a tree at full speed.

Del focused on the ground and the line of beam fire extending ahead of him like a unicorn horn. Not quite Nape-Of-The-Earth flying, but still too low for most lunatics at this speed.

Most.

Poor fools on those shuttles were still aiming to rake his underbelly as he went over them, because what fool risked this shit?

Old fighter pilots.

It was over almost before it started. At this rate of closure, he had to watch the hull for hotspots generated by friction. And keep the guns aiming a hose that the other guy would be flying through.

Oh, and a Mach one-point-seven shockwave trailing as he went right under them.

Because **Navarre** had demanded a personal statement, in spite of the fact that most of the folks he'd left dead had been someone else pulling triggers.

Team effort.

Del pulled up and slipped into a nasty-ass barrel roll as he deployed airbrakes and reversed his thrusters.

Ion weapons also didn't work for shit at any kind of range, so if he kept his distance, those punks were handicapped.

Up, out, over, down, sideways. Throw in a sideslip just for the extra points from the *Merankorr* judge. Drop below Mach and look around. Take a pretty picture of one of those two shuttles on fire and falling out of the sky.

The other one wasn't far behind it, but that was some smart pilot down there realizing that he was next and there was nothing he could do to keep from getting his ass splattered across the forest.

Or whatever happened to be below him at the moment of impact.

Del rolled into a wide starboard turn and glanced over at Navarre.

"You want them exploding in the air, or landing and running like hell for bomb shelters when Djamila kills their chariot?" he asked.

Nobody would have any other expectations after this, save dying.

Javier was back.

"Down and then kill it," he ordered. "Let them surrender to local authorities and go to prison for a while."

Del nodded and continued his circle. Nobody on the ground had launched anything, so he was reasonably comfortable that they lacked the necessary firepower.

He was still making his next pass at ludicrous speeds, just in case.

PART IX

"Zakhar, this is Javier on the shuttle," the Science Officer came over the comm. "Whatever you had planned, I have eliminated the threat from the ground."

Zakhar grinned. He'd been watching on an encrypted feed from Del's console. That barely covered what those two had just done. Three with Djamila, though she hadn't been doing more than holding the fire button down.

"Roger that, Science Officer," Zakhar said. "Stand by for our surprise here, now that you have focused all eyes on the surface."

He paused, noting that the war probably started as soon as he spoke. Up until this moment, they had generally remained defensive. Reactive, in spite of everything he and Suvi had done prior.

Javier had just launched the assault.

Excalibur was about to carry it forward.

The *Extermination* of the Pirate Clans.

"Suvi, initiate your jump and unleash the hounds of hell," he ordered.

It began here.
Now.

PART X

Suvi had a running calculation showing the location of every one of the bad guys. And which pilots were handling things manually versus having their autopilot systems maintain their formations.

Three squadrons. Clustered by clan. Keeping the sorts of respectful distances you got when you mixed three packs of wild dogs and nobody was sure who was about to start some shit.

And Zakhar had laid out for her quite simply the meanest thing she thought she'd ever heard, which was saying something with this crew.

She jumped.

Like last time, lined up like pigs at a feeding trough. Except that this time, she'd deliberately put herself in the middle of the scrum.

This was going to be a mess, even if it did work. If it didn't, she might be dead, taking all of her friends with her except for the team on the ground.

Best to not fuck it up then.

Every weapon with arc got broadsided into *Para Bellum* from close enough that she thought they might be able to breathe on her. Certainly, there was almost enough atmosphere at this altitude, however tenuous, that sound would conduct.

Except that she was already making a terrible racket herself.

Shields were reinforced some, but she was pouring every spare erg of power into her jammers instead. Hopefully, she looked like a spotlight on any scanners pointed at her. Whatever would buy her a few extra seconds of missed beam fire.

Suvi nodded as her wavefront caught up with her location. Everything had been fired blind on a heading for nearly a second. A lot of it had hit. And nobody had been expecting this crazy-ass stunt, so they weren't ready.

Local thrusters pushed her closer to *Para Bellum*, like she was about to dock with them manually, which was about the dumbest thing she'd ever heard of.

Except that all of those Ion Pulsars were pointed at Walvisbaai and H & W ships, instead of everyone maintaining a stable perimeter against her pulling a stunt like this.

Dumb-ass move on their part, since she'd already done it twice, but a smart girl didn't look gift horses in the mouth.

Every Pulsar that could was busy pounding the living shit out of *Para Bellum* from point-freaking-blank range. Almost close enough that her own shields might catch splash damage, except that *Para Bellum* wasn't really a warship.

Zakhar had pointed that part out. It looked to have been a cruise liner that someone had bought and upgraded. Or maybe purpose-built with the extra firepower, but still on a much more civilian hull.

Hammerfield had been designed from the keel up as the

Flagship of the *Neu Berne* fleet, back when those folks were fighting a war to the death with the rest of human civilization. Just short of a Warmaster Mark III with her most recent mods and upgrades.

Crossways, she lit up the Walvisbaai folks with anything to starboard that couldn't bear on *Para Bellum* and her friends. More noise. More trouble.

Suvi had counted to fourteen, then hit *Para Bellum* with every single Ion Pulsar she had left over from the Khatum's drydock. Caught them by surprise, too, because she hadn't bothered using them much until now.

Didn't do any good to stun an enemy warship if you were about to run like hell and give them time to recover.

Timing was everything today. And taking extra damage as the other ships woke up, slewed around their turrets, and tried to drive her off.

Suvi kept firing, watching on her boards as her various shields started to overload. Weapons were overheating to the point that she had probably shaved five years off her armaments in the last week.

But Zakhar had told her more than once that ships—including sexy, awesome ones like hers—were tools, just like their crews, and that sometimes, it was necessary to use them up in battle. To leave everything on the game field, rather than holding anything for later.

She had to do this. And do it right now. Because this was her last change to kick somebody in the nuts before things moved on to whatever evil shit Javier and Zakhar were planning.

And she knew it was evil because he'd identified himself as *Navarre* on the comm when talking to the ground folks.

That was a name a lot of folks around here would know.

Para Bellum was starting to shed parts. Shields blown to hell worse than hers. Hull not nearly as durable or well-designed to take the sorts of abuse that the two of them were facing.

Helped that she was using *Para Bellum* as a shield against all the H & W folks. None of them had decided to just open fire into the scrum and damn the consequences, though it would have helped.

If anything did.

Blackstone finally spoke. Finally. Suvi felt a smile creep up her cheeks as she did the math.

Bastard had over a thousand launch tubes. And had just sent more than a quarter of it at her.

Close range, but not point-blank.

Shadowing the skies with arrows, as Xerxes might have appreciated.

It was like watching salmon coming upstream to spawn, except that a horde of rabid rats was probably a better description.

Suvi didn't even bother trying to engage that mess. She'd turned on everything to blind them in the first place, so someone had gotten smart and launched them blind. Aim and shoot. Detonate on impact. Didn't matter if they didn't know what was in front of them.

She counted down. Held her breath.

Jumped sideways as the first one got close.

Leaving a sadly ionized *Para Bellum* behind, right in the path.

Whoopsie.

EPILOGUES

EPILOGUE: ZAKHAR

Zakhar watched the replay and couldn't help but smile. The image wasn't that great, because Suvi had gone straight down instead of out or around the planet to escape.

Just far enough to not be in the way when all those torpedoes started slamming blindly into the Belfast Group squadron. *Para Bellum* was a tin can someone had stomped on. The others hadn't been in much better shape, blindsided. And caught in a box because H & W had decided to pile on when they thought that Walvisbaai had sprung an ambush on Belfast.

And Suvi had kept up her fire from a distance, hammering *Blackstone* a few more times and taunting him to launch more.

He'd been playing possum, though, because that ship had fired off another five hundred or so torpedoes, then jumped away into the darkness, *Royal Gamma* and *Western Sentinel* jumping with him and leaving Belfast to deal with missile overload.

Badly.

The replay ended with all three squadrons running different directions, all badly mauled. Zakhar sipped his coffee.

"Yeoman, I'm pretty sure I can put you in for a few awards from the *Concord Navy*, in spite of your decommissioned and civilian nature," he offered. "That was the sort of thing—this entire situation has been, really—that tactics classes will spend years dissecting. Extremely well done."

He liked that she took the moment to blush and nod. Still the most human *Sentient* system he had ever dealt with.

Zakhar turned to Javier next. Djamila and Del had largely sat and watched. Not impassive, but not having steam come off their ears like the Science Officer. Piet and Mary-Elizabeth had been sober and involved. Bethany and Afia really didn't have the background to understand every subtlety.

Bethany waved a hand to distract, drawing all eyes onto her.

"I presume, in spite of what we've done here, that it isn't enough?" she asked the group.

Her eyes were on Javier.

"I do not feel that honor has been satisfied, no," the man replied in a crisp, didactic tone that ought to tell any fool how angry he really was.

"Then I need to know how badly Suvi has been damaged," Bethany replied. "And if we trust the *Concord* to repair the ship, or some third-party entity who won't immediately sell such information to our enemies while we might be indisposed to resist them."

Also angry. She got technical when that happened. Outcome of being a librarian by training, he supposed.

"Suvi, how much can you and the crew repair in flight?" Zakhar asked.

He already knew, having talked to her in the immediate aftermath of the battle as they'd waited for Del to locate and pick up his last three stray chicks, then run hard to orbit and safety.

The locals were getting a little antsy, but they also understood that *Excalibur* had just shattered an enemy fleet, leaving five mangled ships behind to be salvaged and several hundred soldiers on the ground in the process of surrendering. After pissing themselves.

Suvi's offer to fly low enough that her Pulsars could reach them through the atmosphere had done wonders to break their will. Zakhar was pretty sure she had been bluffing.

Pretty sure.

Not something to tempt today.

"If you wish an extended campaign, I will need a significant drydock," she replied. "Not as much as when I took this vessel over initially, but time with things shut down and torn apart, preferably with expert mechanics and engineers working to reassemble and potentially upgrade a few things. I could get us home to *Altai*. I could fight a series of battles from here. I do not think that I can do both."

Zakhar nodded.

This was when it got tricky. Possibly ugly. He still intended to send Bethany and Kibwe into the *Concord* with messages for the few old friends of his who might listen to their proposal without immediately throwing them in prison.

It was still a risk they all faced.

Zakhar turned to Javier, ceding him command. In the

end, Javier owned the ship, and the rest of them were employees, including Suvi.

"Gonna get ugly," Javier growled.

"You think I'm feeling merciful?" Afia snarled from her corner between Djamila and Bethany. "Think there's any forgive-and-forget left in me?"

She stood up from the table and pulled her shirt and jacket up, showing off the scar she'd acquired, nearly dying at *Nidavellir* when her escape pod had been fired on.

"They had their chance to let it go," Afia said simply. "And chose not to take it. My only fear at this point is that even *Eutropio Navarre* might not take this to the rightful and proper conclusion necessary to see MY honor satisfied."

Zakhar shuddered in spite of himself. That was a line in the sand that exceedingly few folks would ever consider crossing. And many of them sat at the table with him.

Javier studied her for a long moment.

Then he nodded.

Turned to Zakhar.

"Put your plans in motion," Javier said simply. "We'll depart *Drako* shortly, doglegging several times so nobody can be sure where we've gone. Eventually, we get to *Purton*, either directly or stopping and dropping that team off while we do what we can here."

"I know a few places we could go raid, if we were feeling ornery," Zakhar offered. "Places we could score repair supplies, though not people I'd trust."

"We'll talk," Javier acknowledged, leaving that on the table for later. "In the meantime, everyone remember that we managed to pull this one out, in spite of ugly odds. And that they started it. Again. This time, I intend to finish it. Entirely."

Zakhar nodded as Javier rose. Meeting adjourned, because how do you top that?

Possibly by lining up a whole bunch of heads on stakes as a warning to future generations.

And Javier was probably the man to do it.

EPILOGUE: JAVIER

Javier had joined Zakhar in that man's office. The rage was a constant heat, keeping him warm. He studied the Captain.

"Am I going too far?" Javier asked.

Zakhar was about the only person other than Behnam he could say that to.

Zakhar considered an answer.

"If anything, I think Afia's right," he finally said.

"Burn it all down, salt the earth afterwards?" Javier asked.

"What's to stop Slavkov from putting a huge bounty on all our heads, then sitting back and laughing as we spend the rest of our lives hiding from assassins?" Zakhar grimaced.

"Nothing," Javier acknowledged. "Nothing at all. Which is why I think we have to do something so incredibly ugly here that it makes the history books. I'm just not sure what that is, yet."

"You'll figure it out," Zakhar nodded. "And we'll be right there with you, because all of us are on that same line, forever watching over our shoulders."

"You honestly think that the *Concord* will help?" Javier asked, finding some element inside that didn't immediately discount the idea.

"We're the good guys, Javier," the man said, rapping his class ring on the desk like they always did as a way of acknowledging one another. *Concord* Academy on *Bryce*.

Heroes.

"I haven't been on the right side of things for a lot of years," Javier started to say, but Zakhar's laugh intruded.

"*Nidavellir*," he said, tapping his desk. "*Ugen. Kimmeria. Syntha. Sovereign Nakhimov.* I think you undersell yourself a bit and need to get over that shit. Am I clear?"

Only Zakhar could go hardass with him, but Javier supposed that the man was right. This whole voyage had been intended for exploration and trade, but they'd gotten themselves into and out of trouble along the way.

Occupational hazard for former *Concord* Navy officers, he supposed. Bred deep into the bones, and etched into the soul.

Javier appreciated that. He needed to get over himself. How many people had told him that, over and above both ex-wives?

And none of them were wrong.

"Annihilate piracy in this meta-sector?" Javier asked.

"At a minimum," Zakhar agreed. "Maybe everything between here and *Altai*, depending on how stupid other people get while we're doing that."

"I'd ask if we're doing the right thing, but that's a load of horseshit," Javier said. "Will it make any difference?"

"A century from now, Suvi's likely the only one of us still around," Zakhar said. "And Dorn's Rising Storm might scour everything back down to the bare stone anyway. Best if all the bad folks were already destroyed first, so the innocents have a chance to build something that might survive."

Javier sighed. How many hours, how many discussions, had circled around that topic over the last year?

He'd been looking forward to going home. To being home. To spending the rest of his days with Behnam, making her laugh and enjoying her company.

Wasn't going to happen anytime soon.

"Behnam saw this moment coming," Zakhar said abruptly. "Told me to wave a hand under your nose when it arrived, in order to get your attention."

Javier studied him, but didn't speak. This might be the first time he'd ever heard Zakhar call her by her first name, instead of her title, so it must be critical.

And she was that smart a woman. She probably had foreseen it.

"She understood who you are," Zakhar continued. "And that you would be called upon to do certain, stupid things. She wanted me to remind you that the man she'd fallen in love with couldn't help but rise up right now and punch someone in the mouth. Just remember that you aren't alone."

"Even if means exile for all of us forever?" Javier asked.

"Exile forever," Zakhar agreed. "But not that. For most of us, coming home."

Javier breathed deep, suddenly holding back unexpected tears. She really did get him, in ways nobody else did.

And yes, he had friends. Surrounded by people he could call on to make the galaxy a better place.

Javier leaned across the desk and took Zakhar's hand.

"To victory?" Zakhar asked.

"No," Javier shook his head. "To justice."

Yes.

Justice.

ABOUT THE AUTHOR

Blaze Ward writes science fiction in the Alexandria Station universe (Jessica Keller, The Science Officer, Phil Kosnett, etc.) as well as several other science fiction universes, such as Corsac Fox, Operation Marrakesh, and more. He also writes odd bits of high fantasy with swords and orcs. In addition, he is the Editor and Publisher of *Boundary Shock Quarterly Magazine*. You can find out more at his website www.blaze-ward.com, as well as Facebook, Goodreads, and other places.

Blaze's works are available as ebooks, paper, and audio, and can be found at a variety of online vendors. His newsletter comes out regularly, and you can also follow his blog on his website. He really enjoys interacting with fans, and looks forward to any and all questions—even ones about his books!

Never miss a release!

If you'd like to be notified of new releases, sign up for my newsletter.

http://www.blazeward.com/newsletter/

Buy More!

Did you know that you can buy directly from the KRP website?

https://www.knottedroadpress.com/shop/

Connect with Blaze!

Web: www.blazeward.com
Boundary Shock Quarterly (BSQ):
https://www.boundaryshockquarterly.com/

ABOUT KNOTTED ROAD PRESS

Knotted Road Press publishes dynamic fiction set in exotic locations and unique non-fiction voices in genres such as autobiography, business, cookbooks, and how-to. Our authors cover a wide range of genres including science fiction, fantasy, mystery, literary, and poetry, appealing to all readers. We offer both DRM-free ebooks and print books for a global readership.

Knotted Road Press
www.KnottedRoadPress.com
www.KnottedRoadPress.com/Shop

www.ingramcontent.com/pod-product-compliance
Lightning Source LLC
Chambersburg PA
CBHW060307100726
47907CB00002B/316